FORGOTTEN RUIN

NEVER SHALL I FAIL

JASON ANSPACH
NICK COLE

WARGATE

An imprint of Galaxy's Edge Press
PO BOX 534
Puyallup, Washington 98371
Copyright © 2021 by Galaxy's Edge, LLC
All rights reserved.

ISBN: 978-1-949731-93-4

www.forgottenruin.com
www.jasonanspach.com
www.nickcolebooks.com
www.wargatebooks.com

TECHNICAL ADVISORS AND CREATIVE DESTRUCTION SPECIALISTS

Ranger Vic
Ranger David
Ranger Chris

Green Beret John "Doc" Spears

Rangers lead the way!

CHAPTER ONE

TIME was of the essence. Why? Because there was no time to spare. Time was thin now. At Sûstagul, or what I'm calling the Second Battle of Sûstagul for purposes of this account, time was the most valuable commodity on the market.

And no one had any to spare.

Least of all... me.

What follows is the conviction that I walked among giants who deserved a lot better than me on their six. But I was determined to do my best, if that might help in some way.

Or, as the creed makes clear...

In those hot, worst-ever days after the deaths of Kurtz and Brumm, I whispered it like a prayer as the enemy closed on the walls and the incoming was beyond belief.

"Never shall I fail my comrades. I will always keep myself mentally alert, physically strong, and morally straight, and I will shoulder more than my share of the task, whatever it may be, one hundred percent... *and then some.*"

Never shall I fail.

CHAPTER TWO

WHAT we were facing at the Second Battle of Sûstagul as opposed to what we had faced before was… laughable.

I know… recycle due to *Lack of Motivation*. But facts are facts. And all of it, everything coming at us from out there beyond the cracked and broken walls, overrun with terrors from the desert, was like a raging fever in my brain as I beat the living hell out of the orc we'd taken prisoner that morning. We had no time left. We had no walls, no army, and very little ammunition to burn. Yeah, we'd taken Sûstagul in the first battle. Defeated a Saur expeditionary force. We'd won in fact. Barely. But that was the first battle. That was yesterday. A month ago when it started.

As they say in Ranger School, yesterday doesn't count.

Now, the battle in the port, for the walls, the deaths… it felt like ten years easy. And some days I felt as old as Old Man Sims looked when some quiet moment caught me unawares and hammered me with stuff I needed to settle up.

Chief Rapp calls it *grief*. He also said there would come a time for it, but now wasn't it. Now we were surrounded, knee-deep in expended brass, at times down to pickups and knuckles, knives out to save rounds, and more of the enemy marching toward the wall every new day.

But it would come. The grief.

The Rangers at the Second Battle of Sûstagul were out of tricks and surrounded. That is the situation. Yes, we had two understrength legions of Accadion infantry supporting, and supposedly more coming in by ship, by galley. But no one had seen any white sails of Accadion on the horizon. And now the air was hot and windless and what wind did come sweeping through the piles of death that surrounded the city came up from the dead-smelling south, or what the map calls the *Desert of Black Sleep*. The *River of Night*. Once called the Nile. That hot dragon's breath of foul-smelling corpses pushed against us and off and out to sea and you didn't need to be one of those faithful Portugonian sailors to know that whatever galleys were coming with more desperately needed Accadion legionnaires for the walls we were losing by the hour, or even the smaj's supply train from the Forge... were gonna have a hell of a time coming into port against those hot devil winds coming up from the south.

So, we had that against us too.

But as every Ranger said that month, and this is how they are when it looks real bleak, "Sucks, Talk. But honestly... I wish it would suck more. You know?" And then they would move off, determined and overloaded, usually wounded to some extent lesser or greater, to either help the Legion hold a portion of the crumbling walls of that old desert city or pull the captain's midnight raids out there in the trenches and lines the enemy had spread out across in the desert out there as they came at us holed up inside Sûstagul.

From three directions no less. Mornings were for recovery and chow. Afternoons for redeployment. Nights for fighting. Late nights for raids. You slept when you could catch it. But it was never much.

I hammered the orc one more time right across the side of the head. *Knock some sense into him*, I almost grunted. It was late afternoon. We needed intel. Little time, really none, left to redeploy to whatever portions of the wall were gonna get hit hard tonight.

"He gonna talk, Talk, 'cause we runnin' outta time," muttered Tanner from the side of his face that was still... *human*.

He's turning into a corpse a little more every day. My friend. No one cares anymore. He's Tanner. In fact, everyone smells like death here in Sûstagul and it's something you try to ignore except Jabba going on and on and suddenly getting all goblin-religious about it all.

Rangers now ask the kid who can draw over in mortars to sketch them a tattoo of Tanner's face, helmet, carbine, plate carrier, the whole horror show, because as they say, "That's some cool ink right there and I'm gonna wear it when we find some tat artists."

"Smell like death comin', Rang-aars. Big bigga death," babbles Jabba.

"Big bigga death?" Tanner will ask, just because he likes the game of messing with the little gob. We've all gotten over our irritations with this play if only because we're so dog-tired. And so it goes on between the two of them. "Or bigga *big* death, Jabba?"

Honestly, linguist that I am, I don't know the difference. Maybe there's some nuance between *big* and *bigga* and how they're stacked in the sentence in gob patois. Old me, linguist me, Sidra Paredes boy-toy plaything to piss off her shipping magnate dad me... woulda cared.

But…

I'm not that guy anymore.

Not after Brumm. Not after… Kurtz.

"I don't know…" I whisper to Tanner when the orc leader doesn't talk after the beating I've just handed out. My voice sounds like a croaking hiss in the late-afternoon African desert heat. The part of my head that tracks the intel, the maps, the situation constantly, all that fever, reminds me it's called *the Land of the Black Sleep* now. On the maps.

"I don't know" is my grave-whisper reply to Tanner's question. My voice sounds like Tanner looks.

I suddenly, and savagely, lunge at the orc I've been interrogating. I punch him in the jaw again, hard. I connect with a wildly over-bitten, fanged, gash of a mouth using my assault gloves. I've already knocked out other teeth. They lie on the ground broken and bloody all around us. His eye is swollen shut. Pretty sure I did that too.

But things are getting hazy. I'm starting to take ragged drags of the hot dry air and I don't think I'm even sweating because I'm not hydrated… because there isn't time. There's no time and someone's gonna die.

That's when I realize I have stopped hitting the orc. Savagely. As hard as I can. Again and again.

We need to know where they'll attack tonight, just after dark.

I beat the living hell out of him… again. And again. There are no war crimes here in the Ruin. No rules of engagement. This is survival for all the marbles, and we need to know right now where we're going to get hit just after dark because the Guzzim Hazadi always hit the walls just after dark. That's when they attack out of the shifting sands to the south and the west of the city.

There are too few of us to be everywhere and all at once here under siege. Too many points along those cracked walls to defend. We've come to call the places we defend and have lost... *Observatory. The Crack. Tower Six. Gatehouse One. The Pile.* And others, many others. Places where scared-to-death determined-to-hold legionnaires, young kids who all kinda look like Soprano the two-forty gunner, stand toe-to-toe, shield-to-shield, spear and gladius, ready to hold out on those crumbling points on our crude maps and rough sand tables. Among them, as the darkness gathers and the sorcerous sandstorms roll in rough as nails, often one-eyed, very scarred Accadion NCOs maintain the rank by bark and reminder of what their emperor expects of them, instilling fear and respect... and a commitment to hold the line for Accadios and all these young kids have left behind the walls there.

Mothers, fathers, wives, children... what passes for human civilization in the Ruin.

I am outta time.

I pull my knife and cut off the orc's index finger just like that. So fast even I can't believe what I've just done, only knowing I've done it in some other distant part of my mind. I've hit that brute so many times he just flops over in the small dusty and weed-overrun cemetery we're interrogating him in, hoping for some slice of intel, plans, or just gossip that might tell us where the Guzzim Hazadi are going to hit us tonight. Around us, ruptured graves a hundred years dug up lie like gaping mouths screaming in horror among the piling dust and sand. Marking stones, crooked and turned over, whitewashed long ago which is custom here, watch over these gaping tomb mouths screaming in the heavy silence of the place. Horrified at what's been done to them all along the way and over the cruel years the mind calls *Time*.

Or…

Or are they horrified at what I've become here, beating the hell out of the prisoner because I have reasons that seem just and right?

Horrified.

Yeah, I have that thought and I push it away when I remember why I'm doing what I'm doing.

It was bad, Talk. Real bad.

Tanner dead-walking where Kurtz and Brumm died. Me looking at rust-colored stones already fading in the desert sun.

Dead-walking is what we call it when Tanner gets glimpses of that other nether world of unquiet ghosts and horrible crimes.

Thirty minutes and it'll be twilight. The Guzzim will be on the move for the walls, pushing through the body-littered dunes and active siege units along the hasty fortifications and badly dug trenches. No horns or war cries for the Guzzim Hazadi. They're pros. They're the Rangers of orcs. Forgive me for my blasphemy, Ranger God in the Sky. But even Captain Knife Hand has put it this way during our briefings. Their field craft and ambush skills are on par with us, and that is not lightly taken and is, in fact, as the captain has put it, "to be respected, Rangers. Only so we can murder them and get clear of this mess."

They'll come out of the purple sands of the south in the quiet of the twilight. The Guzzim Hazadi. And if they're lucky they'll have a witch-made sandstorm or some kind of sorcery to create this effect. Then they'll hit the walls and more legionnaires will die. And so will the Rangers who rush to stand in the breach these orcs have created.

We've lost eleven of us so far. Eleven Rangers killed since we took the port city.

Eleven since the battle started. Eleven along the walls, hacked to pieces.

It was bad, Talk. Real bad.

Not counting...

Brumm.

And Kurtz.

"Damn, Talk," says Tanner once I've stood up from the pain-shrieking orc I have ruined. Holding his grotesque and misshapen bloody finger. A foul thing that was already grotesque and made not much more so by my taking.

There is no time left.

THIS IS WHAT YOU MADE ME DO! I want to scream at the whimpering, sobbing thing.

The only resupply we've got are the birds coming in from the Air Force who still can't get the C-5 Galaxy on the ground here in Sûstagul. The dwarves are still trying to build the runway to the west just outside the Gates of Death along the west side of the port city. Under fire. That's another story.

There are three gates to the city.

The Gates of Death where the Ninth Accadion Legion marched out of and never returned.

The Gates of Eternity which lead to the south and the tombs and the Grand Pyramid of the Saur along the Royal Road.

The Gates of Mystery which lead to the east from the eastern edge of the city.

Every day we get an ammo resupply run from one of the still-working Black Hawks. It ain't much. But if we know where the orcs are gonna hit us then we can get mines and explosives down and destabilize their push on our defenses. Using canalization we can push them into killing fields overwatched by the gun teams.

So we save our ammo.

Most of it goes to the snipers and the gun teams.

On the ground, along the wall, in the trenches, we work with swords, axes, and pickups just like the Legion carrying their spears and small swords. Fighting in ranks behind their large shields.

That is how things are now.

"*Hadith!*" I shout angrily at the ruined orc. My face is hot and red and I'm feeling... *giddy*. Dangerously giddy now and that's... *dangerous*. Like any bad thing is possible now that I've crossed some river in the long dark night of the soul.

All I've been feeling since Kurtz and Brumm is nothing but rage because... no more...

Kurtz and Brumm. Brothers.

Talk.

"*Ahduth alan! 'Ayn hadhih allayla?*"

Talk now! Where tonight?

The orc moans and tries to roll away from me, but he's chained and I'm in his face shouting and spitting.

I took his finger because he kept fighting me.

And because he wouldn't talk.

I hear Tanner saying something in another world not the one I'm in now. Here it's just me and the prisoner. But I'm not listening to my friend. The sun, which has been torturing us all day, is down behind the top of the high brick walls to the west. They're coming and there's not time to even get Sergeant Kang and his team in before the Guzzim hit. No time for mines and Ranger trickery.

So why am I doing this?

Why am I out of control? Lost control.

I lunge at the orc, calling him a *pig* and a *dog* because that's the only thing that comes into my madness, barely. I'm snarling and my teeth are gritted to the point I feel like I'm going to break them myself, and I feel that dangerous, giddy rage carrying me and showing me other horrors I can do to get what I want.

Calling him a *Schweinehund* in Gray Speech, now, seems laughably ridiculous. But at the time...

The language of the enemy.

The Guzzim Hazadi speak that too. Words here and there appear in their horrid barking speech.

I want to laugh as I write all this down a little later, but in about one minute within the account I'm going to blow the orc's brains all over the tombstone we chained him up on.

He should have known...

But he begins to babble when I tell him in a mix of Arabic, Gray Speech, and some of the weird snarling orc I've picked up, that I'm gonna start cutting other stuff off PDQ.

"Tonight! Where is the attack tonight?" I bark at him, sounding just like one of his own. Tanner has a hold of me, and the horrid thing is just cowering away from me, trying to get behind the tombstone but he can't because of the chains we have him in.

He talks. He talks and he doesn't stop.

He doesn't want to lose other things and I've certainly shown a willingness to cut... and worse. To him... I don't know what I am, but it's something real bad.

Babbling, barking like orcs do, he tells us, tells me, the Guzzim Hazadi attack tonight is going down at the Observatory. That's where Corporal Chuzzo's men are. Tanner releases me and I put my knife into the orc's ragged flappy throat and push, and yeah, there's blood but not a lot and I'm wearing my nearly shredded assault gloves, so they get covered in orc blood too.

Remember when I was all shiny and new once? Area 51. These were just issued. Kurtz showed me, after that first attack... how to run my carbine.

Remember... some voice that sounds a lot like an elf girl I once knew... *Remember, Talker.*

Well, I'm not that guy anymore.

It's the truth. What the orc is barking as I cut more, just a little, has got to be the truth I need to save lives because it's all I've got time for. So I push her voice away from this because I can't have her see what I've become.

She was too beautiful, too perfect... for this.

All Chuzzo and the legionnaires have time for is a QRF to support their defense.

"*Maebad aleayn maebad aleayn maebad aleayn!*" the orc shrieks over and over, again and again, and we know that's the Observatory. It's a small, cracked and ancient tower near a small fallen gate along the south wall, west of the Gates of Eternity. Carvings inside along the walls indicate ancient stellar positions. And there's a big carved eye in the roof. Half the tower is missing. It's high on the walls and if they can break through there, they can take the walls to the west at least as far as Tower Six and get into the Necropolis near the old Legion fort.

"*Maebad aleayn maebad aleayn maebad aleayn!*"

The eye temple the eye temple the eye temple he's screaming over and over, his ragged bloody throat going hoarse so that his voice is nothing but a hissing, pleading, silent scream. The orc screams until his voice doesn't work.

I am convinced. They're hitting the observatory.

I'm already standing. Giving orders.

Yeah. I'm a corporal now. So is Tanner.

I run intel. I'm not with the weapons team anymore. Kurtz's gun team doesn't exist. Anymore.

Tanner and I are with the scouts now.

Soprano and Jabba got folded into Sergeant Rico's section.

We're thin like that now. But Rangers gonna Ranger no matter how much suck.

Things aren't swinging our way on this one.

"Get to Sergeant Thor!" I tell Tanner. This is my show now. "Tell the snipers which way it's comin' and where it's going!" We're the same rank. But... I got the intel.

"I'm going for the Observatory!" I shout at Tanner as I start to move.

"Hardt's got the QRF in that section, Talk. Go there first. I'll task the snipers and head your way."

"Good idea."

Yeah. What the hell am I going to do? Be a one-man quick reaction force? No. I need more guys. We don't have the time to get Sergeant Kang in there with demo. We'll just have to augment the legionnaires trying to hold the Observatory.

That's SOP as determined by the captain.

Our comm is gone now. Hence all the running around and telling the snipers and getting a QRF headed in the right direction.

Enemy sorcery abounds.

"What about him, Talk?" says Tanner, indicating the silent screaming bloody orc chained to the tombstone. Tears and blood running down his face.

Yeah, orcs cry. The Ruin is a cruel place. Just like it always was.

I shuck my Glock and blow his brains all over a tombstone so old with time and the wind that the epitaph has faded, erased whatever was written there by someone who loved someone a long time ago.

I think Tanner said something like, "No, Talk!" just before I did it.

Like he was trying to save my soul from what I was about to do. From where I was headed.

But there isn't time.

And I'm not that guy anymore.

CHAPTER THREE

I ran. I ran fast. As fast as I could, even though I heard the first ululating horns and shouting war cries out there beyond the walls of the orcs coming out of the trenches, intent on continuing their attacks against the main hardpoints, gates and forward walls where we were visibly holding defensive positions.

A new night was coming on and this is where they always hit us along the southern walls. There were no surprises here, this is how their evening mischief started as they tried to breach Sûstagul. Above, swarms of dark-feathered arrows whistled through the upper twilight, arcing just over the walls to fall almost straight down on our side. Enemy spells from their shaman went off like sudden thunderbolts or flares, illuminating the madness surging toward Rangers and legionnaires on the ancient desert walls of the port city.

At the same time, their siege engines, lugged out of the desert sands and assembled near the walls as trench and siege works got underway, strange machines we thought we'd destroyed the night before by the captain's raids, began to sing out as they launched at us. Massive stones, huge, or sometimes shotgun blasts of smaller ones, arced out from there and overhead, smashing into the city behind us.

These were nothing but terror weapons. And it felt like the enemy knew it and did it anyway because they couldn't push us off the walls.

Orc artillery was awful as targeted fire in support of their attacks on the walls. So instead, and you had to give it to them for this, they just hurled huge desert stones into the city itself. Sometimes landing among the graves in the necropolis or smashing into the decrepit old Legion fort looming above this section of the district. Or reaching as far as the marketplace along the eastern edge of Sûstagul where the strange wizards who'd once ruled the city had abandoned their old towers and just disappeared into the east one night. They were all gone save for a few crazies that shambled about, casting spells, telling fortunes, and dying in or near the street battles that erupted when the orcs inevitably broke through and our gun teams repositioned and murdered them. Or the captain dropped some of our precious iron on them.

Or perhaps the pretty ponytailed Air Force co-pilot was on station piloting a drone all the way back from the Forge.

That was becoming rare. Strange things were going on back at FOB Hawthorne. But that was beyond our ability to reconcile, and so the Rangers and Air Force personnel that remained would just need to handle that.

A huge boulder, a seemingly impossible sight, careened overhead through the blue twilight and smashed into some section back near the port. I heard the citizens of Sûstagul screaming as it came in, watching from their roofs and higher towers, screaming like they were on a rollercoaster from the times we came from. Their cries of horror when it landed. I thought of Amira and Aaila and their father, as I always did when death went crashing down inside the city.

Their coffee bar among the portside tents and pavilions, no doubt swollen with rough legionnaires waiting to go for the night missions to save the city. I tried not to think about her. But I saw her face anyway, hopeful and dark, flashing white teeth, a beautiful determined-to-be-happy-no-matter-what smile expecting good to happen at any moment, proud of her teak box of sugar, or what she called *cīnī*. Hindi for sugar, from Kungaloor, wherever that was. I saw her and remembered her father, the small man who worked the hot sand and made the beautiful dark thick syrup of coffee saying, *"It is good we came here, Amira. I still have the magic to seduce. Things will be different here now. Things will be good."*

I knew some of their story in the moments I'd stolen just to sip their brew. She would tell their story and place her long cool hand on mine and that was it. Or at least that's what I told myself. But it was a lie, and it was more and I knew it…

I had no time for that, and I ran for all I was worth and heard my battle rattle and how it could have been tighter, and I should have seen to that. But I'd been too busy beating information out of the orc… losing control… and now gear banged, flopped, and rattled as I carried my MK18 carbine with one hand and ran for all I was worth through the old necropolis south of the Legion fortress with the main southern and western wall intersection ahead.

I'd reach it and go left to find the QRF rally and then move on the Observatory with the intel, knowing the Guzzim Hazadi would hit it soon.

First came the line troops, orcs and siege and archers, coming out of the trenches. Then the Guzzim to exploit some target. Then... the darker forces of the Saur and the tribes of the desert.

Above and ahead a giant bird creature, later I'd find out it was another wyvern night raider, swooped in over the Gates of Eternity and tried to take out the Ranger gun team there. Claws reaching, huge leathery wings like the offspring of the dragon we'd faced reaching for the Rangers there. Soprano and Jabba were acting as the secondary gun team in support of that critical spot.

It could be them this time, my frantic mind screamed as I ran for all I was worth knowing I was about to take the long way, going through the necropolis and moving slow so I didn't break my neck in an open grave. Instead I chose a faster route, one that was more dangerous, as that section hadn't been cleared and we'd already lost one Ranger there.

Chief Rapp was working with the dwarves on exactly how to... and this was their word... *cleanse* the linear danger area we'd identified in our midst.

The *otherworldly linear danger area*.

Reinigen. That was the word the dwarves of Wulfhard had used regarding the LDA we called the Alley. In once-future German, or what the Ruin called Gray Speech, that meant clean, purify, purge.

I could cut that way and get to the QRF rally faster. But like I said, we'd already lost Alvarez in there.

The wyvern screamed above, a dark silhouette in the early night.

At almost the same moment the desert wyvern came out of the twilight, a shadowy mummy rider astride its back, bandages and ragged burial cloak flapping in the night, definitely a Saurian asset, a Ranger Carl G gunner who must have been nearby fired an ADM munition and smoked both rider and wyvern in midair. The round exploded near enough to airborne mount and ride and shotgunned both beast and undead terror in a sudden moment. Even as they went down, their eyes glowed demonically red against the blue twilight and the greater purple dark rising above them. They plummeted in beyond the wall, the wyvern screaming in pain and terror as it fluttered like a broken-winged bird.

Trust me, that is a sound you'll never forget hearing. And... never want to hear again. It stands out above the orc catapults, their roaring screams as they try the wall once again. The two-forties patiently murdering them with effective fields of plunging fire. The thump of the gun, the wet slap of seven-six-two breaking wooden shields and finding hulking bodies to tear apart.

I crossed out of the dangerous necropolis full of open graves, taking the fastest route, and hit the Alley that led straight to the wall ahead where I'd turn left to reach the rally and get the QRF pointed at the Observatory. The Alley wasn't really an alley other than the fact that it looked like one. It was actually just more graveyard, but an area that wasn't *as* dead as the rest of the place. If you know what I mean...

Here were once-notable worthies, high servants of the Saur when the place had been known as the City of Pythons, who'd been buried, or entombed really, along the two walls that formed the Alley in great rotting stacks of badly shaped tombs and rotting scrolls that seemed to spill out from the sealed tombs every night.

Vandahar had indicated, in his typically grand eloquent fashion, "The Saur have seen their Death Priests forward among the hordes. I have no doubt that even at this hour they are conducting their unholy rites to cause the slumbering dead among us to come forth and attack us in our midst."

Tombs there popped like pustulant blisters and spilled ancient rolled papyri all over the bones and stones. In the evening the wraiths came out.

This was danger central and the smaj had advised us to avoid this as a *linear danger area* since it was not uncommon for the dead corpses of the centuries-old priests to suddenly come to life, crawl down into the Alley, and go after anyone passing through.

Strange stuff like this was going on all over the city.

We'd lost PFC Alvarez that way on the first night of the Second Battle for Sûstagul. He'd been sent that way by Sergeant Joe to get the Legion repositioned from the Western Gate and supporting the sudden attack on the Southern Gate. Joe and his platoon were holding the Gates of Eternity as the first of the orc cav, camel riders with smaller goblin archers on the backs of the camels, rushed the gate from the sandy twilight of the desert. At the same time, some kind of invisible force had blasted the gate off its hinges in a sudden violent thunderclap. So, at that moment Joe was holding the gap and burning belts from both gun teams when he sent PFC Alvarez and Rocky to get the Legion shifted from their staging position and over to supporting the gate.

Alvarez was a younger Ranger, not in much before me. Rocky was a corporal in the assaulters who liked to box. Hence everyone calling him Rocky.

Rocky made it out of the Alley. Barely. We didn't know it was dangerous then. Alvarez got pulled into a tomb as a whole section of these tombs suddenly gushed strange ashen-cloaked dead priests, floating and rattling their bones as they hissed spells at him. Each of them had a golden cobra headpiece around its mummy-wrapped head.

Like I said, Rocky barely got out of there alive. We didn't pull Alvarez out of there until the next day after we burned a bunch of the dead priest burial shelves with the thermite we had on hand in order to keep them down and dead. Eventually we found what remained of PFC Alvarez. He looked like a desiccated husk turned into a two-thou-sand-year-old mummy man sucked of what he'd once been.

We dragged him out of there on a collapsible litter at noon, sweating and cold from the otherworldliness of the Alley. Yeah, it's strange in there.

"They drained him," said Kennedy, who was on hand in case anything worse came out of those dark holes along the walls. Our resident wizard and master of possible Ruin lore explained what *draining* meant. "Life force, or levels, just gone in the game. Sometimes aging like what happened to Old Man Sims. Only way you can get it back, if your character still has hit points, is a *Wish* spell."

Sims was there and reminded everyone he was still technically just "twenty-four, guys." No one cared. He'd always just be Old Man Sims now.

I thought of my two wishes from Al Haraq. I'd been thinking of those a lot lately…

For the most part Kennedy had given up adding his standard disclaimer of, "Guys, it was just a game I played. It may not even translate here," to every instance of Ruin lore we tried to get him to download on us in order that we might survive just one more day.

He got tired of everyone telling him, "We know. Get on with what's gonna kill us today, Gandalf!"

And the funny part of this is that later, when the smaj was having one of his blue percolator sessions with Vandahar, and because there was coffee of course I was lurking and listening, the old wizard asked who, or what, a "Gandalf" was.

The smaj gave a rare smile, blew on his coffee a little, and took a sip.

"I fail to see the humorous part, Sergeant Major," said Vandahar, slightly indignant at the chuckle. "You Rangers do seem to have a very grim sense of humor, and so I can only guess that this *Gandalf* is someone you horribly killed, what with your standard Ranger Smash tactics, and that his death has amused you in some way to this very day."

The smaj set his old canteen cup on the small burnt stones of his little fire.

He adjusted himself.

"Negative, Vandahar. It's funny because *you* are basically Gandalf. It's a literary character back where we come from. But... if I was to be makin' a movie here in the Ruin, I'd basically cast you for the part."

"Ah," said Vandahar, musing on his long-stemmed pipe as small smoke rings escaped his mouth. "He was a wizard, you say?"

"Yes," replied the sergeant major.

"And what is a... *movie*? The casting part I get. Sorcery. But I am unfamiliar with the *movie* word."

Even I had to laugh at that.

According to Kennedy's game we had to consecrate Alvarez's body so he didn't become a wraith. So we did. Chief Rapp saw to that.

Now, as I ran down the Alley, full name Alley of the Dead, watching all the shelves stacked with bones, cracked burial chambers, and gaping dark holes for any of the older mummies to crawl out of, I remembered the look of pure suffering and horror that had been carved on Alvarez's frozen older-than-dirt face. He'd been a *swole* Mexican-American Ranger kid who was quiet and smiled a lot. He had a thing for the girls in the port, but he was shy and sometimes I'd see him over there trying to use a few phrases on them. I'd taught him some words and pickup lines in the local Sûstagulian dialect. Which is basically a mix of Arabic, French, and Gray Speech. A lot of desert orc words have worked their way in and occasionally you'll find some Greek and even Chinese once or twice. But such has always been the way of port cities across all times and all over the Ruin.

Or what we once called the world.

Alvarez was content with telling the girls he could get into a conversation, as they went about their tasks of water drawing and washing, that they were beautiful. That was it. That seemed to be his go-to pickup line. And he was content with that and trying it out whenever Joe didn't have him off on some task.

When I remember the dried-out thing the wraiths in the Alley had turned him into, I forced myself to remember the kid carrying some girl's massive water jug in the afternoon near the port. Him telling her over and over how beautiful she was. Still using words from his family Spanish even though they didn't understand them. Calling them "*mi novia*" as he trailed after them. Doing his best. Their smiles he couldn't see. Flattered and knowing they were totally in control. Enjoying it.

Me thinking of Autumn and feeling old.

When I think of Ranger Alvarez I think of those moments.

I ran as fast as I could now and felt *Coldfire* on my assault pack bang against me as I did. I could have been better tightening my gear. But it felt like I'd been running around all day. And every day lately felt like that since the second battle had begun.

Using rounds on the undead was a waste of time. Yes, you could get it done, but running, moving fast, and then nailing the kill shot on a dusty brain-bucket skull, in the night, with no NODs now as batteries were going to the snipers and the gun teams... Even with Chief Rapp's school of legendary gunfighting, my abilities to do this were exceeded.

I'd begun to get better with *Coldfire*.

And honestly... I was starting to get a taste for *Coldfire*. Especially on orcs.

Like... *it made it more personal.* Me telling myself... *Maybe this was one of them.*

Kurtz. Brumm.

I'm a mess. There's too much that needs to get done and too little of me. So... you do dumb stuff and take shortcuts like the one I was taking now because maybe... *just maybe...* someone was gonna make it because I took another risk I couldn't afford. Rolled the dice. Wrote checks I could only cash in death.

The sick feeling knowing all this... and doing it anyway.

"Worth... it..." I grunted and ran faster because speed was life now in the Alley. They may be otherworldly undead... but they ain't fast.

Bones rattled all around me as I moved as fast as I could, seeming to come to life in their dusty alcoves. But like I said, I was moving too fast.

I placed my hand on the dead SEAL's sword, *Coldfire*, grasping the wrapped hilt as I moved. I had the ring too. Verdict was still out on whether the dead could see invisible stuff or not. Listening to Kennedy debate this with Rangers just getting acquainted with the rules of his game made my brain hurt. And I wasn't the only one.

In the distance, as I ran down the Alley as fast as I could, the gun teams opened fire at the main gate. The orcs had crossed the fifty-meter line there. They were pushing and it was do-or-die time. But I was headed somewhere else tonight. Where the real battle would be and only Tanner and I knew it. The snipers would be able to support it faster. But the QRF team would make the difference for legionnaires forming up to hold the Observatory.

I made the end of the Alley, turned to check my six, and saw three dark-cloaked specters, their shadowy forms ragged and floating, coming down the Alley slowly toward me.

There was nothing I could do about that. I was ahead of them now and they generally stayed here in the Alley. "Past behavior is a predictor of future performance," I said to myself like some bizarre life skills coach for all the madness of the Ruin. But that's how I Ranger. I constantly chant everything I've learned regarding every Ranger task, skill, and piece of data in order to do my job and keep as many Rangers alive as I can by doing my small part in all this. Yeah, I coulda been a natural at this stuff, but I'd seen naturals, great Rangers, get straight-up smoked just like anyone else by stray arrows in the night and the surf. Like that kid when we hit the mermaid tower. Arrow right through the throat. Every NCO said he was the best Ranger they'd seen in a long time. That he was going to be a great one.

I think about that. A lot.

Kurtz.

Brumm.

Tanner says I think too much now.

I moved on fast, running alongside the great southern wall of Sûstagul now, racing for the quick reaction force rally point just ahead on the other side of the abandoned section of the city.

Everything along the walls and near the necropolis is abandoned.

I gave one last check back on the wraiths at the next turn, even though I didn't need to, where the crumbling old houses and buildings that had once been the merchants of this abandoned quarter had stacked themselves along the wall.

They usually stayed right here. In the Alley. But...

The three specters weren't staying put tonight. They were following me. Slowly, but steadily. And now that I think about it that had to have freaked me out on some level. Three floating... dead things... just following you like some movie serial killer. But that, as a Ranger, wasn't what I was thinking. What I was thinking was that now they were my problem if only because I'd somehow activated them, and they were now in our lines and moving around. Which could be a real problem for some other Rangers if they were suddenly attacked from the rear while fighting the orcs on the wall.

So, I had to solve them.

Because all problems are now my problems since if you don't solve problems, they people get killed.

I stopped, breathing heavily, and got my one grenade off my rig. I checked what I could see of the Observatory that I needed to reach with a QRF, high and alone on the twisting wall. I pulled the pin, waited for the floating wraiths to get closer, and whispered "Frag out" as I practically rolled it at them, thinking, *Time to cleanse the negative attitudes.* This was pure Tanner because he says this same thing practically every time we use a grenade in non-dire circumstances.

And yes, there are times when you aren't necessarily using grenades to save you or your buddies. Sometimes you're just tossing them into "a bunker" that others in the Ruin might call a tomb, or maybe a den, or just a danger area, to make sure anything harmful can't come out and jam your *chi* while you get your Ranger Smash on. In these times Tanner will laugh, which is now, as a becoming-undead thing, more like a Halloween Frankenstein croak, and say, "Sometimes you gotta just let go and cleanse the negativity all around you, Talk." Then he pops the spoon and tosses the frag in.

And it's funny.

First time I ever heard it I almost threw up I laughed so hard. Like heaving and gasping laughing.

How do I know I'm a Ranger now? Because that's funny to me.

I tossed the frag, timing out three seconds, covering in an old doorway that had once been someone's home as I did so.

The blast rocked the area, and I was instantly aware that the building I was covering in was so desert-sucked rickety that it could come down with me inside. Dust and spiders rained down on my gear in the explosive aftermath as I popped out and checked the detonation site and what had become of my wraiths.

Scraps of blasted cloaks and ruined bones lay everywhere, shattered along the desert stone set long ago by ancient builders.

They were done and I had no time for anything else, so I was on the move for the QRF rally and the Observatory once again. As fast as I could hustle.

Ten seconds later… indirect fire arrows were raining down all across the Alley and I instinctively hunched, continued forward because "mission," and tried to use my bulging assault pack as a shield. An arrow slammed down from above, thick and heavy, penetrated my CamelBak and sent warm water all over me as I duckwalked forward.

That would be a problem for most guys.

No water for the night.

I on the other hand had two canteens of cold brew from Amira, and Kungaloorian sugar, so in Talker rationale I was *just fine*.

I could hit the fountains and wells back in the city center at dawn when the orcs and darker Saurian forces faded at daylight.

The arrow storm stopped, and I ran. I ran for all I was worth as incoming siege-engine-hurled stones didn't pass overhead and instead began to slam directly into the upper portions of the wall, knocking great sections of brick and ancient mortar loose. Sending all those sunburnt bricks cascading down into the narrow street I was running along.

Huge clouds of dust blossomed and billowed, and I waved them away, pushing myself forward and through.

I knew I should stop there. Cover for a moment. But *I couldn't* and I tried to find my way through in the dust and the broken brick, seeing phantoms that weren't there within it suddenly coming for me, finding my way forward and blocked by a wall that shouldn't be there if I had my bearings right.

I pushed forward, climbed over crushed building and shattered rock, and found the other side of the debris pile and a street, small, that I'd never taken before. But I knew the QRF rally point was just ahead and so I ran, ignoring the singing other-side-of-the-wall *twang*s and heaving thunder above as siege engines beyond the walls tossed more Bronze Age artillery into the city. Or the whistling chorus of arrows coming in. Or the hiss of their flights. Or the *thunk*s and shatterings as they splintered all over the walls all around me and I just kept running, rifle pulling me forward, sure I was losing gear along the way.

I slipped, turned an ankle and told myself it was bad, hobbled forward and ran more ignoring real pain. Ahead, I saw the ChemLights the QRF marked its position on the line with and the shadows of three lean and mean Rangers, and Sergeant Monroe, obvious by the hulking shape and wide curling horns of the minotaur-revealing the Ruin had done to him.

The sixty on his back. His axe in his hands.

"They're hitting the Observatory!" I gasped, sliding onto my knees. Fumbling for my cold brew, telling myself it was just for hydration and to get the tomb and brick dust out of my mouth. Knowing I'd never spit it out.

That I'd swallow it.

Where was the two-squad QRF?

Or Hardt's scouts?

"On your feet, Talker," rumbled the Ranger minotaur sergeant. "We'll move on Observatory to support with pickups. Hardt and the captain went out early. It's just us."

CHAPTER FOUR

ORC artillery—don't get all excited, it's just their siege catapults out there in the trenchworks of desert and sand dune—began to range the Gates of Eternity off to the east of our current position as the QRF got itself strapped for the counterattack on the Guzzim surprise attack.

Yeah, the orcs had Rangers, but we were gonna see who Rangered harder and surprise-ier. And that's not even a word.

I get that.

Don't @ me. I'm working on two hours, at best, sleep, and a whole bunch of coffee. I'm beginning to smell colors and see atoms vibrating.

And I'm fine with that.

This was standard for this battle so far. The orc artillery, the feints, the surprise attacks by their "Rangers." The desert orcs and their khans always attacked in the same manner every dusk. Throw everything they had at some point along the walls, get cut to shreds by our gun teams and snipers, or slaughtered by Accadion spear forming in the gaps, then leave piles of their dead, pull back, possibly maybe hold some portion of the wall we'd spend the next morning dislodging them from with extreme violence of action, then do it all again come nightfall.

Or as Tanner liked to put it, "One more time, Rangers, but with feeling this time." Like he was some hack stage director of the most violent community theater production of *War and Peace* ever put on.

Meanwhile, their "Rangers," the Guzzim Hazadi, hit their selected target that night, hoping we'd committed everything we had to the main assault when it came at some other place. It was smart on their part, and it probably worked against Not-Rangers, like every Accadion Legion who'd ever tried the deserts of the south and disappeared like the Ninth Legion had. Unfortunately for them, we were actual Rangers, and this is something we totally would have done ourselves.

So we were wise as bubble eyes to what the Guzzim were pulling, and we had our own tricks to play on them. And if it was anything that kept the Rangers interested in the battle, other than their sheer determination to find more suck and embrace it so they could show who was who in the *I'm the Biggest Baddest Ranger* competition of all time, it was their mischievousness at thinking up new things to destroy the Guzzim surprise attacks.

This game, that battle, even dislodged *Ranger Dead Orc Toss on the Objective*, which had been the reigning favorite everywhere we'd laid waste and conducted slaughter. Don't get me wrong, *Dead Orc Toss* was still the game that got played every day and never seemed to bore. I even won once. But *Ruin the Guzzim's Surprise Attack* was the latest *Call of Duty* drop, back in the world we came from.

Ten thousand years ago.

So the Rangers dedicated much time to getting inventive about Violence of Action.

The SF operator had thoughts on this, and in his own pleasant way, he made them known.

"Surprise, Ranger Smash!" Chief Rapp liked to chuckle every time he sat in on the day's planning of malevolent Ranger fun and games.

Our plans to harm the enemy surprise attacks seemed to give the jacked SF operator endless delight every time any one of our plans invariably failed to deviate from that constant theme of "Surprise, Ranger Smash!" In hindsight, when I think about it, at times, he was, in his own affable way, challenging us to make sure we weren't getting complicit and teaching the enemy exactly how we fought every night. This was after all his specialty as an SF operator, since besides being a field-surgeon-grade medic, he did doctrine warfare and planning for the Green Beret A-Teams.

Green Berets are, at heart, trainers. And they challenge the units they fight alongside to up their game, be them indigs with basic weapons, communication, and medicine, to highly trained special operations units like Rangers.

A Green Beret is always a combat multiplier in the deadly math of war. And what they say, whether barked or softly spoken, should be listened to. The Rangers knew that, and soon it became another game to try and not just meet the chief's expectations for planning mayhem and violence but exceed them.

Because of course… Rangers.

The small unit leaders of the Ranger detachment knew this well, and whenever they approached the "War Council," which is what we called the morning brief at the command post with the captain and the smaj, they'd set themselves thinking up some new way of doing what needed to be done the next night to defeat the orc hordes and keep the massing Saur out there in the desert from taking our walls. And as I said, invariably they failed and simply came up with increasingly elaborate plans that were still, in essence: *Surprise, Ranger Smash!*

Rangers love to hit and fade.

But pinned down in a desert city, you had to hold for a number of reasons. You couldn't fade. You had to hit and hold. We had to hit and push.

And AAR'ing all of us here in the warts and all that is my journal, we struggled with that. Yes, many times I am their biggest fan. But Rangers aren't fans, and *I are one now.* Rangers are brutally, relentlessly, honest. And that's what makes them modern Spartans in ways many are not.

Never shall I fail my comrades. I will always keep myself mentally alert, physically strong, and morally straight, and I will shoulder more than my share of the task, whatever it may be, one hundred percent and then some.

It's that *morally straight* part that sergeants like Chris will deliver short, terse lectures about on the *integrity of communication* to younger Rangers.

"Lie to everyone else if you like. Never lie to another Ranger. Because every Ranger's life depends on the facts of the situation we find ourselves in," he has said to me and others before.

Then he'll spit some dip into a bottle, looking you in the eye the whole time like he's driving a sharp blade into your brain, slicing away all your weakness and leaving a scar tattooed with that lesson on that specific part of the creed. And he'll nod because something *clicked* inside your switch and you get it, believe it, and will do it, or he, or the ghost of Sergeant Chris, will come make you pay for ever forgetting it.

May I digress here more than I already have…

I sucked at my cold brew right there in the middle of the quick reaction force rally point for that section of the wall as I set myself and my gear up for the attack to support the Observatory the Accadion spear were holding. We had time still. We didn't attack until the orcs made their "surprise" attack. Right now, the orcs were still hitting the main gate off to the east and leaving their dead everywhere the two-forty teams chose to lay the hate there in the killing sands. "Never mind our dead," the orcs seemed to roar out there, "this is where we're really attacking tonight!"

But here's my digression. We, the Ranger detachment, were coming apart at the seams. We'd crossed the entire Med, or the Great Inner Sea as the Ruin calls it, on foot, fighting a running battle most of the way. The walls we'd just got behind after the first battle of Sûstagul, walls being the thing that separate the living from the dead in the world that has become the Ruin, had depleted our resources and left us with a lot of wounded.

And that's what we thought as a fighting unit. Get behind the walls, get safe. Reload, rest, go out and kill some more. We were here, after all, to run that strike on our high-value target… Mummy, or what the denizens and citizens of the Ruin call Sût the Undying, Lich Lord of the Saur Pharaohs.

No problem, we'd already smoked one lich back during our fight with the army of the dead east of FOB Hawthorne. Side note… apparently Sût was the Supreme Lich of all liches. Or, as one of the Rangers put it when we got the brief on the HVT from Vandahar on our soon-to-be-dead jackpot, "So, this Sût… he's like Andre the Giant if all the other liches were just Mexican midget wrestlers and all?"

Vandahar's only response was a very serious, "He is not a giant, if that's what you are implying. And I have no idea what a *midget* or *a Mexican* is. Some kind of horrible monster with big fangs I suspect. Sût the Undying has no known equal in his necromantic craft. His powers are... *quite formidable.* Some say he is as old as the Ruin itself and was perhaps one from your days... if that can be believed. But I do not know if this is true. I do know he is not a giant. And probably not those other things you mentioned which sound very silly and made-up. *Mexican.* Perhaps you are... as you Rangers say... perhaps you are just *messing with me?* Silly old wizard that I am. I warn you, I could turn you all into toads if I so chose. Tread carefully, little Rangers. Old men and wizards exist because they have survived many young dead men, and much treachery in general."

So, as I was saying, we're a mess. As a fighting unit, that is. We've broken down into skeletons of teams, barely squads at times, and our mission nonetheless is to be every-where, all the time, supporting the Accadion defense of the walls of the city we barely hold.

"We're a hatchet force now," the smaj told the NCOs during a briefing. "You boys who've studied 'Nam, you know this is part and parcel of how we became Rangers back in the day. Back then we were just division scouts. SF before it was SF was called MACV-SOG. They'd take large units of indigs usually classified as Rangers, who'd come out of our Recondo School, and lead them into the bush on what amounted to little more than suicide raids deep into enemy territory. Groups of sometimes maybe two hundred Rangers engaging entire divisions of the enemy. You wanna talk about studs, that was them back in the day, and we're deeper than they ever got and still stacking.

The one thing they were doing that we can't, is they were mobile, on the move, and fighting running battles for days at a time. Unfortunately for us, here, we gotta hold these walls no matter what, and transition to leading our indigs to hold those walls. And these Accadion legionnaires, they may talk funny and look real *purty* in their shiny armor and all, but believe me, they're as lifetaker as they come.

"So you are, and this is no surprise to Rangers, leaders now. There's too few of us to get this done the way we normally do it. And what the chief is doing when he challenges our planning, is getting us to think Bronze Age warfare like it gets done here in this Ruin. Which ain't necessarily our kind of warfare. But it is now. We'll be back on mission and doing what we do better than anyone else when we see clear of this hot mess and get our hit on Mummy down in that big ol' pyramid of his he's quakin' in. But right now, we're fightin' a fixed battle like something out of the Civil War and we ain't got the numbers to hold all by ourselves. So we gotta lead hatchet forces of the indigs and understand how they fight, hold ground, and push the enemy off into the desert to die badly of the gut wound we gave him for his troubles."

The sergeant major looked around at every Ranger there, checking in with all his sergeants. So that's where Sergeant Chris got that from.

And me too for some reason. Oh yeah… *I are Ranger.*

"But we're still gonna do our thing," the sergeant major continued. "And we just need to know their thing, how they do it, to get it done with maximum violence. Yeah, we can let them take some wall in the dark. But by daylight we're gonna creep back in there when these forces o' darkness seem to be at their weakest and cut their throats and tomahawk their skulls wide open or Robert Rogers never lived. We are gonna do that, Rangers. And when the battle's thick, we fix 'em in place with those spear units the Accadions are forming up, like a chokehold… and then we lead the QRFs in fast and cut the enemy bicep so he can't hold on to us and all he's got is a chance to flee. And *then* we're gonna let them run back into the desert to die out there. Badly. Gun teams will get them on the way out, or Thor and his boys will red mist some skulls at distance to put the fear of skilled marksmanship in them. Either way, it's still hit and fade, but different. We hit, *they* fade this time.

"And that's what the chief is trying to get us to do now, Rangers, with all that Green Beanie big brain planning they do. Chief Rapp is trying to get us to understand that most military fighting units don't have the luxury… of bein' *Rangers.* Ain't that the truth. Fighting where you didn't expect us to be. Most soldiers throughout history didn't get that luxury. Most guys out there on the line for all times known, go where they're told to go, stand there in full view of the enemy, drive down some dirt road filled with IEDs, hold a watch on a wall, or at some lost crossroads, and know the enemy knows they're exactly right there. And believe me, even if they are dirty legs, takes a certain kinda real live stud to get into a fight the other guy's totally ready for the time and place on. Ask them Stryker boys back in the 'stan about it some time. But hell, that was ten thousand years ago, and an old man forgets a thing or two never mind the ten thousand years between then and now."

He held the stump of his missing hand up and rubbed his cheek with it, a faraway look in his eyes for a moment as he went somewhere, or when, else.

"We're still Rangers. You find yourself in a fair fight… then your tactics suck, Ranger. Get good."

And then the smaj was done, and it was up to us to know if we had attended and known wisdom. Or if we'd die with our skulls cleaved in by an orc scimitar out there along the wall.

I reconcile all that with where I found myself as QRF Feelgood rolled on the Observatory to effect a counterattack against an imminent "enemy Ranger" attack. I got my gear tight for the fight, sucked the last of the cold brew, and made sure I had loaded mags. I knew I did, but lately it was easy to forget some things with little sleep, too much adrenaline, and… Brumm and Kurtz needing to be avenged.

And no more Kurtzes or Brumms. Not if I could help it.

If it was only that… yeah. But shortly the stakes, or my participation in the stakes, would get upped. And suddenly I felt that sick feeling in my stomach that always seemed to be writ large over Captain Knife Hand's face.

Like you ate something that ain't sittin' well.

Of course Sergeant Monroe, our fully jacked minotaur who carried a huge double-bladed battle axe and strapped a specially modded M60 E3 with a belt ready to go and two belts around his immense traps and shoulders, would tag our QRF as *Feelgood*. As in "Dr. Feelgood," the Mötley Crüe song. He jams old-school metal when he stacks plates and gets swole, as the Rangers say. *Stacking plates* in the Ruin is just mainly lifting heavy things he can get his workout on with. Not a lotta gyms in the Ruin so far.

But hopes were high.

Stacking plates seems to be squatting impossible amounts with heavy things he finds on, or near, the battlefield. This is another Ranger game, but not as popular as *Toss the Dead Orc*.

I kid you not, though, he does it. I heard he squatted a dead orc captain that must have had some eastern hill giant in him. In ornate battle armor, the dead orc chieftain, taken out near the Gates of Death during an enemy night raid against the dwarven sappers trying to construct the airfield, must've been approaching eight hundred pounds in weight. Sergeant Monroe squatted it just to see if he could the day after the battle where he'd personally led the QRF that killed it and its six bodyguards.

Most of the bodyguards were wiped out by an MPIMS claymore. Then it was hand-to-hand as the gun teams were busy with Guzzim Hazadi slavers who were driving a herd of cockatrices into the dwarven trenches and got prioritized as urgent targets because Kennedy had worked with Hardt's recon in identifying the approaching monsters. Apparently a cockatrice bite can turn you into stone. They look like a weird amalgamation of a lizard, a bird, and a bat. Dead, I thought they looked like giant roosters bloating in the desert sun. Kennedy had to burn them with his dragon-breathed staff as we couldn't take the chance of touching them.

Back to the QRF I'm about to participate in...

It's good to be going in with Sergeant Monroe. It's hard to tell which one has become the detachment murder machine: Thor or Monroe. The minotaur Ranger sergeant gets more opportunities, as Sergeant Thor has to run the snipers up in the old fortress battlements. But Thor did get that god in the old temple we burned after the first battle of Sûstagul.

Then there's Otoro, the samurai gorilla. But we'll get into that later. He is death incarnate with those two massive samurai swords. Plus, he's an eight-hundred-pound humanoid gorilla who can tear your throat out with his fangs or just pull your arms off your torso no matter how jacked you are as an orc.

He is... a whole other thing for the detachment.

So like I said, it's good to be going in with Monroe on the QRF. He's a competent Ranger, an excellent NCO, a total cold-blooded killer, and... he promptly offloads the sixty on me and says, "Gym Fail, Corporal. You're running the QRF this time. Take lead, set up a base of fire with the pig once we're in. Suppress their flank and then hold their edge of the Accadion line so they don't get rolled up."

I say nothing because this is an order. I just take the sixty's weight, the two other belts around my shoulders. Like they say at Kurtz's Ranger School—hey, two-time survivor here—I got me some shoulders. But I am already carrying a lot tonight and so some has to stay here at the rally. I ditch the carbine, but I keep *Coldfire* for the up close and personal it always becomes lately.

"Hardt got retasked by the captain, otherwise they'd be handling the QRF," says Monroe as he hefts his thick double-bladed battle axe and begins to flex like he's Conan the Barbarian or something. "So I had to get Feelgood together to pick up the slack until they get back inside the wire tomorrow morning. Captain spotted a high-value asset he wants to knock out ASAP, so they went Reaper."

The other three Rangers going in with us are Gill, Specialist White, and PFC Dylan. Specialist Commons, you may remember, ran screaming "I got bit!" from the water when we came ashore against the medusa's tower, and is now known by every Ranger, the dwarves, and various others who've attached themselves to our show, simply as "Gill."

You can guess why.

He has gills now. He can breathe underwater. Yeah, he got bit, and there was something in the mermaid's... let's call it *venom*... that turned him into a merman. The question now is—and there's serious Ranger currency, dip and good knives, riding on this—whether he's gonna grow a mermaid tail as the Ruin keeps doing its... *revealing*.

Rangers will ask him, "Grow that tail yet, Gill? I got two cans on it, man. Get a hustle on. Dip ain't cheap these days now that the Forge is on the other side of the world."

"I'm not growing a tail!" Gill will shout back. Fuming and stomping off, his worn boots caked with dust because he has to be in and out of the water so much.

For now, gills have appeared just under his jaw and along his long neck. And to boot, tiny translucent scales are starting to flake off of him when he's been out of the water too long.

It's hilarious and horrifying if you think about it too much. But hey, what can you do but laugh about what's become of us.

If they knew what was going on with my mind, the psionics... I'm sure the names would be hilarious, and I'd hate them. So... for once Talker keeps his mouth shut when he has a headache and can see pictures of what people are thinking.

And that's not always as fun as you'd think it is. Especially if one of the local girls has just walked by with hips swaying and a clay jar filled with water atop her pretty head.

Rangers gonna Ranger. Know what I mean?

During the long march across the desert of North Africa, or what the map calls No Man's Land, east of the Lands of Sût the Undying, we mainly clung to the shore to keep the various monster tribes, orcs, and the occasional sand kraken out hunting, off our backs. There were dangers in the shallow waters, too, so we had to be careful from both sides and sometimes it felt like threading a needle or walking a tightrope. But during those long marches, Gill, or Specialist Commons as he was once known and is never to be known as again, was able to get wet, and along the way he learned the arts of combat diving from many of the Rangers, and from Chief Rapp, who'd attended actual US Army Combat Diver School. And then when we took Sûstagul, working with Monroe's merkids, Gill was able to run amok inside the shallow translucent aquamarine harbor waters, get explosives on the ships we'd tagged as problems, and hole other ships with a trident version of the Ranger shank Sergeant Kang had put together for him.

Gill will often say, posing with the trident, "You know you guys could call me something cool like... Aquaman, I don't know?"

As if he'd casually thought of that tag just in that moment. Not carefully selected in advance at all.

But of course... that's not gonna happen.

Now that the battle was south of Sûstagul, in the seemingly endless deserts of the Land of Black Sleep, the port wasn't a priority as the Accadions were now running naval operations there. Commons, I mean Gill, did daily patrols through the waters and noted the various denizens: mainly sahuagin tribes and their two-headed sharks like hunting dogs, plus a coven of sea hags who'd been swimming close and trying to cast witcheries on the harbor waters and the Accadion triple-decker galleys and crew. But that wasn't the worst to be had there in the deeps of the shore of the port. Beyond the shallow waters of the harbor, there were old sunken ruins within sight of the city. Gill said they were like an ancient Greek temple or something. But even weirder, there were these things out there and, the way they were described by Gill, Kennedy said made them most likely something called "kraken priests." And if they were anything like what was in his game then that was bad because those things worshipped something called...

"The Horrors of the Deep."

"What's a Horrors of the Deep, Specialist?" the smaj had asked our junior enlisted wizard in his typical stoic you-couldn't-tell-if-he-believed-half-this-stuff-or-not way. "And why is it," emphasis on *it*, "pluralized, Ranger?"

See, that's what our senior-most NCO did, and if there was anything I wanted to learn from him it was that. He paid attention to everything, even the details your mind glossed over because even more fantastic things had been mentioned, or your mind just made assumptions about while missing the buried treasure. You see, I would have chalked up the pluralization of *Horrors of the Deep* as merely Kennedy using slang as many young kids often do in pluralizing things.

The smaj did not. He caught it. And now he wanted a good look at it.

Kennedy cleared his throat readying an answer and expecting to get busy digging slit trenches for the latrines.

"Hard to say, Sergeant Major..."

Yes, his voice cracked.

The smaj hated when Kennedy did that—you know, answered—and he gave his standard look that said he would murder Kennedy later that night... *and get away with it.* But to be fair, the smaj looks that way most of the time. Still, Kennedy got the message and got busy with an actual answer with actionable information in it.

"Mind control beings, Sergeant Major, like that aboleth we ran into back in the swamps. Very powerful creatures that make slaves out of many beings at a time, and may have access to..."

Again he cleared his throat, and I'd learned this was a Kennedy tell when he was gonna lay something totally unbelievable on you, but you had to believe it if you were gonna even have a chance at surviving the Ruin. Even Kennedy didn't want to believe half the stuff we'd run into out here ten thousand years later.

And he'd played the home version of the game!

"... like... uh... things from... the Outer Dark... Sergeant Major."

Total silence.

If the smaj had shucked my Glock and just drilled Kennedy right in the skull with his remaining hand I would not have been surprised.

Instead, the smaj just went "Humph..."

Then...

"Like Lovecraft stuff, PFC."

Kennedy nodded, and before he could stop himself, incredibly and fatally, he actually corrected the sergeant major on his rank.

"Specialist, Sergeant Major," said Kennedy timidly.

Mic drop.

"Yeah," muttered the smaj. "We'll see about that."

CHAPTER FIVE

SO that's where we're at as I get ready to lead a QRF into a hot battle. We are wounded, falling apart, having to adapt to a battle we didn't necessarily want to fight, and determined to come out the survivors anyway.

Ranger gonna Ranger.

Are you new here or something?

My time in the Rangers had taught me this was every day. And that there was no easy day. Ever. And yeah, as I took charge of the QRF, I wasn't thinking about the linguist who'd shown up at the last second trying to collect a meaningless merit badge, to show Sidra or whoever it was I was trying to prove myself to, that I was worth more than I'd been appraised at.

No.

At that moment as the desert wind came moaning through the cracked and broken walls of the rotting desert city, as Bronze Age arty streaked overhead and into the city, or sometimes smashed into the walls, I was thinking about Operations. And Leadership. Specifically, taking control of a small unit about to move on the fly to change the course of a battle that had already been predetermined by the enemy.

This is pure Ranger School stuff. And yeah, for all of Kurtz's abuse and endless torture in the biting insect swamps and the sides of the nasty climbs he could find, he'd drilled Operations and Leadership into us along with the other instructors. So here I was, I'd been ordered by a Ranger sergeant to take command of a small QRF and lead it right into the developing battle against enemy "Rangers" who just happened to be black-cloaked cutthroat orcs who could scale walls effortlessly and cut throats just as easily. That's all.

No big deal, right?

Or, as Sergeant Joe says, "It's just Tuesday, because Monday is already a day in the rearview and I'm on the way to Friday!"

Then why are my hands shaking as I hold the cold brew?

I drain the last of it, ditch what gear I can't hump with the sixty, and get my procedures organized in my mind for taking command of the QRF. Stuff I learned from the well-thumbed, dog-eared Ranger handbook dangling from a length of five-fifty dummy cord I'd gotten real serious about in Ranger School, and deadly serious about after Joe tabbed me.

I stopped. Reminded myself I knew this from both sides of the equation.

Now just do that, I told myself and my hands got steady as I slid my threadbare assault gloves back on. Or maybe they just covered the shaking.

I'd received the order from Sergeant Monroe. Now give the order to the QRF.

But first…

Now is a great time to have a word about Sergeant Monroe, the uber-jacked minotaur Ranger thumbing the edge of his bright shining battle axe.

For purposes of the account. Warts and all. And sometimes... it's other people's warts. And all.

Sergeant Monroe, the jacked minotaur Ranger who'd once been known as the Batt Squat King back in the world ten thousand years ago, had acquired a taste for battle. Specifically, hand-to-hand combat with Ruin-local weapons. Or what we Rangers affectionately called *pickups*. Just like lifetakers and heartbreakers from our modern wars a long time ago went dry on ammo, Winchester, and picked up the AKs of the dead to use against their former owners' allies and close friends. "Hey, that's war. It comes at ya fast," says Tanner. "Guy got up that morning never thinking he'd get killed by his best friend's weapon, but hey... surprise, surprise. Better he than me, Talk. Always better that way when the other guy gets dead, and you get to go home. Always. Every time."

Pickups in the Ruin are the same, but different. Of course. Rangers now had swords, axes, knives, and even the occasional spear they'd taken off their victims or found among the treasure hoards we'd sacked along the way from there to here.

Then three steps happened to making the found weapon the Ranger's pickup for use going forward.

I'll explain.

Of course, the Rangers had their beloved tomahawks. And they are, as I have mentioned before, also conscious of knives of all kinds like no one you've ever met in your entire life. Even lifers in prison would be like, "Whoa, you Rangers do like your sharp stabby things. You guys got probs."

Understatement.

But hey, we were going *Lord of the Rings* here, or Kennedy's little game of dice and paper, monsters and Bronze

Age basements, your mileage may vary. So of *course* we were going to use the scroll-worked battle axes, spears that sparked lighting when struck against enemy armor, or swords that glowed when the enemy was near, a soft blue usually, brighter as the enemy got closer even though Sergeant Chris had a fit about noise and light discipline and forbade their usage among his platoon. Still, they were cool weapons to have. Imagine running through some gibbering horror with a light medieval lightsaber, sorta. And there were other weapons. Monroe's axe. *Coldfire,* which I'd taken off the dead SEAL.

Still, not every weapon was magical. Some were just well made and looked pretty cool in that Ruin epic fantasy kinda way. And now that Forge resupply was getting trickier and trickier due to the fact that our Forge was in France and we were in Egypt, or the Savage Lands and the Lands of Sût the Undying, respectively, our carbines, sidearms, and light machine guns were beginning to break down from overuse and probably the last gasps of the nano-plague that had forced us through the QST gate.

Carbines, sidearms, and light machine guns, these are the stock and trade of Ranger units. These deal death violently at the small unit level, and the Rangers are pure street dealers of the most dangerous kind of that drug. But Rangers are ready to get it on without these things even so. They train hard on combatives, on pickups back in the world, haji AKs or whatever. In the Ruin, it's scimitars and bows. Swords and battle axes.

Like ya do.

So, the three steps toward making your own pickup… yours.

First, the Ranger finds a pickup he wants to make his own. Sword, bow, spear, mace, axe. Other weirder weapons we've run into. He then immediately seeks someone in the unit who's trained on this type of weapon or something similar. No matter how weird, someone is usually to be found. Again, the Rangers study causing death like it's a bodily function, so this is easier than you'd think. Then the Ranger heads off to Kennedy, or Vandahar if Kennedy doesn't give them the answer they like, usually convinced the weapon they took off that dead orc chieftain, lizard man shaman, troll tank, or asymmetrical shadow wraith operator that came out of the undisturbed grave, is indeed magical.

Rangers, for all their practical stoicism, are always convinced they've found a weapon of great power. Fifty percent of the time they'll want to know if their new sword they pried out of some dead lizard man's claw has a vampire or some horrible creature embedded in it and how they can make it do their bidding, and the powers they'll get from it.

They get excited about this.

Our wizards, Kennedy and Vandahar, run spells that inquire of the great arcane, or whatever, regarding the magical properties of said weapon. More often than not, the very cool—and to Rangers "cool" means deadly and wicked-looking—weapon is not actually magical, in fact.

Bummer. But not a deal-killer for the Ranger. After all, it looks cool. Read: *wicked and deadly*. Especially if they're younger.

That's step two: deal with your magic weapon.

It's actually better that it *isn't* magical or special, if you've decided you want to make this weapon your pickup, the one you'll be relying on when it's Winchester on mags and the enemy is close and looking to tangle with sharp sticks. See, magic is dangerous.

Vandahar and Kennedy can tell you if it's magical. Sure. But telling you what it does, if the effects are positive or negative, is a whole other thing. It involves a series of tests. Vandahar usually takes charge at this point in the investigations as this surpasses Kennedy's apprentice skill level as a hedge wizard, or fledgling wizard, or whatever he is at this point. And, I have noted, at this point Vandahar gets real serious about his job.

Meaning he doesn't blow smoke rings and talk about lore and *the nature of things,* or what the Rangers will call *boring stuff.*

At this point Vandahar wants to know what the magic is in the item the Ranger has found, and if it's gonna cause general or specific harm.

That's a good thing for us. Generally and specifically.

A lot of times the weapons are what Kennedy calls *cursed.* Surprisingly more often than you'd think. But then when you think about it, the guy using it did die at your hands, so maybe that's not all that hard to believe. Cursed as in you can never hit. Or maybe the thing will make you feel tired when you use it and slowly sap your "life force." Vandahar's words.

And worse. Curses can be much, much worse.

Those cursed weapons get tossed in the nearest river, bog, or swamp. Some Rangers want to save them and find a way to get them into the hands of the enemy, but the plans become too elaborate and there just aren't the resources. Again, despite the brilliance of the concept, it will still end in, "And then Surprise, Ranger Smash!"

Cue Chief Rapp's gentle chuckle.

So. Before we get to the good weapons, the ones that smite extra hard, or make your opponent catch on fire— more hilarious than you would think—or spread frostbite all across the strike area even here in the desert...

... and yes, I have asked the guy over in Joe's platoon to use his frost axe to make my cold brews... colder.

You would too.

Don't @ me. I'm doing my best.

So, before we get to those cool weapons, wicked and deadly, we have to discuss the weird ones. Like...

Soprano's *Dagger of Giggling*.

It's a weird blade, short and stubby, almost like a small samurai sword, or what some have called a *tanto* although other Rangers who know better say that's a made-up word and then they use the real Japanese word.

But it's like that, and it has a handle instead of a grip or pommel. Like *Coldfire* does. A normal sword. Soprano's weird dagger is more like a tool you'd use to turn something off. The handle is more like a T-bar than a hilt.

You'd think it wouldn't do anything but make a small and not very deep cut. Which it does, by the way. Soprano even took some cracked plates—and by the way, all our plates are cracked or useless—and went straight through them "like buttah," he exclaimed joyously in Mario *voce*.

Again, we need resupply.

Still, you'd think Soprano's blade wouldn't do anything much it's so small. Then you'd find out why Vandahar exclaimed, upon magical investigation of the weird item, "Ahhhh... this is indeed a Dagger of Giggling!"

"What's-a that?" Soprano asked in his Italian-American wise-guy voice. Not his Mario voice.

Then Vandahar swiftly and deftly pricked Soprano in the arm with the blade and Soprano laughed for thirty minutes nonstop.

Funny at first. Then when he began to cry, still laughing hysterically, his eyes pleading for us to help him stop, it was downright hilarious. Eventually he started gasping and Chief Rapp was summoned. Running Under the Moon followed the SF operator, her huge aid bag banging against her slender form and the Crye Precisions that swallowed her delicate frame.

"There's nothing you can do, Cleric," stated Vandahar from his seat on a cracked stone above Soprano's hysteria. Smoke rings rising from his long-stemmed pipe. "This Ranger has been pricked by one of the fabled laughing blades of the Circus of Death, in the black heart of Parvaim, deep in the Eastern Waystes of the Silent Desert. The effect will stop soon, and he will live. But now he knows what the blade does. And now that he knows... he knows what to be wary of, which is the best way to teach a weapon of such power to its wielder. Trust me, I have much knowledge in this area."

Chief Rapp therefore watched, standing patiently by, and in the end Soprano lay in the dust, panting and chuckling pathetically in little spurts.

When it was over, they gave Soprano an IV to rehydrate him, and later he told me he felt like he'd just done a month's worth of white-line cardio, ab work, and wall-to-wall counseling, in thirty minutes.

I had to admit, his abs did look pretty cut afterward. His obliques were on point, and he will dive in on anyone's carb-heavy MREs at the drop of a hat despite being a tiny triangular hurricane of muscle. So yeah, I thought about trying out getting pricked by the dagger not just because my obliques could use some work, but because it was an *edge*... and I was starting to get a taste for edges lately. A taste I hadn't told anyone about.

Warts and all.

Hopefully there's not more about that later and I will just learn to be careful about edges.

After all this, I asked Vandahar what a *Circus of Death* was.

"The Circus of Death," he grandly told me later, sitting down excitedly in his old man wizard way and getting out his pipe, "was once a powerful order of assassins in the desert kingdom of Parvaim. With these weapons, their highest order of assassins was able to slay one of the greatest emperors of Accadios on a mission from the east whose paymasters were never quite discovered in the bloody end of the matter. In return payment, Accadios marched eight legions through that cursed desert, sacked the city, slaughtered the disciples of the order wherever they could find them, and put an end, officially, so they say, to the Circus. But... I have always had my doubts regarding the matter. There have been other... curious murders... since those long-ago times."

So that's the second step in the three steps to a Ranger making a pickup his weapon. Third step, after magical detection and training, is the invariable tacticooling it up. Which they would never admit to calling it that. And that's not what they're really doing. Mostly. Usually they'll find some spare grip tape, or bandages, to wrap the hilt in. They might add some battlefield trophies. Or carve something tough into it. Improve it in some way they feel will make it more effective in close-quarters hand-to-hand combat.

Cold-blooded.

And that's the three steps.

I tell you all that to tell you this…

Monroe, Sergeant Monroe, the Ranger the Ruin had revealed to be a bull-headed giant of a warrior, had already gotten into a number of hand-to-hand engagements. And, as he'd confided in me because we'd been working a lot together, he was starting to go red mist in the middle of fights and prefer his pickup to leading Rangers and working our various systems to maximum killing effect. And further, that there were times when he should have gone to guns, and instead kept hacking away with his shining double-bladed battle axe, or in one particularly gruesome case, goring a Saur with his sharp, and I mean needle-sharp, horns.

"I think, Talk, I'm goin' full… minotaur, man."

And, as the good Ranger he was… he was being honest. In other words, in the middle of a fight he was losing his ability to lead effectively because he just wanted to get it on, hand-to-hand style.

Nothing wrong with that as far as the Rangers were concerned. The fighting part, that is.

The leading part on the other hand…

Big problem there. Rangers are all about leadership, and everyone gets thrust into a leadership role regardless of rank. Hence the corporal linguist running the QRF to relieve Corporal Chuzzo's legionnaires at the Observatory at the current time.

Monroe and I had discussed this previously. In the event he felt himself losing the ability to lead in combat effectively, or, as he put it, "Well duh, Talker, the Ruin revealed me to be a man-bull. Bulls go all blind rage in a fight. That's why matadors exist. So we gotta adapt and overcome what's happening to me."

We picked a code word to alert me to the fact he was losing control.

I picked *Matador*.

He picked *Gym Fail*.

I'm a linguist. He's a minotaur. *Gym Fail* it is.

When he called "Gym Fail," I took over so he could run his killing machine game on behalf of the element while I concentrated on getting the mission we'd been given, done.

But this was unusual. This was the first time he was surrendering control *before* it even got started, and so as I got ready to skip issuing the tentative order step and just move on to making a plan and initiating movement… I issued the tentative order anyway because I was a little shook. These are steps in leadership. All I could do was fall back on them and do something.

Monroe and I had discussed this situation with Vandahar and Chief Rapp. Vandahar had said nothing, merely leaning back, intently studying Sergeant Monroe. Chief Rapp had suggested some control exercises to keep the sergeant's mind focused despite the urge to slaughter hand-to-hand style. SF understood this kind of exercise to keep a soldier in the battle even when they went all suddenly Terminator.

The verdict had been, before taking it to the command team, that we'd try these exercises for Sergeant Monroe. And continue our solution to the problem. The sergeant's and mine. *Gym Fail*. Command had enough on its plate right now.

Not SOP, but we did it anyway.

Chief Rapp convinced us it was kosher for now.

But now at the QRF rally, the minotaur was heaving, snorting, pawing at the ground to get on the move, as I stood, hefted the sixty, and said, "Tentative plan... we're gonna move on the Observatory... coming in on the preplanned flanking route. We'll move in, recon, assess, METT-T, then roll on the enemy attack as it develops and attempt to destabilize their push and get them to beat feet."

We knew all that.

That was the plan for the QRF already.

But I needed to start somewhere, so I started with what I knew. I was leading my first combat mission, after all.

I took a deep breath and got ready to initiate movement to contact.

"What?" White yelled at me. He'd had his ear drums blown out when an orc shaman of major voodoo level set off a thunderclap spell on his squad. White took the brunt of it and had been shifted back to the QRFs until, or even if, he got his hearing back.

I gave the necessary hand signals and White nodded that he was following and in. Then went back to softly singing, "Froggy went a-courtin' he did ride with a pistol and sword at his side."

He always does that lately. Maybe he did it before. I didn't know him well.

"Where'd you learn that old-timey song?" I asked him one time recently, being a linguist and interested in such things and their origins.

"What?" he'd shouted at me.

There are no Ranger patrol hand signals for *Where'd you learn that song you're obsessively singing.*

Chief Rapp says it'll help White's hearing come back if he keeps in touch with his voice. So, White sings. The same song. Over and over.

It's not as annoying as you'd think.

But it is… constant.

I check in with everyone as we get ready to move.

Our squad minotaur is impatient and ready to get it on. Snorting and flexing. Pure menace. Might possibly go berserk and go on a killing spree that may, or may not hopefully, kill us all.

White is deaf-singing, nodding, spitting dip. Smiling like he hears what we're saying even though he doesn't, but ya do what you can because that's how ya do it.

Then there's Gill. Specialist Commons. Ranger Merman.

"Ready to go, Talk. I got the suicide ruck this time."

And then I think… *Oh yeah, there's that.*

Then we're rolling on Observatory, and apparently, I'm in charge.

CHAPTER SIX

WITH Sergeant Monroe on point and leading the way into the action we were about to take, I was barely able to control how fast he moved as his huge nostrils scented the developing battle ahead and it was clear... *he wanted right into the bloody middle of it.*

A hulking minotaur who happened to be a Ranger was a frightening thing to follow in the early dusk as the wind swept in off the desert, sending sand and dust everywhere, mixing with the sound of slaughter all along the walls. His huge strides threaded the narrow path up along the slope of broken wall that had fallen into the city long ago, and entered sections that took us around and into the flanking side of the Observatory. The rest of us followed, my head on a swivel, watching for killers in the shadows and keeping my element cohesive despite the battle-mad Ranger minotaur practically leaping forward to get it on.

But we were Rangers first and he seemed to remember that, stopping and hustling us along, his dark eyes forward as he watched the approach, then signaling us forward impatiently. We made our way along the identified route into the Observatory flanking ambush spot, already scouted via the various battlefield recons, and now the objective for the QRF was to defend that section of the wall.

We were about two minutes away from insertion when the battle lit up hard in the Observatory above us. The old rotting structure, once an ornate small fortress, lay along one of the highest parts of the old southern wall. We could hear the legionnaires up there already shouting as the first arrows of the Guzzim Hazadi came at them from the shadows and the deep cracks of the outer bulwark of the shattered Observatory that had fallen five stories below.

It wasn't an easy location for the Guzzim to try and storm due to its elevation, but then again, if they were the enemy version of Rangers, of course they were gonna go for it.

We would've.

So we'd planned accordingly. We were prepared to murder them if they did what we would have done.

Side note… war teaches you a lot about understanding the other guy and what he's going through, even if he's an orc, and what he's planning to do to you with what he's got. Or as Sergeant Joe put it, "The other guy's shoes, one day you might be wearin' 'em. So try real hard to kill him before that day comes around. Anyone can conduct an L-shaped ambush. Hell… even that Jabba thing can set one up. And for that matter, anyone can walk right into one. So don't be that guy I gotta go get burritos for someday."

Jabba smiled, having no idea what we were talking about. He was nearby eating what remained of a can of dip someone had given him.

Eating it.

Let that sink in.

I ran through my actions as the QRF leader as we made our ascent up the rough scree of what remained of that ancient section of collapsed fortress that led up the Observatory along the southern wall. First thing I needed to get done was to get us into our ambush site, set up security in the short halt position, and get an analysis of the situation inside the objective.

Thankfully Sergeant Monroe was running Chief Rapp's self-control techniques as we moved, even though he kept switching the haft of the huge double-bladed battle axe between his giant leathery hands, snorting and grunting as he did so like he was working himself up for an old-school Conan-style murder spree. He got us into position at the ambush site, which was off to the right flank of the legionnaire spear line now formed up at the back of the high Observatory.

The legionnaires were taking arrow fire from all across the front and holding their own with sporadic return spear fire.

We established security, Commons and White running either flank and keeping an eye on our back trail. The Guzzim Hazadi were known to use smaller orcs, goblins like Jabba really, to get into the flanks, work their way through areas and objects thought impassable, then lie in wait with poisoned blades to come out at the least opportune time.

Least opportune for us, that is.

"You see anyone back there," I briefed Commons, who was working suppressed as we all were for right now, "burn 'em and make sure there's no more. Last thing we need is a bunch of murder jabbas with knives out and running amok in our six."

Commons nodded. "Watch our six. Burn the murder gobs," he back-briefed, the hump of suicide ruck on his back glaring at me with all its apocalyptic and unspoken destruction. "Affirmative, Talk. I gotta frag I'll lay on the dead bad guy and that way if more come in, they'll probably loot their buddy like they do and trip the explosive. That'll give us some warning if they push the six when we're in it."

Thumbs up.

I crawled through the fractured scree and rubble of this side of the ruined ancient astronomers' fortress that was the Observatory to get a better view of the battle taking place below us in the main well of the old place. Sergeant Monroe, like some hulking demon in the dark, chest rig open because it could not contain his swole, crouched near the fractured base of some archaic statue of no one we knew that had once served as one of the major support columns for the roof of the structure.

We'd chosen this route into the ambush because it was a difficult approach, and we'd thrown down some knotted five-fifty, hidden in the dirt and rubble, that allowed us to pull ourselves up onto the Observatory ledge we'd flank from while still humping all our gear for the attack.

I set the sixty down on its bipod after making the ledge, got down on my belly, slithered over debris past Sergeant Monroe, and made my way toward the edge of the old dais that had once watched over the inner sanctum of the ancient stargazers' chamber.

This was the battlefield I saw.

The tower that is called the Observatory is almost like the remains of some fractured bombed-out cathedral I'd seen World War Two pictures of a long time ten thousand years ago. The outer and inner walls, outer being what faced the desert, inner facing Sûstagul itself, were thin skeletons up here of what was once an ornate structure. The arched windows that looked out on the vast enemy-overrun desert to the south or the spreading port city behind us, were empty and tall, like church windows. The roof, which once was a high dome constructed of hammered bronze, had collapsed and shattered down into the well of the Observatory, which was quite large. About the size of a chow hall. The bronze had long since been salvaged and taken away, the Observatory having been long ruined even before we showed up to wreck it more.

The shattered walls had fallen in along the sides of the structure to mix with the rubble of the lost roof. Ancient stellar frescos and charts painted in faded, once-vibrant colors were still just barely visible, and one of the local sages who'd made a study of the mystical place told us that long ago, fantastic gems with powerful magic had been placed in the walls where the stars and planets had been represented in the paintings. But all of that had long since been looted, and now, as I peered down into the developing Guzzim Hazadi attack against Corporal Chuzzo and the legionnaires, I could see the main floor of the building already littered with the dead.

Orc and legionnaire.

The Legion had been maintaining a watch fire in the well when the Guzzim came up through the fractures in the outer wall, scaling rough and uncertain stone under artillery fire. We were about five stories up, here along the southern wall, east of the Gates of Eternity. Where the Guzzim had not come through the open fractures to the desert, they had swarmed though the gaping portals that had once been fine stained glass. The doddering old sage told us this was glass from the Lands of Oblivion, wherever that was, supposedly a distant place little visited and probably mostly myth, which lay deep in the desert beyond even the Grand Pyramid itself. It was said, according to the sage, that the stained glass showed scenes of Sût's initial rise to power, and his questing for the dead gods to attain the great powers he would eventually wield. All of this was from an age the sketchy history of the Ruin records as "The Long, Long Dark." Which as near as we can tell was shortly after we departed the scene ten thousand years ago.

Pretty dark times apparently. Even that Delta team lost their way, or so we think according to the rumors and ruins we've found along the way.

The dais where we were was the highest occupiable space within the Observatory. From the viewpoint of the body-littered battle royale along the floor, the area we'd set up the ambush from was not identifiable. Of course the Rangers had climbed all over the place to find this, the most inaccessible point, from which to launch their ambush should this spot on the wall come under surprise attack.

"Surprise, Ranger Smash!"

The discovery of the raised dais—once part of a greater fortress that lay west of the old Observatory and had since collapsed—had caused the doddering old sage to delightedly exclaim in his high-pitched whisper of a voice, "This area was barely mentioned in the ancient texts I have long pondered, my friends. But I had thought it lost to time and ruin, or not a reliable piece of information to even be savored. This dais was once home to... the *Chorus of the Damned*."

He told me all this in a mix of Arabic and Chinese, a little Gray Speech, and the desert patois of Sûstagul itself, which I was quickly learning more and more of despite the battle and my obsessions.

But the coffee tent, even when I just sat and drank cups and stared off into things I could no longer change, had a way of making the language part of my mind... learn harder.

Despite even my dark wanderings.

"It was here that eyeless slaves sang praises to Sût himself in a language not of the Ruin, or even known under the sun or moon. A language that came from the stars, or so some say, and that is now lost or known only to the dragons themselves," ranted the wild sage.

Normally the thought of an undiscovered language would have had me drooling. But this was just after the first battle and I'd been... not *checked out,* but... I don't know how to describe it. More like *checked in* was the actual answer when I think about it now.

Languages had begun to... fade. For me.

I had *other things* on my mind now.

The djinn had made me an offer. But it had come with a warning. And apparently, when wishes are on the line... words really matter.

Like... *a lot.*

What I wanted in those days, after Kurtz and Brumm... what I wanted was payback really. Or so I told myself. And even as I wanted it, it was already morphing into something else... like things do. They twist. What I wanted was that what happened to them, didn't happen to anyone else. Any other Ranger. Ever again.

It was then I began to work relentlessly at any task I'd been given, thinking somehow...

Somehow...

I could prevent death... from calling again.

What's the old poem?

Because I could not stop for Death –
He kindly stopped for me –
The Carriage held but just Ourselves –
And Immortality.

I pushed the words of that dead woman aside and vowed…

I shake my head even as I write this.

But I made a vow that things would be different. Somehow.

And they weren't. Other Rangers died and Tanner talked to me about that as I blamed myself for even those…

"I had to learn that, Talk, back in the sandbox. Everyone's death ain't your fault. I was like you. I remember bein' so, and I'm not sayin' I ain't now. Sometimes I am. Hell, look at me, Talk. I am death now. And I think about it different now too. Someday… someday you'll all see what I see now. Then you'll know. Then you'll see…"

I still loved languages.

But I'd become obsessed with death. With beating it. Somehow. Some way. Making things right.

I went to Joe.

He said, "Well, if you gotta be obsessed about something, death ain't a bad one to wanna lay a beatdown on. He's got a great record. But even the champ gets a beatdown someday, Talker. Maybe you're the guy, Ranger. Maybe."

I just needed everyone to make it now. And I was gonna lie, cheat, fight, gouge out eyes, and steal smokes from the devil to make it happen.

Psionics, or waking dreams from the sleep I didn't get, even when I had time, a few minutes here and there really, told me... or rather showed me... she was still saying Shadow Elf vespers over me back at the FOB. For my protection. That I would still be *me* no matter how many scars and dead buddies I acquired on the long march toward wherever it was we were ultimately headed.

I felt bad for her.

I was changed. Now. Me... me was gone.

But maybe that's not the Ruin revealing. Maybe it's just wishful thinking.

The djinn came to me one night.

"Just seeing how I may serve you, Master?"

The girls were gone. Not there. Somewhere else. That's a small blessing. It's hard to think... when they're around.

Ranger gonna Ranger.

I asked Al Haraq. If there was a way. If what I was seeing was just... *wishful thinking*.

Al Haraq. Fire.

He watched me with his burning blue eyes, white smiling teeth, and chocolate skin. Rich silk clothing.

"Ah, Master... wishful thinking... maybe that's the greatest magic there is."

I asked him a question.

He gave me an answer.

And a warning. The most dire warning I've ever received.

I heard it. And then I remembered Tanner telling me.

It was bad, Talk. Real bad.

I have dark obsessions now. So, a Chorus of the Damned singing in an unknown language from the stars that maybe only dragons know, from the long dark age when the Ruin was becoming what it would become... it didn't grab me like it once would've.

I'm different now.

I'm not that guy anymore.

The Accadion legionnaires had taken some losses already as I assessed the situation, ran the METT-T, and got ready to make some decisions. I counted two dead on the floor, pincushioned by the sudden arrow fire from the creeping, pressing, cloaked, and ragged Guzzim Hazadi coming out of the early night, scaling the impossible walls while the battle was elsewhere along them. Suddenly lighting up the legionnaires who'd fallen back, turtled behind their shields and lobbing spears. Chancing arrows from some of the Accadion irregular troops, unarmored archers that had come in on the last galley.

Young men and boys really, answering the call to the ramparts of civilization's last stand against the dark.

Many of the archers were now already dead. The Guzzim Hazadi carried short yet powerful bows and fired them as fast as a rifle on semi-auto.

With deadly accuracy to boot.

Those bows had claimed five of our dead so far.

The poison they used didn't help matters.

But the Legion shield wall held despite the surprise attack from the other side of the wall.

I slithered back to Sergeant Monroe.

"Situation?" he rumbled in the darkness. Keeping down as best he could. If he stood, or even slightly exposed his hulking form, they would have known we were up here and ready to do extreme violence to them.

I'd analyzed the mission as I'd studied the attack, and I already knew our courses of action from the planning phase we'd prepped for this particular QRF knowing an enemy attack would eventually come for the Observatory.

The mission, as I ran the METT-T through my brain at fever-of-battle speed, was to disrupt the enemy attack, only now beginning, and get them to shove off back into the desert, letting the snipers and gun teams know their location as they faded. Those elements were still working thermals and better optics and so they had a great chance of picking up some kills on the bad guys.

The enemy, as it stood now, were Guzzim Hazadi harassers. Or at least that's what we'd tagged them as when we'd analyzed their tactics.

Typically, once the main attack started somewhere else along the wall, they sent in their ninjas. The harassers. These were usually shrouded archers carrying those powerful short bows. They'd get close and start shooting targets with poisoned arrows. Since they were used to dealing with the Legion for centuries, they knew the Legion would form their legendary shield walls and become all but unhittable.

The Accadion Legion had the shield wall down to not just a science, but an art. Once turtled, they were nearly impossible to move or break, unless you were going to spend a lot of troops doing so. Remember, I'd seen them in the desert, where they'd destroyed psycho elves and giant war spiders by the score thanks to tactics, positions, and the leadership of Captain Tyrus.

Knife Hand had advised us on this. "The Legion is an excellent defensive fighting unit. Which… is understandable given their tenuous position here in the Ruin. Ten centuries have taught those people how to use walls and defenses to survive. They're not conquerors anymore. They're survivors. And I'll grant you, Rangers… this is just what we've seen so far. They may have maneuver armies and heavier units closer to their main cities, but in the field… with what we've encountered so far… they move into defensive formations and try to wear out the enemy. Once the commander in charge has determined an enemy is sufficiently weakened, they advance in kill lines, sweeping the battle and dispatching the dead. Talking to their commander, it seems they have an entire philosophy for this and adhere to it religiously, as their very survival depends on its precise implementation."

Joe would tell some of us later, "See, these leejes have gotten smart. Back in the day, when the barbarians like the Mongols used to pull this trick on the Greeks and the Romans, the civilized guys with armor would get all cocky in their defense, break ranks, or leave their walls, and chase the horse archers out into the desert. Where *they'd be sitting ducks.* They get surrounded… then *mollywhomped.* These Ruin legionnaires don't get carried away like that. For all their *I-talian-ness…* they got cool heads in a fight. I've watched their NCOs literally club the rankers back into shape to prevent them from getting too strung out in a bad position. Gotta admire that in this little slice of hell. One mistake… Ruin'll make ya pay, Rangers. Note it well."

The harassers, or the ninjas, that's what we were getting now as they attacked the Accadion legionnaires on the floor of the Observatory. But the Guzzim, for all the Legion good tactics, weren't stupid. They'd learned. Once they got the Legion to play defense, they would send in some kind of heavier force in to peel shields and stick legionnaires with sharp things in order to create a breach.

We'd seen a few variations on this. Normally they sent in squads of orcs with long hooks or swinging grappling hooks. They got these into the shield wall, exposed an opening, then concentrated arrow fire trying to widen the breach they'd created. They threw acrid smoke pots to choke and confuse and didn't mind dying en masse to get that breach made.

And once they did get a wedge in… the Legion got rolled up and it turned into a slaughter.

For both sides.

But the Legion couldn't afford the losses.

A few times the Guzzim had actually sent in huge… *monsters.*

I mean, c'mon. This is the Ruin. Monsters are like calling in air support or armor.

The Guzzim seemed to have a whole military unit dedicated to enslaving animals and using them as weapons against their enemies.

Kennedy was on hand to identify the first monster attack they used on the Legion holding the wall. He was with Joe's platoon when a displacer beast came in through a hole in the wall the Guzzim had broken open with a giant demon-headed bronze battering ram they'd been repeatedly ramming into the base of the wall over and over, again and again. Their assassins were shooting from the walls above but the Legion had responded, turtled, and were guarding the street and preventing the enemy from swarming into the city. The Guzzim sent in a few squads of orcs and those guys died on Accadion spears and some sniper support from Rangers nearby. Then the displacer beast came in.

I saw what it looked like afterward. Talk about a total freak of nature.

It was like a puma. But it had six legs and four tentacles coming out of its back and shoulders. Huge, powerful tentacles. Its eyes, even in death, were like burning green emeralds.

It's one of the freakiest things I've ever seen.

According to Specialist Kennedy, resident Ranger wizard, the beast has an innate "phasing" ability that basically acts as a defense for it. Its features, fur, or eyes, or even *psionics*... maybe... bend light, so the Legion and snipers *thought* they were stabbing and shooting it, stabbing from behind the shield wall, long spears out and thrusting, sniper support from the nearby fortress, but instead they were missing it by not just inches but feet because it wasn't really where it was indicating it was.

The phasing light-bending trick it does as a predator.

It got close to the shield wall, used its tentacles to rip shields right off legionnaire arms, and then went in destroying them right and left once that happened. The beast punched straight through Legion armor and tore the troopers inside their breastplates and greaves apart, limb from limb, while grabbing others with its tentacles and biting off more limbs.

Real horror movie stuff as I heard it.

The Legion broke, and Kennedy fired off a salvo of magic meteors that went everywhere *but* into the raging beast. The thing saw Kennedy do that, like it knew or something, and went straight for him, bounding over broken stone and destroying ancient desert columns in that portion of the city just to reach him in a sudden mad fury.

The legionnaires think Kennedy is the bravest Ranger ever. Apparently it was pretty impressive, the displacer beast's attack. Ranger Wizard held ground and got ready to fight.

Even the smaj thought that was pretty baller.

"Told you I'd make a Ranger out of him even if it killed him in the process," our senior-most NCO muttered over his Kindle with a cup of coffee on his knee.

Kennedy fired off a fireball at the last second as the beast came in, marking the wave of destruction coming straight at him instead of the false read of the big hunting cat's position his eyes were telling him. The fireball from the dragon-headed staff wiped out the crumbling columns, sending flaming stone in every direction, but the cat just leaped out of the way and circled through the dead ranks of the legionnaires to get to Kennedy from a new angle of attack.

Ranger Wizard, seeing his fireball was too slow to get the agile cat, slammed his dragon-headed staff into the dirt and cracked paving, sending up a ring of magical fire the killer freak cat couldn't get through. Then Kennedy did another spell Vandahar had taught him with the brief break he got because of the ring of fire surrounding him, and that revealed the displacer beast's position to everyone.

Kennedy threw a broken ChemLight at it, and at the same moment, staff planted in the dirt, he held out his hand and sprayed the tumbling ChemLight with sticky, almost ghostly webbing shot from his splayed fingers. He told us later he'd cast "spider web" to get the ChemLight caught on the beast's back with some of the webbing. The cat broke free of the magical strands in an instant, but the snipers now knew exactly where to fire because of the dancing ChemLight.

Mjölnir and Sergeant Thor hit the displacer beast center mass and tore out its heart, sending black fur, cat blood, and broken bone all over the dusty stone behind it.

It stopped, took three tentative steps, tentacles suddenly dragging the ground, and died in a smelly heap.

It smelled awful.

Like death warmed over.

Shades of Bag-of-Death Taco Bell Island.

The Legion rallied in the next moments, retook the street, and later Vandahar caused a small earthquake to collapse two abandoned buildings and the remains of a tall monument statue of an old Saur, some pharaoh, across the fissure in the southern wall the orcs had created, effectively sealing off that portion of the wall.

So right now, the orc harassers and their death poison arrows weren't the problem for the QRF. What we were waiting for, what I needed to make a decision about, was the heavy, or second wave that would play its hand shortly.

Seriously, I was on pins and needles.

As I studied the developing battle the Legion was being forced into, the harassers staying in the rubble along the outer skeletal wall, the Legion turtling in a semicircle shield wall near the entrance to the Observatory and the carved steps that had once led up into the building from the city wall and the city itself, I had yet to see the second movement of the enemy. The heavy. Either an orc massed push, or some kind of wild weird magical monster straight out of the deeps of the desert.

Come on, Ruin… let's get weird. As usual.

That was what the sixty was for, and if Tanner had reached the snipers by now then at least one team, spotter and shooter, had eyes on the Observatory and were ready to lend support by fire.

We had no mortars. We were down on A-T rounds. Kennedy was somewhere and Vandahar was too, but it was hard to say what the wizards could do and where they could be. They kinda, unusual with Rangers, ran themselves. I'd seen Kennedy two days ago and he looked pretty beat.

We split his Rip It and I told him to be safe. We each got one on the last supply run. Courtesy of the Air Force Forge on the C-5.

I traded mine for instant coffee out of the MREs. I was still king of the market and old habits die hard.

"Ha, Talker. Ain't no safe in the Rangers. Even I know that. Plus, man, I'm a wizard."

Then he did an NFL end zone dance and we laughed.

The OODA loop was running in my brain.

Observe. Orient. Decide. Act.

I saw one of the orc archers, a harasser garbed in desert sand robes and totem-laden grey rags, a black mask about his face like a ninja, suddenly go down. One of the snipers had taken a shot and turned his head to red mist flying away in the night wind and dust. Bows clattered and arrows spilled out from his thing you carry arrows in.

There's a name.

I don't know it… I'm tired. But I can't sleep.

The dead orc without a brain went sideways, slumping by the light of the fire in the well and the various torches among friend and enemy, and arrows spilled out of his… *quiver*. Aha! I did know it.

Yeah, *quiver*. That's it.

So, Tanner had made it and the snipers were engaging now. Good. SOP said they were always cleared to take the harassers. It was that second wave I was waiting for to show its face as the OODA loop ran through my brain like an unquenchable fever that couldn't cool down.

Did I mention I was mumbling, "No one dies tonight"? Over and over. So low no one could hear it.

Except the hulking minotaur next to me did, tapped his axe, and directed me to the heavy coming in.

You ever see *Indiana Jones and the Temple of Doom*? The evil priest. Mola Ram or something. One of the Rangers would later describe their heavy, an orc shaman, as very, very powerful in the same way. If that guy, Mola Ram from *Temple of Doom*, had been an orc... then that's what we were seeing come into the battle all smoke, fire, and curses of annihilation.

He had flaming skulls circling him.

Yes.

Read that again. He had flaming skulls circling him like some kind of defensive shield.

One of the snipers fired, and a skull, a bone-white human skull with flames in its eyes, intercepted the high-caliber sniper round speeding at thousands of feet per second, and it exploded in a dusty *smaff* of bone and annihilated lead.

The round suddenly just consumed in a fury of magical defensive energy.

Mola Ram was chanting something. He was tall, taller than most orcs. Grey where they were green oftentimes. He wore bloody red robes and a necklace of bones and other weird stuff.

He was chanting like he was in a trance. I heard his baritone voice on the wind like he was the lead in some unholy opera.

He carried a staff. At the time I would have told you it was nothing ornate. Later I'd tell you different.

He raised it high and a powerful spell went off and the entire shield wall of legionnaires exploded in every direction. Whether they were killed outright or just knocked over, at the time, I had no idea. But they busted our defense, and the Observatory was wide open for the taking. A key position on the wall.

Then every orc in the world came flooding up through the skeletal remains of the outer walls and the desert beyond, through the shattered spaces, firing arrows, waving huge scimitars, throwing barbed spears.

Shrieking like angry demons.

Instantly the odds were a hundred to one, faster than I could have thought possible.

"It's on!" shouted Monroe, raising the huge double-bladed battle axe and leaping down from the hidden ledge we'd staged on into the swarms of orcs already racing pell-mell for the steps leading down into the city.

I didn't think.

I just did.

I turned, grabbed the sixty, stabilized the bipod on a cracked feature that must've been part of some old wall, and opened fire.

CHAPTER SEVEN

I opened up with a solid blur of bright gunfire from the pig. If you're new to the light infantry game and just tuning in to this account, soldiers since Vietnam have called the venerable M60 light machine gun "the pig" since it entered service. And often using it in the sentence *Hold the pig steady!* as once it starts working it can cut everything in its outgoing cone of death to little more than the remains of a well-mowed lawn. Which is great when you're the grunts that have to go in and kill everything hiding in there that the pig didn't kill. Plus, it's heavy. I shouldered it, stabilizing on the bipod, picked out my target group, and sent outgoing hot seven-six-two downrange. Instantly I lit up a cluster of snarling orcs, just pushing into the well where the battle would've been taking place had the legionnaires not been blown in every direction by the powerful magical blast of the Mola Ram orc shaman with the shaven skull painted with bloody red symbols. That cat stood head and shoulders above the howling Guzzim Hazadi surging all around him and pushing on the well for everything they were worth.

We'd seen some big pushes before, and some probes which are just lesser lighter attacks to find out how dug in we were. This felt from the get-go like a major push and within seconds, feeding the belt, getting hit by flying linkage and watching the brass trail away in burps, I was pretty sure this push was legit bigga big.

Thank you for that, Jabba. Rangers now speak gob and don't even notice half the time. On the other hand, the younger Rangers love *Big Bigga Big* and some have even added scroll tattoos of the phrase on their sleeves usually around their swollen biceps when they can duck away from details and hit the merchants on the Street of Ink and Beauties deep in the Mystery Gate Quarter.

The smaj has given several warnings about this street.

But hey, Rangers gonna Ranger.

Meanwhile the little gob assistant gunner has a basic command of Ranger battlespeak though he sometimes stares at us in bewilderment, which I suspect is occasionally feigned, when he doesn't want to do something in particular.

I'm not kidding though: one time the stoic Sergeant Kang actually briefed the captain and used *Big Bigga* to describe the emplaced explosive he'd set off in a narrow street we were losing in order to collapse the buildings there on a major orc push that breached the outer walls for a few hours.

The face Captain Knife Hand gave was the equivalent of serving someone a lead omelet at a Waffle House just after three in the morning. Too many dirty tables and dead drunks to comment. But you're hungry so you eat it anyways and ask for the bottle of ketchup.

Once the blast went off the Rangers went reaper, crawling through the dust-blooming rubble and slitting the throats of the half-buried and torn-apart orcs who'd managed to survive the blast. Sometimes calling out "fire in the hole" and dropping grenades into some of the harder-to-reach buried rubble where they suspected some of the enemy was still stuck, buried alive, and awaiting a better fate than the one they'd been dealt.

I would've called that *mercy*. But the Rangers don't understand that word. Nor do they expect it. So it wasn't.

It was just war.

Don't make it more than it is, don't expect anything different than what comes with it. Your mileage may vary. But in the year I'd been at this, I'd found that was the best way to stuff it in your emotional rucksack. On the other side of all this, there'd be time to deal with… let's call it… all that *stuff*. But for now, to simply make it to the next day was enough. And of course, you were going to have to do your best and even then… that wasn't always enough.

Eleven dead had done their best.

I asked for nothing more of the day ahead every morning and expected nothing less than that I would do my best and accept the results as best I could when the time came.

So. There I was machine-gunning orcs to death with the pig. Tuesday.

Sure, a Ma Deuce would have been great right at that particular moment. But all the QRF had was Sergeant Monroe's sixty and three expensive belts of high-power armor-piercing seven-six-two to burn as fast as we could to stop the push.

Belts weren't cheap in Sûstagul when everything came in on the supply birds in the morning and got used up that night holding the walls and the thin lines on the map.

I'd seen the map.

The lines were so thin sometimes it was like they weren't even there.

Corporal Cassio's platoon. Strength thirty percent.

Three legionnaires on Straight Street. Pre-planned fires or pre-plotted targets plotted already right where they held, just in case we lost that thin spot in the line and the last of our doomsday break-glass-in-case-of-emergency rounds were needed to buy us some time to get a QRF in there and seal the breakout.

"This ain't no way to fight, Rangers," Sergeant Chris muttered nearby one night when I was on watch. "We need to be out there shooting up supply lines, smashing their siege engines, and taking scalps. Make them afraid to even get near the walls. Hit with the night, fade with the dawn."

Then he spat dip on a dead orc that had been too long in the rubble and said nothing more. I followed and listened, updating the math of our survival as I went.

We had no comm now and our gear was falling apart due to the residual effects of the lingering millennia-long nano-plague. So even if there was a drone on station, run by the cute little blond ponytailed co-pilot back at Hawthorne, we had no idea if it was coming in to assist our defense with a couple of AGMs or a strafing run.

When it happened, we were as surprised as the dying orcs were.

We had no mortars on call for fire support unless the captain fired the replotted positions because there was no way to adjust fire support across a city filled with leaning desert brick towers, tumbling dried mud houses, and a series of walls that turned streets into blind alleys and kill zone prison yards guarded by the desperately angry and very frightened denizens of that district.

They knew there was only one way out of this for them now that the enemy had surrounded the city on all sides of the desert. It was fight or die, and no one had any fantasies or illusions about what that was gonna take. The locals ran water to the legionnaires on the wall and carried the wounded away back to their own houses, doing their best to patch them up and get them back on the line, spear in hand.

In short... the answer to every question was violence. And the faster you could get more violent than the other guy, the orcs, the better your chance of seeing the dusty dawn.

So Sergeant Monroe, sensing the moment to get his hack on, driven into... *bloodlust* by what the Ruin had revealed in him, landed eight feet below the ledge we were fighting from with a heavy thud from both of his gigantic boots. Then he went in hacking and slashing without hesitation.

So juiced up was Sergeant Monroe to get it on, he'd cut the first, and yes, I'll use the word *unfortunate* here, *first unfortunate orc* right in half with a sudden savage stroke of his massive double-bladed battle axe in his first seconds among the orc push. He'd landed on both massive feet, hams and quads even more huge than anything the premium batt gym back in the world we'd come from had been able to do for him, and the orc came streaming, or screaming in, right for him, scimitar raised and dancing for a swift cut. Monroe switched hands on the battle axe because he'd gone down with the mighty weapon in his off hand, I'm guessing to stabilize himself during the drop in case he needed his good hand free to catch himself if the ground down there was uncertain... so at least that part of his mind was still thinking rationally. The part that should have naturally done a roll, or at least a solid PLF, parachute landing fall, on the other hand didn't care and so he landed on both feet ready to deal death in economy-sized doses.

He switched the haft of the battle axe with a small flip, and I swear that thing must weigh as much as a heavy barbell, took one step, and then swung the razor-sharp axe, burying it deep in the oncoming orc's side lightning-fast.

But he didn't stop the cut there.

The orc screamed bloody murder as Monroe dragged the leading edge of the battle axe right out of him. The guy fell away and I saw the cut as I tried to track Monroe's progress into the battle below now that he was exposed and ahead of our battle line in the well of the Observatory. At the same time I fired another burst into a group of orcs moving straight through the remains of the ones I'd just cut to shreds.

I had the best of both worlds with the pig at that very moment.

Plunging and traversing fire even though the sixty was mounted on a broken stone with its bipod. I could still lean and traverse and run a light of devastating fire across their assaulters as they surged forward to get onto the tumbled and blown-apart Accadion legionnaires.

But... I didn't want to hit the jacked friendly, our Ranger minotaur, who was now wading into the orcish press, slaughtering right and left like he could do it all day long and not get tired in the least. Even the orcs must've thought they'd just walked into a nightmare as the seven-foot-tall horned demon worked that battle axe over and over on them, slashing and cutting two and three of them sometimes at a time.

I wondered how he could do it, but then I heard a voice from my own past. At the beginning of all this that

I'd set out to do, never understanding at the time how far it would go, and where it would lead...

You don't mind, it don't matter, barked Drill Sergeant Ward in my mind from ten thousand years ago in Basic Training when he was smoking the hell out of a company of new recruits who thought they might be soldiers or something. Like I said earlier in this account, I trained hard just to show up to Basic and even at that moment when he said that I was questioning how long I could last in the summer heat inside a stale barracks, getting burpeed to death with all kinds of other fun nuances like rolling around on the floor, flutter kicks until you felt like you were going to vomit or spit up blood, and sometimes "resting" against a wall as though you were sitting on an imaginary chair. Your quads screaming, you told yourself you couldn't make it much longer.

Then that drill sergeant said it and... it was true. If you didn't think about it, didn't set a line you couldn't pass, well... then you could go for longer than you ever thought you could at first when all the torture started.

It's as though the universe had known one day that Kurtz would get ahold of me. Many was the extra-duty PT run down through the crag below FOB Hawthorne when I gasped *You don't mind, it don't matter* as Kurtz ran like a mountain goat and screamed at me to keep up.

I did.

I didn't mind. It didn't matter.

As I ran the gun and tried to abate the swarm of orcs through sheer outgoing death by kill pill, I understood how a Ranger with a battle axe can slaughter, and not get tired knee-deep and surrounded.

You don't mind, it don't matter.

The first orc Monroe had sliced in half... I iris in on the moment for purposes of this account because, as I have stated, *warts and all.*

You need to know.

I need to remember everything because some days it's so much, even in all its brutality, and beauty, yes there is that and maybe it's there because something about all the death and impending mortality makes everything clear and more real than it can possible be, but sometimes it's all so much and I want to remember everything.

So.

The Ranger minotaur cut an orc in half with one stroke of his deadly weapon. And it wasn't a movie, or a sketchy memory, or even hyperbole... it happened.

I have marked it down for the permanent record. I was there that night.

Writing things down... it banishes all the lies of time and recall, and even contrived deceptions. And the Ruin is so fantastic on its own on any given day, never mind its sorceries, survivors and sinners... that I find writing it all down like this is like putting on a plate carrier that keeps the lies, even the ones I want to tell myself sometimes... *out.*

It's armor for the truth. There are things I don't want to remember but I must. Things I want to forget... but I can't.

It was bad, Talk. Real bad.

Warts and all.

The orc Monroe cut in half as the QRF got busy taking lives and breaking orc girl hearts, that guy was still connected by his back and maybe even parts of his spine that survived the savage cut of Monroe's axe. *But...* the two halves of the body fell away in different directions. At odd angles not meant for a body that's still whole.

Important?

I don't know. But I write this down because I need you to know the level of savagery required to hold the line that night in a world gone completely Bronze Age and filled with real live monsters.

We hadn't planned on this particular game when we went through the QST to save the world we once knew, but we were here to win anyway. And that's what winning looks like. Your team sergeant cutting monsters in half with a razor-sharp battle axe, surrounded and raging like a... bull. A mad bull.

If I had been those orcs I would have turned and run from that towering horned murder machine working the axe like a weaving scythe of death. But, to their credit, our enemy was in it to win it that night. So they got close with high hopes, sharp things, and clearly bad intentions. And died anyway.

We both understood the game. No quarter would be given. None was expected. Sometimes you were the bull, and sometimes you got your throat cut in the dusty remains of an IED as grenades got dropped down holes to get your buried buddies.

And sometimes you were our eleven dead.

Good, I thought at the time, as Monroe cut that dude in half with a titanic effort that seemed effortless in the watching, then I opened fire again and burned the last of the belt, brass and linkage flying psychotically in every direction and hot smoking lead screaming from the barrel of the beautiful pig, smashing enemy skulls, destroying their bones, slamming into the thick muscled orcs surging for the downed legionnaires who were our allies. My hot streaking rounds hit the massing enemy with wet *slap*s and thick awful ripping that sounded horrible even through ear pro.

Yeah. We still got ear pro.

It's the little things you need to be thankful for when the slaughter comes in adult-sized doses.

I don't know how long I'll live here in the Ruin. How long I'll make it and when I'll join the eleven. *Mortality* has gotten ahold of me, and not just my own personal supply of the stuff. But if I get known for anything with what time remains I'd like to be known for the good things I learned along the way, and took the time to share with others.

I doubt there is one thing in this account that meets that criterion. Yet. But as my mom would always say to me, *You can start now.* You can start doing the next right thing… *at any moment.*

So there's my first contribution to a better tomorrow, and I had that epiphany during plunging and traversing fire on masses of orc light infantry punching a big old hole in our line that would be bad for the rest of our defense of the outer walls.

The Observatory had elevation and fields of fire. It was key to the defense. Hence an entire platoon of legionnaires and near-at-hand Rangers to relieve by QRF.

It's the little things you need to be grateful for. You can start doing the next right thing… at any moment. What a strange time to have such a thought, while machine-gunning my enemies. But… warts and all. Your mileage may vary. That was the thought I had when it went down there at the Observatory, and all that would follow.

Meanwhile Sergeant Monroe's next victim died violently when the jacked minotaur overhanded his double-bladed battle axe and slammed it straight down through the skull of the next orc to think it had even half a chance against him.

Oof.

Then Sergeant Monroe was on to the next victim and pushing forward into their midst, working the blade quickly back and forth, just catching orcs with glancing blows that instantly removed limbs and generally devastated them like grass being cut with a swift savage finality.

Bet you guys didn't think that was going to happen when you woke up this morning. But there you go. Life comes at ya fast.

As the slaughter continued I saw what Sergeant Monroe was doing—and it wasn't *all* battle-mad-minotaur-gone-totally-berserk. In Sergeant Monroe's push right into their massing midst, he'd created a straight line, or was creating, through double-bladed chaos and stunning dismemberment, a sudden on-the-ground interruption to the push on our downed legionnaires who were groggily getting to their sandals and grabbing their spears and shields with not as much haste as I would have liked for purposes of their continued safety. But in some cases the quicker ones were coming up with their razor-edged gladii out and delivering thrusts at the first fast-movers to reach their line, all snarling teeth and orcish battle roars, scimitars upraised and not ready to defend their suddenly slashed guts.

I could hear Corporal Chuzzo barking out orders above it all, leading his men and alerting them to action in what seemed a hopeless situation as they were being overrun even as he called out to them.

"On your feet, Dogs! The enemy has come to die on our spears! Bite off more than you can chew, Legionnaires! *Andiamo! Andiamo!*"

Let's go! Let's go!

And now, as QRF leader of this particular mess, machine-gunning as many orcs as I could, getting a belt change done, swearing and positioning the links in the feed tray, Commons taking shots from cover at orc archers off to the right, White picking up our six, watching and mumbling that weird song he kept singing, checking in with us and the action forward… it was time to pull some Ranger-level leadership voodoo.

Go me!

I slapped White on the shoulder, hard, three times to get his attention, yelling, "Take the gun! Unlive that guy!" while pointing at Mola Ram Orc, who was spinning up some new spell to release on the legionnaires.

Then I shouted, "Commons, you got the six and all flanks, I'm going down to keep them off Monroe *now!*"

I'd seen the plan the minotaur Ranger sergeant was running in his blood-fever brain. Keep the orcs from reaching the legionnaire line so our allies could re-form under Chuzzo's leadership. Draw fire and create chaos. But his back was exposed and the swarming orcs were seconds from figuring that out.

I swapped for White's MK18, checked the mag, half-empty, rounds were precious, and went down eight feet PLF'ing into a roll.

And yeah, *I came up firing like a boss.*

Kneeling, I had no time but to put a bullet into an orc's head, taking off half his scalp at less than five yards and sending bone spray and red mist away on the night wind.

He'd been too close and too fast for rounds center mass. So I'd gone for the switch kill and it worked as I domed him.

My success rate at switch kills wasn't great. But Chief Rapp, Ranger marksmanship drills, and the imperative not to get stabbed a lot at ranges of up close and personal, forced me to take the head shot at that range.

So I did, and the check cashed.

The orc I'd just shot reached for what remained of his skull, eyes crossing even as he went down by the firelight of the huge bonfire the legionnaires had kept for their watch. I pivoted, picked up my next target, on my boots now and shifting left to keep them off Monroe's back as he hacked and slashed further and further into their ugly charge. I shot two more orcs. A lot. More than I'd've liked to have done, ammo being as expensive as it was these days of re-supply by bird. But it took that much just to get it done and they were dead as I moved closer, working the carbine fast, swapping mags and closing the gap on my team leader's six.

Above, White went full kinetic murder on the Mola Ram orc who'd thrown up some kind of magical shield in addition to the flaming skulls that air-defensed my first bursts of fire.

Ear pro dulled the thunder of the pig in the echoing space of the well of the shattered Observatory and let me hear everything under thirty decibels. That's how I heard, just barely, a woman's soft laughter coming from the gun position behind me and just to the left.

Instantly I was like, *C'mon, Ruin. How about just one break today.*

The laughter... at first it made me think we had some kind of invisible, or near-invisible, assassin in our midst.

But as White worked the gun and I drove forward, shooting down orcs with every step and burning rounds too fast on my second-to-last mag, the laughter sounded... *different*.

Let me explain, now that I've had time to digest it, and *no I won't do one of my rants or digressions*. I mean, hell, this isn't about coffee so it'll be short.

Hey... Coffee... It's Fantastic! Brought to you by Talker.

The soft gentle feminine laughter coming from just around White on the sixty, above and behind me, as I swapped a mag... was like... *adoration*. Like when a giggly girl goes gaga over thick quads and jacked biceps on some Brometheus.

I mean, whoever she was, she even cooed for a second as White continued to shoot everything, a lot.

And then it was gone and I didn't have time to consider it more as a lot of orcs were trying to kill me at close range now that I'd closed up the gap with Sergeant Monroe. I slipped on dead orc guts made by Ranger minotaur and swung the carbine back to the right to pick up more targets coming in our flank, pulling that trigger fast and now just shooting every orc I could until I got the dry click I knew was coming.

Then I was out.

One kill stick left. Right now we were getting three mags per night. Then it was pickups.

But the orcs were pushing on the flailing, chopping, instant death machine of the minotaur ahead of me. One clubbed him with what looked like a spike mace, and Monroe roared like an enraged bull, instantly stopped the chop he was handing out on another orc, and backhanded the axe onto the mace orc who'd just punched a hole in him.

That ugly caught it right in the face and I got blood and bone all over me as I, at the same badly timed moment, called out, "Winchester!" letting every Ranger know I was out of kill sticks after the next thirty rounds.

We were doing that a lot lately, and we'd gotten over the dire-last-stand aspect of it. True to form the Rangers had embraced the suck, looked forward to being out of rounds so they could get their kill on with the pickup of their choice.

It was as though they *wanted* to be out of rounds.

Rangers.

An orc knocked me to the ground in the next instant, and flat on my back, I shot him through the jaw, killed him through his brain bucket, and barely avoided getting "maced" by another orc with a giant, demon-headed mace that slammed right into the cracked and dusty old mosaic tiles of the Observatory floor.

I rolled and then shot that guy in the gut. A bunch.

Thanks for your troubles. Die already.

He didn't. But he was over trying to kill me after a few rounds in his gut and just ran off through the other orcs trying to kill me right now, clutching his drooling guts and howling unholy hell through my ear pro.

At that instant Monroe went down in front of me and I had no idea if he was dead or alive still. All I knew, at that point, was that Mola Ram Orc had shouted out something that sounded like… and I have no idea what it really was but it sounded like… *"Supersize me!"*

It wasn't that. It was some kind of spell in the arcane language of orc sorcerers of the deep deserts beyond the land of Black Sleep.

It sounded like that.

Mola Ram Orc shouted and Sergeant Monroe went straight down in a huge clump of minotaur, and the orcs he hadn't slaughtered yet went right after him with knives and other sharp things out.

He got cut a lot until I shot everyone, pulling them away and firing into their wild-eyed skulls then went dry not counting my rounds. I felt more than heard the *click* of an open bolt with no more kill pills, then let go the rifle thinking it was on a Vickers Sling about me like the one I usually carried was, and not remembering that I'd taken White's gun and that I hadn't slung it in the mad rush to get down and in the fight to keep the swarming enemy off my team sergeant's back.

The carbine clattered on the dusty stone floor of the Observatory and I felt stupid as I got ready to die with Monroe, three or at least four orcs with various weapons pushing forward on me there standing over the giant black-furred heap of Sergeant Monroe.

Yeah, I'll admit, at that point I felt like my first leadership experience in real live combat had gone... *less than smoothly.*

My team was strung out. I'd just dropped my basically empty weapon, and we were getting overrun. That about covers it.

Those thoughts didn't matter as my right hand pulled *Coldfire*, the blade I'd taken off the dead SEAL McCluskey, from my back-scabbard the dwarves had sewn for me. It pulled effortlessly free and came out like a bright winter day full of terrible cold death.

Yes. The dwarves sew.

And yes, they are quite proud of that skill.

The orcs were pure snarling murder as they closed in on us. I changed their minds about that as I threw myself right into them with *Coldfire*. I didn't back up, didn't retreat, didn't relent. I just started handing out slashes because that's how you fight with swords and other Bronze Age weapons.

It's not like... anything I'd ever imagined. You just start swinging and some of the things you've learned along the way from when you first picked it up, your weapon, to right *deadly now*, are there. But mostly they're not and you're just trying to cut and stab everything before they can do it to you.

Those are the terms of the deal, and all involved seem to accept the stakes.

We'd trained that when outnumbered it was best to get close and start working like a frenetic jackhammer to get it done fast and get some space. Especially when overrun.

The dwarves had become our *de facto* hand weapon trainers, and as I have mentioned before, if the Rangers had a collecting knives problem, then the dwarves have a downright full-blown junkie addiction to blades. They are good at "knife verk," as Max the Hammer tells us in the German-accented English he has learned since we joined forces. "Ve are in fact... very gut vit zhe knife, Rangers."

And all *Coldfire* really is... is just one big knife.

And it cuts like butter when it connects.

I closed with my enemies, turning my shoulder and lowering my jaw to protect my head and throat because everyone involved in this little skirmish over Monroe's prone body was knives out and looking to cut.

Best not to get slashed in the throat right about now I thought to myself, some nugget of training surfacing in a sea of fear and anger.

Did I mention Mola Ram Orc was now firing necrotic bolts of magical energy at the massing legionnaire line behind me? Chuzzo's men held their shield wall, dragged their casualties back behind it, and I heard, as I thrusted and ran the first big ugly orc straight through with *Coldfire*, I heard the Legion corporal issuing the command to advance on line forward to our position.

They were coming for us, forward of their line, and our flanking QRF. Spears out to save us from getting chopped up.

The dying orc I'd just cut gasped and covered me with a blast of its breath so foul I wondered which was worse: Bag-of-Death Island back when we first got here... or this guy's last meal.

Stale Doritos covered in bad tuna fish vomit is how I recall it now. Please enjoy my descriptions and don't complain so much when I wax eloquent on a nice Arabica Roast pour-over, dry and nutty, hints of tobacco and leather with a little molasses and butter in the aftertaste.

We now return to our regularly scheduled slaughter by Bronze Age weapons and up close and personal distances.

But like I said, *Coldfire* cuts like butter and the two-handed thrust I ran the orc through with felt more like one of the exercises Max the Hammer had shown me than a full-blown savage fury.

The effects were devastating nonetheless.

The relentless blade met no resistance, and I kicked—just as I'd been shown and trained to do by Max the Hammer—the dead orc right off of the blade, pulling *Coldfire* free at the same time.

Did I mention this was an upward thrust? I went in just under the orc's bulbous sternum, pushed the blade through his pump and pipes, then came straight out his back.

Like I was cutting into some sponge cake. Enjoy that the next time you attend someone's afternoon tea.

See, I told you we didn't mind going Winchester on mags. This was where the real fun started. I had to admit that.

Admit what?

That it was intoxicating.

Yeah, I ain't that guy anymore. The one that wasn't sure. I had… from the start to now… embraced the suck in ways I'd never thought even possible when at first I began.

I was… not that guy. Anymore.

Now I looked forward to sharp implements at close range.

Laugh. Out. Loud.

Coldfire called to me more than I liked.

Blade out of the dead guy, I slashed hard and away on the next one I needed to clear off. I'm not sure where I hit him because it happened fast, but he screamed, and an orc's scream is bloodcurdling in the hearing and straight-up nasty with the spitting and bad, really bad—this cannot be understated—with the breath. Then that guy was spinning away, his flying blade falling at my boots.

Blade now wide right, I shifted my feet and basically slashed across the center of the battle over Monroe's inert prone hulk.

I was thinking… just keep them off him. He's not dead. Just… keep them off.

Some poor orc lost gnarly green fingers, black nails. A fourth orc had backed away, wisely, and now pulled a dagger and flung it right at my chest.

No, I did not block it with the blade. Come on, this is real life.

It caught me center mass, and if it hadn't've been for the plate carrier it probably would have punctured a lung. Instead it glanced away harmlessly and I *roared*…

Yup.

I did.

Then I took three steps forward and chopped that guy from the shoulder to the sternum in One. Angry. Cut.

Not cut in half.

But he was done for sure.

White was coming in now and that told me that in my own sudden battle lust we'd burned our last belts for the pig and he was coming in now to help me get Sergeant Monroe clear of the fight.

Behind him, laboring like a stud under the suicide ruck, Gill picked up targets and burned more rounds keeping the advancing orcs back.

White was on me. One-handed I shouted and motioned for him to grab Monroe's arms and that we were going to drag him back to the legionnaire line as best we could. He nodded fast, grabbed, and we began to drag. This was not easy as I can't even make a guess at what his minotaur weight is now.

It was like trying to drag a bag full of wet concrete. I heaved and told myself he wasn't dead.

More orcs were pouring through the windows and cracks along the outer skeletal cathedral high walls of the High Observatory. My mind was running all kinds of math, and none of it was good. I didn't even have the space to check his breathing. And nothing was moving.

"Commons!" I shouted, forgetting to use his hated tag. "Frag out to cover us! *Now!*"

Gill nodded, pulled his grenade, shucked the pin, and tossed the explosive right at Mola Ram Orc and his personal bodyguard at least twenty yards away near the raised steps at that far end of the well of the main floor of the Observatory.

The imperious orc sorcerer glared at us with knowing, bitter eyes, waved his hand, and opened up…

… *a negative space in the universe.*

That's the only way I can conceptualize it now.

It was like looking at something you couldn't look at.

I had no idea what happened next as I threw myself over Monroe and White did too. The frag was out, the results imminent.

I saw the legionnaires moving swiftly in tight formation right up on us when the grenade at the other end of the well suddenly and underwhelmingly detonated.

I had no idea where Gill was. Or Commons if you prefer. But he'd thrown the fragmentation device and so he knew to cover in the next instant.

If you ask me… I'm terrible at leadership.

This was all nothing but badly managed chaos. And apparently I was in charge of it.

I thought I'd gotten used to battle up to now. Pretty cool when it was just me fighting for me. Taking care of just me and doing what I was told to do along the way by someone better than me. In the moments before this fight I would have told you that I'd come a long way from that first QRF to save the Bravo gun team when the hill giant came for us and Brumm killed it dead, saying, "Carl G don't care."

Just so you know… I went and had a smoke after writing that.

Warts and all.

So… I would have told you that I'd become a pretty cool customer in a fight since my time with the Rangers and here in the Ruin.

But, put me in charge and I felt like I was wearing two left-handed gloves keeping track of everyone, fighting the battle, and chanting my mantra that everyone needed to live for me to get through this. For them to get through this.

Just before the det I wanted to scream, or pray even though I don't believe in anything in particular, that the fight needed to stop just so I could get a handle on all of it and catch up. Then we could start killing each other again.

If only just so no one else died.

Then the grenade went off and my ear pro whined and whistled.

Strange energy snapped and spat in all directions that usually didn't happen during the deployment of a live grenade.

Hot metal death fragments went flying, streaking past our protective gear and exposed skin. So, I knew the grenade had detonated. And it should have ruined a whole bunch of orcs in doing so.

Then, just for fun, I realized I had a hot fragment in my leg.

Duh, that's what happens when you cover your lifeless sergeant from a live explosive detonating nearby and danger-close.

But the orcs that were supposed to be dead... weren't dead.

If anything there were more of them pushing forward now. Hard. Coming through the windows of the outer wall of the Observatory, and up the ladders they no doubt had stabilized on the sand-dune desert floor below the wall, as fast as they could.

More archers taking shots.

Arrows hitting the Legion shields like tin cans getting shot.

Poison arrows your mind tells you as you get to your boots, shout at White and drag Sergeant Monroe for all you're worth. Sergeant Monroe who'd gotten as heavy as it gets, pulling for all you're worth for the legionnaire shield wall just ahead and to the rear of the battle line you're on.

You're in, really.

Corporal Chuzzo was suddenly there, shouting something. Bloody. Frag and spall cutting his gawky face and frame.

Something roared from the outer wall.

I turned and saw it.

"Commons!" I shouted as we yanked and pulled at the several-hundred-pound Ranger minotaur.

"Deploy the suicide ruck! *Now!*"

CHAPTER EIGHT

TWO giant floating demonic eyes peered in through the cracks and fissures of the delicate, almost cathedral-like outer walls of the Observatory that faced the desert. The *X* we were fighting for.

The spot on the papyrus maps marked with our markings indicating we could not, at all costs, lose it.

The giant floating demonic eyes caused me to call suicide ruck "Out!" Meaning deploy our last chance right now because it's clearly game over in the next few seconds if something that huge is creeping into the battlespace right now.

To be honest… and this is warts and all… I was freaked out. At first I thought it was a giant. The next minutes would reveal it was something far worse, and nothing we needed right about now.

Two giant floating demonic eyes peering in through the cracks and fissures of the delicate, almost cathedral-like outer walls of the Observatory that faced the desert… that shook me. The Rangers now affectionately call what came at us out of the desert night storm of that battle… "Shagbag."

It's their way of dealing with it. Their way of being hard in the face of incoming suck. Or as Drill Sergeant Ward would have put it to young Basic Training recruit Talker, "Ain't nothin' but a thang, Private."

And of course his eternal, *You don't mind, it don't matter.*

Amazing how those words echo… ten thousand years and lifetimes later.

Calling it something diminutive was the Ranger way of diminishing their enemies into manageable-sized bites for consumption, and ultimately… destruction. Even if that thing you were supposed to "bite off more of than you can chew," to borrow from Captain Tyrus and the legionnaires, was considered a god on some level or other.

Other being the operative word perhaps.

Shagbag.

To be fair, a lot of *true orcish*, the language the orcs actually speak to one another and none of it having anything to do with any known language from the time we came from, seems little more than riffs on what sounds like *"Shagbag"* anyway. *"Rish rash garble gash"* is probably something in orc. It could mean something like, *"Get me another skull's full of enemy blood!"* Or basically orc Rip Its. Maybe it's their overbitten fangs or something that makes them sound this way. Maybe it's the fact they're as close to humanoid monsters as it gets here in the Ruin. They seemed to embody all the worst humanity had to offer back in our day: slavery, bloodlust, terror, savagery, unrepentant swipe-left ugliness, and it's not often I throw this word around because I get a little, or rather I used to be, gray on topics like good and evil… but pure evil.

Like diabolical. They've dragged our dead through the streets, jeering and shouting, tearing them to pieces and… yes, eating them.

The group that did Kurtz and Brumm had to pull back. They didn't have time for that.

There are things I am thankful for.

But back in the Ivory Towers of Scholarship and Higher Education I would have told you, because I had been told, that those terms, Good and Evil, were antiquated. Outdated. Not relevant anymore in those halcyon days of self-proclaimed enlightenment.

They are not. They were not. I know that now.

I've seen evil. It exists. It needs to be rooted out and croaked wherever one finds it. Trust me… it's better that way in the long run.

Unfortunately, the orcs seem to have an affinity for it. Evil. They're real bastards about it. I've left out some details because I'm run right now. Run hard and I'm trying to manage and keep functioning. It's warts and all, I know that. But right now, I just can't stand to write some of it down, much less see it. So, mercy on a poor historian is requested at this time. Later… later I'll write it all down, haul it into the light, unpack it, exorcise it.

As soldiers must do. And wonder why.

Our Ranger wizard, Specialist Kennedy, thinks this particular being, Shagbag, that came through the fracturing walls of the Observatory we're fighting over, was called Shaargazz. *Two giant floating demonic eyes peering in through the cracks and fissures of the delicate, almost cathedral-like outer walls of the Observatory that faced the desert.* I write that passage again because the moment was so stark, all those descriptive terms got stuck in my mind. Like I said, at first I thought this was just some giant, some monster, some new enemy heavy being brought to bear against our defense. Instead, this was something completely different, something flirting with that concept of... *other*.

Shagbag we call him.

Rangers. They gonna spit in your face and laugh even when you're beating the hell out of 'em. I understand that now, more than I ever did. More than at first.

According to his long-ago game, Kennedy thinks we went up against a very powerful, or what he calls "very high-level," enemy.

We asked him to define terms during the AAR. He said some nerd stuff.

I translated nerd stuff.

"What's a Shaargazz?" I asked the Ranger wizard holding court, his face smoke-burnt, his RPGs scratched and cracked. Tanner was there with me, as were a few of the other Rangers. Tanner was, of course, smoldering a half-burnt smoke between desiccated and rotting lips and the revealed bone of his becoming horror-show face of an undead bounty hunter or something, and just muttered, "Yeah, Kennedy. What's a Shagbag there, stud?"

And after that, we simply called it *Shagbag*. It was best that way. I won't lie to you: if you were gonna get shook, then Shagbag was something that would *shake* you.

That concept of *other* more real now. When it shouldn't be. We had enough to deal with.

Shagbag appeared, entering the battlespace during the flat-out brawl for the Observatory, just behind and above Mola Ram Orc dominating the enemy attack across the well facing the Legion line and the Rangers I was leading. Again... two massive glowingly malevolent eyes like the eyes of some huge giant peering in at us with a... *darkness*... that cannot be described right now.

And honestly, when have you ever known me to be at a loss for words on any subject? Hey, Talker here. Have I written three pages lately on a Guatemalan pour-over I once had that changed my understanding of the concept of *earthy* and hints of malt?

Their appearance was shocking to me, the floating demonic giant eyes. It was so sudden that I felt a wave of pure arctic night cold sweep through me like I'd just been electrocuted for a brief and almost endless second. Those words are somewhat at odds… yes. But those are the words that make sense now. Ten thousand volts of sharp ice floe running down my spine and loosening my bowels in a sudden instant that threatened to ruin me forever. Like some player whose girl just checked his DMs. For me… this particular moment would be like *Rise and shine no coffee in the cupboard for Talker*. Yeah, we all have our Armageddons. Mine just happens to revolve around ground beans and hot water being endlessly unavailable before the day starts. You have yours. Don't judge me and I won't you.

You know that horrible feeling when the bottom drops right out of your petty schemes and you're caught without any kind of pitiful excuse for your behaviors and addictions? It feels like… *the end of the world meets a PowerPoint term life insurance seminar*. Forever. On Zoom. Cameras on, folks.

That's what those hate-filled eyes felt like glaring in at us small creatures fighting for a patch on the Ruin.

Other Rangers felt it too. I asked. Even ones not yet at the battle, but closing in and getting close, near enough, responding to signals from the snipers who were engaging, felt that things were going seriously sideways for us on the *X*.

Kennedy would later tell me that was one of Shagbag's innate abilities, apparently, adding his standard Ranger wizard nerd gamer's disqualifier that events in real time might not match the game he plays and *"Please don't bet your life on this, guys!"* You know, like when you tell someone how to do something that might be a little sketchy, change a car battery, clean some rain gutters, that sorta thing, and then you add, *"But hey, I don't know,"* because you don't want to be responsible for their possible death. His game was invented ten thousand years ago, and Kennedy again reminded us to, *"Please don't bet your life on this, guys!"*

The Rangers ignored that because it was information and they'd take it. They liked betting, but they liked winning more. *You ain't cheatin' you ain't tryin'*, they'd say, and laugh at the dead orcs they tossed off the walls the next morning. Watching their stinking bodies hit the sand and rocks below like the stench-filled bags of death they were.

Winning has its benefits.

Yeah, normally all of us would have groaned like we always did, shouted Kennedy down, or threatened the Ranger Wizard Specialist with violence of some sort, on some level, if he added his warning ever again, but... Shagbag had been a real-deal fight and most of the Rangers, having just encountered the real-deal *other* supernatural in ways we hadn't before, weren't necessarily feeling like shutting down the flow of info coming from Kennedy because he wouldn't stop his particular version of, *"But hey, I don't know."*

See... Shagbag was a new thing. A bad thing. A, in fact, very dangerous *other* thing. And if that was the case, new bad very dangerous things for the Rangers to play with, then things were getting weirder and weirder by orders of magnitude here in the Ruin the closer we got to our intended high-value target: Mummy. Much weirder here in the desert sands of the south than at first when we started out from the Valley of the Island of Bag of Death, or Ranger Alamo if you prefer. It gets called various things in the retellings and AARs.

Kennedy says that's standard on *quests*. Tougher, weirder, *other* things coming into play.

So… we're on a quest now.

Quest. An expedition undertaken in medieval romance by a knight in order to perform a prescribed feat.

Apparently, in Kennedy's little game of pens and paper and strangely shaped dice, rulebooks, and manuals with crazy drawings, a Shagbag, or *Shaargazz the Night Lord*, if you prefer, is a god. Of some sort.

A god of the orcs, to be specific. They seemed to have more than one.

If you believe in that sort of thing, that is.

Now, Shagbag wasn't the Ranger detachment's first go-around with this level of supernatural Ruin weirdness. Sergeant Thor had iced a "god" back in the temple within the city when we took it off the Saur.

But what's a "god"? A powerful being with abilities beyond that of, even here in the Ruin, fantastic creatures and monsters? Something a bunch of monsters view as beneficial to them if they give it stuff? Don't know, don't care. All I knew at that moment was it was entering my battle, and on the wrong side. That meant it, Shagbag, needed to die right now. ASAP.

Get it done, Ranger.

This is how a Ranger would think regarding a haji with an AK, or your divine all-powerful god of endless suffering and darkness. You need to no longer be a problem.

I are Ranger now. And so… I Rangered it.

The OODA loop ran in a half a second just like Kurtz, and every other Ranger NCO, had drilled into us. Observe, Orient, Decide, Act.

Deploy suicide ruck. Now!

Whatever this thing was, right now two giant demonic eyes glaring into our fight right then and there, and yeah other strange shadowy creatures swarming out of the *nepenthe of darkness* surrounding it, needed to die, and I immediately prioritized it for as much destruction as I had access to.

The suicide ruck.

Which was strapped to a Ranger who got bit by some sea hoochie and was now carrying a very dangerous amount of explosives. Gill.

Nepenthe… something capable of causing oblivion of grief or suffering. A very purple ten-cent word I won't charge you for. I shouldn't use it, but hey… this is my account and I'm the greatest writer in the world if only because everyone else died a long, long, long time ago. So I win and coffee, which I've had a lot of, whispers to me now, "Go for it, Talker! Use the fancy words. Time's running out. Shoot your shot."

So… nepenthe.

The *nepenthe of darkness* surrounding Shagbag.

In a way, at that very moment, the fantastic was getting really commonplace, though it was trying very hard to murder us practically every day here in the Ruin.

A small observation here within the account: An orc, back in the world we came from, would have been an incredible thing to see in real life when you think about it. Disney would have swooped right in, bought that orc up, built a whole new "Orc Land" complete with stuffed animals and tee shirts in the gift shop to showcase him after the orc ride in which I guess there would be colorful scenes of looting, pillaging, and general murder. But here in the Ruin, every orc and their mother, along with every other lizard man, a ton of goblins, a bunch of hobgoblins, packs of werewolves, gnolls, or snarling dog men if you prefer, and a bunch of other random and very weird creatures, had tried to kill us just about every day.

Not even every other day. But literally every day I could remember. Plus there was magic, poison, and generally dangerous terrain and weather.

Or, Tuesday in the Ruin.

In the Ruin the fantastic is pretty much commonplace from the perspective of ten thousand years ago. Even though we're carrying machine guns and explosives and eating MREs, that fantastic is creeping, crawling, and sometimes flying right at you in order to kill you dead. And if that's not bad enough... it probably wants to eat you to boot.

Yeah, back in the world we came from, things were dangerous. Gangs. Bad neighborhoods. Shootings and stabbings. General violence. But... it's not like they were gonna eat you, now was it?

The fantastic is fun, until it comes at you with a rusty knife and a hungry look in its eyes. Then... well, it's a different kind of fun and games. But I guess that all depends on what kind of person you are.

For Rangers... it was fun as in *Game on, weird thing. I get finished with you, you ain't gonna propagate the species straight ever again.*

To the monsters... *we* were fantastic—and that had been mentioned in AARs and noted accordingly.

After Kennedy told us what a Shagbag was, or *who* he was, Tanner burnt the last of that smoke he was musing, swore a little like a soft, silent hiss, and tossed the dead cigarette off into the sand near a cracked carved stone probably ten thousand years old. Of course, Jabba scrabbled after it, teased it out of the sand without burning his claws, tried to smoke the butt, then ended up eating it instead like he usually did. Meanwhile, in the silence that followed, Tanner summed up the Ruin even as the little gob gobbled, gagged, and finally swallowed the spent butt in some kind of goblin triumph. And Tanner summed it up eloquently, in my opinion, because that was how I, and I bet a lot of other Rangers, were beginning to feel after a year and a half of trying not to get killed every day by the fantastic and weird here in the Ruin.

"When we… like… gonna meet a unicorn… or a horse with wings, or something cool, Kennedy? When's that gonna happen, man? Something nice, you know."

To which Kennedy, in his standard unable-not-to-be-specifically-precise way silently murmured a small correction to Tanner's abuse of myth.

"Pegasus. That would be a horse with wings, Tanner. Greek mythology."

"Yeah," said Tanner, not bothered in the least by the correction, his dead eyes far away and somewhere else. "When we gonna meet something nice, man? Something good. Something… magical in that way you thought things might be when you were just a kid and someone read you fairy stories you hoped were real, and better than the life you were living."

And of course, there was no answer to that. Kennedy, much less the rest of us, had no idea what would get thrown at us one day to the next. You left the walls of your fortress, like FOB Hawthorne, or the major human settlements like Portugon, and Accadion, according to the legionnaires, and the world was literally filled with fantastic, fanged, poisonous, magical, and very dangerous monsters that would try to kill you one way or the other. And as has been noted… oftentimes then *eat you*. And if that wasn't bad enough, there were more of them, collectively, than humans. Including even if you added in the human-adjacent "good" races, like elves and dwarves and a few others we hadn't run into yet. Apparently, according to Vandahar.

And even then, they weren't always good. See the dark-skinned psycho elves that hunted Sergeant Joe and me out in the desert for example. Those guys were nuts. And murderous.

I mean maybe Al Haraq, the djinn, was… *magical.* But he felt, I don't know… *dangerous* to me and not necessarily on anyone's side. In some way I couldn't necessarily put my finger on quite yet, it felt that way with him. Maybe it was the three demon temptresses who constantly stretched their curvy bodies and undulated in silk gowns of tempting sheer gossamer, casting eyes and whispering soft sighs that promised ten thousand years of damnation for just a moment of pleasure.

The legionnaires argued endlessly over the terms of the deal. So did the Rangers.

Maybe it was those diminutive beauties that told me there was something darker to the smiling djinn. But I had a feeling it was something more than just that. Something more dangerous. Something darker. Something inhuman. Riding around in my ruck. Tempting me with the power to change things. The power to ruin things.

The power to be damned forever.

Maybe...

Have I made it clear I have a lot on my plate?

So Shagbag, or Shaargazz the Night Lord, in that first instant of entering my battle, didn't appear like a god to me as he, or it, peered malevolently into the battle in the well of the fractured old Observatory high atop the desert walls of Sûstagul. I thought he was *just a giant*. LOL. The Legion line had formed around me, White, and Sergeant Monroe who was still down and unconscious, or dead at that very moment possibly, we didn't know then. Gill with the suicide ruck, watching our rear and shooting down the fast-moving orcs waving hatchets or strange curved swords with jagged edges, was just behind us, working his way through the slaughtered and hacked dead orcs and legionnaires who'd already gone down, boots navigating slick blood and pulpy guts spreading out over the stones and flooring, outgoing fire putting down fast-movers as he closed up on us.

I saw those huge demonic eyes at that moment, felt that utter coldness of what death and true hate must be like, and thought, "Giant!"

That was my initial impression when I saw those two huge malevolent eyes glaring right in at me. Sending a bone-chilling cold right down into my soul. I felt, and I think this was my ability kicking in, my psionics flipping over from *passive* to *active scan*, which is how I've come to think of them and their usage, I think I felt pure, endless hatred. Utter... utter hatred. For everything.

For life itself.

It was like... nothing I've ever felt before. And yes, I would have told you I'd been around people who hated me for good cause, Sidra's family for example to name a clan of mobsters and high-finance criminals. And also, people that didn't have any reason to hate me other than that they just hated me.

Which has surprisingly never really bothered me.

There was this one drill sergeant back in Basic. Sims. That guy was what I would have called a practitioner of the art of pure hatred. Kinda guy who just watched you and you could tell he was just disgusted with you for even continuing to breathe. But that wasn't the worst thing about Drill Sergeant Sims. Sometimes, when he thought no one was watching, I could see him just glaring at us, like he was in a trance, at all us new recruits just formed up and waiting for the next horrible thing to overcome.

And it wasn't good. Not at all. It was, now that I think about it, a kind of low-grade *other* that wasn't on the training schedule. It was like he was just thinking up all the bad things he could do, given the right excuse, infraction, or set of circumstances… and the utter pleasure that would give him torturing others for the sheer fun of it. Again, I'll add one more wring on the chamois of description here… sometimes, in rare instances, Sims would let you see just how happy your suffering was actually going to make him when he got to work on you. When you failed at some task, he'd stand there, long legs spread and planted, tapping one fist on top of the other, head down, staring into his boots like he was thinking real hard about what you'd just done and how terrible that was, but his eyes were just absolutely glittering with evil as a huge smile spread across his thin dark face.

You were his now.

All his. And there was no one who could rescue you.

That was a pretty scary feeling at the moment and it's still one that bothers me on some level.

That's one of the things about your first real exposure to... *other*. You think it's new and terrible, then you realize it was lurking in the cracks and corners of your life all along. Waiting...

Before that first wave of hatred from Shagbag hit us I would have told you that was what pure hatred was. Sims, smiling, knowing he had you now. But, in hindsight now, after this Shagbag, death god of the orcs, Sims was just an amateur playing at being a devil.

Shagbag... orc god of death. That was the real live hatred devil in the big book of pain and suffering.

That wave of pure cold death hit you like a sudden arctic front you could almost see sweeping in at you and it made you feel, for just a moment, some horrible sharp pain that if it doesn't pass in the next second or two, *if it stays... if it torments...* then that's real bad. Like... what if this is forever now? What if the pain stays? There's a certain kind of sudden terror, utter helplessness, in that forever moment.

If that's what Hell really is, then I want no part of it. Zero stars. Would not recommend.

When I described it to Kennedy later, during the AAR, he said, "If the rules of the game are in play, Talker, that was some kind of saving throw check you made. And again, rules of the game... hold on here I'm not going to say what you think I'm going to say, but if this was some deity, or demigod, or a demon playing at being a god to these orcs... in the game this level of power would have made you save at negatives to save. Meaning the deck was stacked against you not freezing in fear. So, the fact that you 'rolled your save,' Talker, means, metaphorically… you threw a natural twenty and beat the fear- and cold-based attack its very presence emanates. Which is… something, Talk. Way to go. You made your save."

I have no idea what any of that means.

I doubt the rules of the game are in effect here. But, since we need everything, everything we can get our hands on here, just to survive one more day, then Kennedy's lore has become a kind of gospel, or whatever, among the normally stoic Rangers.

Save versus Death.

Or as the Rangers say, *Anything, Anytime, Anywhere.*

The Rangers listen to Kennedy. Imagine that. And sometimes the stuff he tells us is straight-up nightmare fuel. Stuff most people will pull the covers over their heads and hope goes away. Rangers, they'll hear it… then they'll get on with the business of killing it. Regardless.

In that way, they are pure stoics. Rangers through and through. They will try to kill anything. Telling them it *can't* be killed is just a challenge. More suck to embrace.

So that's what I do now at this moment of a god trying to flip the red queen on my force.

I accept the ridiculousness that somehow I "threw a natural twenty" on some metaphysical level and failed to get scared. Then I ordered Commons, or Gill, to deploy the suicide ruck on his back because that giant had just scared the living daylights out of me at first appearing.

Or…

I knew we couldn't hold against one of those, whatever the giant demon-eyed thing was, from the moment I first saw it. If only because the eyes were so… *giant*… and that indicated the rest of the body must be… *huge*. Obviously.

I'd been up close and personal when Kennedy used his powerful magical staff, the dragon-headed gnarled old chunk of dark wood, fireballing a giant right off the side of Ranger Last Stand Hill on Taco Bell Bag-of-Death Island.

That feels like a long time ago.

That feels like another Talker ago.

I remember the next day I'd meet Autumn and the stench of all that killing the Rangers had wrought in their determined defiance of death's meeting, none of that touched her when I first saw her on the edge of the river, the bodies of bloating orcs floating by.

That was... a long time ago.

Another life, not this one anymore.

At that moment I knew we were in trouble, and I ordered Commons to deploy the ruck and blow the death god, and all of us most likely, straight to smithereens. Or hell.

Again, I thought it was *just a giant*. LOL.

If you don't understand why I did that then you don't understand that this spot on the wall could not fall into enemy hands if the Rangers were to survive and complete the mission they had set themselves to accomplish.

Anything, Anytime, Anywhere.

That we and the legionnaires died in the process didn't matter. That it, the mission, was accomplished... did.

I knew Shagbag had to die in order to hold this spot on the wall. That was all that mattered in that moment. Kill the orc death god. Hold the wall.

Do it, Gill. Blow us to kingdom come. Whatever that is.

CHAPTER NINE

GILL knelt. I dashed forward and grabbed his MK18 carbine as he shouted, "Ten rounds left!" at me. He set the ruck down, stripped the Velcro cover off the det-timer cord, and got ready to yank for arming.

We'd get thirty seconds once that happened.

I shot an orc running in at us with a dagger. Three rounds to kill him.

More coming in.

"Firing!" shouted Gill.

There were ten bricks of C4 in the ruck and about fifty pounds of shrapnel that had once been riveted orc armor that had been broken up and cut into jagged pieces in order to rip everything to shreds after the initial *thunderhump* of explosive force from the detonation.

Sergeant Kang said that would give us about seventy-five to one hundred meters of kill. Then he uncharacteristically added, "When dealing with explosives, the 'P' always stands for 'Plenty.'"

One brick can destroy a vehicle. A small house. A rail, pylon, or a support beam. A small light traffic bridge even. Three can do a lot more. Composition C4 explodes at twenty-six thousand feet per second. Add in the Ranger-contrived dirty-tricks shrapnel, and not only are you going to make a large crater, or in this case blow out the outer wall of the Observatory, but you're going to destroy every living being within the radius of said explosion.

The shrapnel wasn't packed to form an explosion cone—meaning a one-direction explosion like a claymore to ruin the enemy and protect the defenders. The intent of the suicide ruck Gill was arming was that the explosion, and speeding shrap, go *everywhere* as whoever was deploying the last-stand weapon was considered to be overrun and that the enemy was everywhere and needed to be destroyed in order to maintain the hold at this particular point in the defense once the next quick reaction force came in to secure.

It was a denial-of-movement munition Sergeant Kang and Captain Knife Hand had cooked up. It was payback on the enemy for getting the position we were defending.

There would be no survivors.

The chances of surviving deployment of the suicide ruck were slim, according to Sergeant Kang, unless there was sufficient cover. Three bricks of C4 were going to turn the walls of the Observatory into yet more speeding shrapnel in an instant.

There was little cover I could see my force reaching in time.

But we could not lose the walls.

Gill ran.

I shouted, "Run!" and we grabbed Monroe. But even as we did, I knew we were never gonna make it in time.

"*Corri per le tue bugie!*" I barked at the legionnaires, gasping and hoarse.

Run for your lives!

"*Correre! Correre! Correre!*"

CHAPTER TEN

THERE was no magic that protected us from the blast. No sudden power of Ruin Revealing discovered when we needed it most. We ran and we dragged Sergeant Monroe for all we were worth with what little few and precious seconds remained to us before we were disintegrated by our explosives.

White, whisper-singing his song about a frog with a pistol and sword at his side, worked fast and hard just to get our sergeant onto a portable stretcher as we'd deployed the suicide ruck. Now it was by that that we dragged the minotaur Ranger and moved as fast as we could, me counting down the det.

Wishing for more time than what had been allotted.

If wishes were horses, beggars would ride. Isn't that right, Mom?

The legionnaires didn't need to be told twice to run. Shields and spears hauling and flailing, they weren't chicken, it's just that they'd gotten used to our particular brand of "Ranger magic." They knew the big *BOOM* was coming. They'd learned to survive.

At the count of five seconds left we made the top of the steps leading out of the wall. At four, the legionnaires were practically flinging themselves down and off the steps leading away from the wall. At three, I turned and saw Shagbag himself manifesting into our reality like the being of utter darkness he was.

He was a hulking orc, rippling with muscles. Shaven-headed like a monk. Like Mola Ram Orc. Grinning like a demon with ears to match. Huge, like one of the western orc giants from where the maps marked the Land of No Return beyond the edge of known Ruin civilizations. We'd fought those there, beyond the map's edge. Now they were just the dead we'd left on our trail of revenge and payback. But now, here, was Shagbag, hulking and jacked, wrapped in a flowing ragged cloak that seemed darker than the night itself all around us. He grasped its edge, his mouth and fangs working, his voice sounding like the creaking giant final door of damnation and Hell itself, and suddenly a winter storm formed and sprang out for us, turning everything to ice as it raced across the floor of the well of the Observatory.

At the count of two I saw panthers of shadowy black ink, phantoms really, slinking over the broken stones and ruin of the well, sliding effortlessly over the forming ice everywhere that was streaking toward us like a winter cyclone coming without remorse or mercy. Huge bats swarmed the night, the size of horses, swimming through the frost and icy mist that had suddenly appeared in the night. Their eyes burned apocalypse red, huge dripping fangs open and moaning like a roaring sea never meant to be heard by human, living, loving ears.

It was the sound the damned make when they want nothing but the end of all good things and that all of us join them in that place of final no return.

At one... someone grabbed me and I fell backward, I never found out who, knowing in that same instant I'd been hypnotized in some sudden way by the very *otherness* of Shagbag the Night Lord, demon god of orcs. I was, in that instant, frozen to the ancient rock steps that led into the well from our defenses along the wall.

I was the last one out...

Then I fell backward, pulled by someone, and was dragged down as the sudden detonation of the suicide ruck went off like dull thunder far off, and roaring horror sudden and all at once.

I have a vague memory, or an image, of the walls blasting away above me as I was pulled down into the walls and mounds beyond and below the Observatory.

My ear pro was on, but the concussion of the blast drove the wind out of me and seemed to slam into my brain and my eyes. All breath was gone, and I wondered if I would ever breathe again.

This was overpressure from the blast.

Flying, spraying, speeding rock went in every direction. The stone steps shifted and collapsed under us. Legionnaires roared, and screamed, and prayed, shouting in Italian to "Hold!" as if they were fighting the line, holding the shield wall, when really, they were just victims of the blast and hoping to see another day. Aren't we all, though? But that was them. They'd run their game no matter what. That was what they'd been trained to do. That was what they would do come Hell or Hades.

Whatever their captain wanted, they would do. For the Legion, for the eagles they wore, and of course... for their captain.

"*Tenere! Tenere!*" they shouted, dumbstruck and screaming, no ear pro for them as all went darker than it should have been, flames and rock suddenly going in every direction all at once and an earthquake unlike any ever before right under us.

"*Tenere per il Capitano, Cani!*" shouted Corporal Chuzzo above it all and was still shouting it when the thunder died and the wall we were perched on and sliding down its shifting piles of cracked rock... stopped even though the raining dust and debris did not.

There was a kind of dull silence.

I was on all fours, panting.

"*Tenere per il Capitano, Cani!*" continued Chuzzo just as harshly and hoarsely as when I'd ordered them to run for their lives.

Hold for the captain, Dogs!

Dust and powdered rock rained down on us like the victims of some terror bomb at ground zero, or near enough. I looked up into the night and could see the dust blossom and bloom against the cold and naked stars up there that didn't care about our petty wars and desperate fights. The night wind and the sandstorm already carrying it away as though getting ready for our next tantrum.

"Rangers... sound off!" I barked just as Kurtz would've, and felt in recognizing that, I must be doing something right.

For once.

"Here," coughed Gill nearby in the destruction. His voice a dry croak. I followed him through the dust and found he was not far from me, lying among a pile of legionnaires who'd covered him with their shields. They were covered in dust and smiling, their eyes and teeth white, their dusty skin like the buried dead. Some even laughing, though I could see fear in their eyes at what they'd just experienced.

As though they were asking whether we were dead, or alive for a little bit longer and a lot more horror now. And wondering if that even mattered, knowing it did not.

They were Accadion Legion. They would give a good account of themselves and have fun stacking skulls until they could not.

"White?" I shouted above it all and got nothing. Then I remembered he couldn't hear. I pushed forward to where I thought we'd been when the blast went off, crawling through the scree of pulverized stone upslope. Through the swirling dust I could see him lying atop Sergeant Monroe.

Covering him. Protecting.

I crawled on all fours to the inert White, tapped him, and hoped they hadn't been killed. White looked up at me, grinning, mouth moving, singing that stupid song.

I think. My ear pro was smashed. Or I couldn't hear now too.

I gave him a thumbs-up and pushed off, scrambling through the debris, pushing upward to reach where the Observatory had been. Out there all along the walls of Sûstagul below, I could see the battle, battles, still raging despite what had happened here. I saw the guns talking. Tracer fire. Legionnaires repelling mass waves of orc fire. Wizards, ours and theirs, firing off their arcane sorceries to prevent, or prevail.

None of that mattered to me.

I had to know if we'd killed the giant. The thing. Shag-bag the whatever. I had to know if we still owned the real estate.

That had been my job. Time to see that it was done.

I had the sergeant major's Glock and my knife. I got to my feet and pulled myself up into the remains of that point on the wall we'd called the Observatory, determined to get it done, if it still had to be, with a knife and a gun.

Anything, Anytime, Anywhere.

What I saw next shocked me to the core, and the only thing I could mutter as I stood there was...

"That's... impossible..."

The Shagbag thing, half his face missing, one arm blown off, skin shredded in a dozen places at least, standing amidst ruined shadows and the minced, explosive-pulverized remains of bats the size of horses, hissed inside my mind at me.

Psionics.

"Come to me, one called... Talker. Come to me and know death. Come to one as old as you."

CHAPTER ELEVEN

I hit Shagbag with everything I had on hand.

Ranger. Me being one.

I bore down hard, just like Vandahar taught me not to, instead recommending I control my power through mental direction, suggestion really, and letting it flow outward from me in its usage.

Use the force, Luke, and all that jazz.

But I had found in times past, like that time I nuked all the headless horsemen trying to push the gun team, really just their horses, that if I gritted my teeth, bore down hard, and thought, "You wouldn't like me when I'm angry!" it really did make me angry, or at least better able to access what I was trying to do with my powers. And yes, I did binge-watch the old series that phrase came from and I always dug it when the star used that line. But really it was when the actor would look at the camera and his eyes would go wide and angry and change color…

Hey, wouldn't that be cool if my eyes actually did change color? I'll have to ask Tanner if that actually happens when I do this.

Noted.

But that look on the actor's face, that was my… key. My key to unlocking this level of the psionic blast I could do.

I knew an actor back in one of the colleges I was blowing through who was taking Italian so he could nail a part in a movie. He was really good at accents. He could imitate all kinds of celebrities like Christopher Walken, Sean Connery, and a bunch of others. I mean… spot on, and when I heard them, those actual actors, later, I thought he actually did them better than they did themselves. Go figure. But that actor told me the trick to imitating someone was to unlock a key phrase the celebrity did, a touchstone, and then build from there in mastering them saying other things.

Which were funnier than what they really said.

That's what I'd done with my psionic blast power.

I have other powers I've unlocked and been taught by Vandahar. And I think more will come. Whether that's a good thing or a bad thing… jury's still out. But the Rangers need me to be all I can be, and me is a guy who can basically shoot a mental fireball at you and fry your mind. A little.

And that was all I had to work with right now. So… game on.

Side note… it gives me a real bad headache whether I do it the Vandahar nice way or go full David Banner.

It's just the David Banner way is the easy path for me, and the key was, "You wouldn't like me when I'm angry."

I'd think that, or even mutter it. Then… stand back. I'm about to give you the ice cream headache of your life. And then some.

Fear me, you know.

So, I hit Shagbag, half his face blown off…

Later, when I told Tanner my end of the story on the *X* at the Observatory, he kept saying, "Face Off!" over and over in that dry dead voice of his that's becoming him more and more now. The Ruin revealing. Then he's laughing. Also, a dry death chuckle. Like autumn leaves rattling around on a windy cold November afternoon when no one seems to be out and the world is as dead as the calendar says it is.

"Ya ever see that one, Talk?" Tanner asked me, smoke between his rotting lips.

I had no idea what he was talking about.

"Face Off!"

I still have no idea.

But back to me using my mind powers on a divine being. If you're thinking this was really cool and all, like a Jedi mind trick sorta... it was, in fact, a very big mistake on my part.

Shagbag laughed at my psionics. Big-time. He had them in spades. And other massive powers.

I mean, I think I hurt him. A little. His face was blown off after all. Half of it. His left arm was missing. His skin was shredded by shrap. All from the blast of the suicide ruck.

The bats and shadow panthers were ruined in every direction spreading away from ground zero of the ruck. He got nuked, as they say. But he was still standing. And laughing at me like Hell's door slowly creaking open.

Not... unlike Tanner, at times.

And yeah, that bothers me too.

The Ruin reveals isn't just all jacked muscles, tiger claws, and minotaur horns. Or gills in Gill's case. Oh, and he says he can talk to fish.

LOL!

Rangers give him no end of grief for admitting this and tell him that's the lamest superpower ever. Chief Rapp says it's actually good, as the fish can give us intel. But he would say that. He always finds something useful in everyone. He's an encourager. I could be like him more.

Gill says the fish have the attention span of a gnat. And that all they ever want to talk about is food, their constant hunger, and their pretty colors. They have no long-term memory and seem surprised when they're hungry every ten seconds or so.

Look at my pretty colors. Oh, hey, food. I'm really hungry. Look at my beautiful stripes. Who's hungry? I could totally eat again. Wow, my colors are beautiful today... Hey, food.

Apparently, this is a conversation with fish.

Or as Gill says, "Fish don't care, Talk."

He also notes they're quite friendly and polite if not a little overly self-obsessed. So there's that.

Not everyone gets superpowers of the Ruin. Some are X-Men. True. And some are just Aquaman talking to fish.

So there I was...

I hit Shagbag with my thermonuclear psionic blast and felt my teeth bite so hard in doing so that I either chipped a tooth or made that horrible grating sound you sometimes make when you're really hungry and chewing too fast. My temples throbbed instantly like some weird mind alien-brain thing in a sci-fi show with bulging head muscles and all. I could feel my blood suddenly growing thick inside my skull and I was like, for half a second, *uh-oh*.

Then the powerful psionic blast shot away from me. I can see it. Mentally. I can also see that no one else can see it. I know... weird, huh? But, like I've said before, it feels like that X-Men character's eye blast thing. Whoever that guy is.

And this one was a good one. If I do say so myself.

It slashed right into Shagbag like a wave of ragged mental energy and knocked him back.

A little.

Then, instantly, a shimmering red gem of darkness grew right out of his skull and surrounded his ruined body like... I don't know... the shields on a starship. And yeah, I know no such thing exists, or maybe it does, hey I'm here in *Lord of the Rings* Land so why not? Maybe there are space marine versions of the legionnaires and star freighters that jump around real fast and some kind of Clint Eastwood bounty hunter pursuing a man in black across the Edge of the Galaxy, I don't know. That sounds pretty stupid like something a couple of lazy science fiction writers would pitch to a film studio that would make anything on a discount.

A couple of real chungos.

But I'm using this account of the Rangers' time in the Ruin, warts and all, to describe everything as it happened and as I experienced it. And psionics... psionics are weird. And that's putting it mildly. It's there. In real-time. And it's not. The users, or "wielders of the mental arts" as Vandahar would say and make you feel like you're in a movie or something, can see it. Psionics. No one else can. I've asked Tanner when he's been around me and I've used them, if he can see them firing off. He's seen nothing.

And he can see the dead!

But I can't. So there's that.

Again, the Ruin is a strange and very weird place.

The pulsing red ruby that came out of Shagbag's ruined skull, one of his eyes was hanging from its socket where it'd been blown out by the blast, that psionic gem, as it were, deflected my blast away from him just as it enveloped and swarmed him. It was as though the gem of ruby-red mental energy was creating a small channel, or making an island, around Shagbag.

My mental blast lasted for a brief second, then it was done.

And then I threw up.

'Cause I'm dope like that.

Ranger working here, folks. Stand back... I'm a professional.

The mental gem faded and again all I could hear was Shagbag laughing dryly, like an opening tomb, at me.

There was nothing but that and a vast dead silence.

Well, that's not totally true.

There was the sound of me heaving up my last meal. Meat on the street just outside the coffee tents before I started interrogating the orc early that afternoon.

Remember that war crime?

But the battle, all up and down the line and all along the walls of Sûstagul... silence. Nothing even existed as we blasted each other with our mental powers.

Vandahar has explained this to me.

"When two wielders of the great powers meet, time becomes... strange, young Talker. A contest can take but the blink of an eye before one of the wielders is dead, and the other lives. Attacks and counterattacks can be exchanged for what seems, to the wielders, like hours, but mere seconds have passed to the external watchers."

So. Maybe the universe stopped as we fought. I don't know. Hey, I'm new here.

To my credit, and not being all... self-aggrandizing here... I shucked the smaj's Glock and walked forward, still throwing up, firing one-handed at Shagbag. Yeah, not pro-level Chief Rapp shooting, but the one hand was all I could do. Half my body felt dead, and when I looked down at my vomit-covered rig, venomous cobras, undead figments of psionics—so they were real, and not real at the same—were slither-crawling all over and up my legs and arms on my left side.

This was Shagbag's opening move. I had to admit, in a distant part of my brain… that was pretty pro.

I dumped rounds, slower than I would have liked, as I walked forward toward the maimed Shagbag. The sound of my boots crunching on the explosive-ruined gravel echoed like the only sound in a completely empty universe. Each bang of the gun was like a supernova of light, noise, and pain there.

A psionic cobra, clearly a mental attack from Shagbag, reared up at me, spit mental venom in my eyes, blinding me, and then, as my vision misted over, dove *into* my eye.

And that's when things got bad, and I got lost in the dark ocean of madness that was the Night Lord's mind.

CHAPTER TWELVE

HE was a serial killer. Shagbag was. From a long time ago. Our time. Ten thousand years past.

What I saw there, inside his mind, as our mental powers connected, was more horrific than anything I've ever seen in the Ruin.

And we've seen some dark stuff.

I'm not gonna do details. Warts and All takes a break here. There are some things you don't want to know. Trust me.

I know them now, and I truly wish I did not.

So… please… trust me.

Shagbag was once a guy named Kenneth Lemoore. Ten thousand years ago as the nano-plague started.

The implications of that statement are… staggering. In a lot of ways. But the thing my mind fixates on is the longevity aspect. If only so I can block out all the true darkness I saw in there, inside his mind, when he sent his psionic cobras through my eye and into my mind after my pitiful psionic mind blast got deflected by his mighty mental ruby shield.

The cobra was a mental probe of some sort that sought to link us. And to enslave me. Now that I think back on it, AAR'ing a psionic battle all by myself—because half the Rangers would think I'm nuts, and the other half would be afraid I could read their thoughts and that's not good—but when I think back... yes. I think Shagbag was trying to enslave me.

The psionic cobra attack did two things. It connected him to my mind, my memories, me. And it connected me to him, his mind... his memories.

Ten thousand years of horror suddenly flashed across my brain. In ways it was moving too fast, and in other ways, in what I think Vandahar was trying to explain to me, slowed down and... and I *lived* those horrible memories of a murderer.

Cold fall nights on his desolate rundown pig farm.

The forty years he spent in prison when he was caught.

The endless cigarettes he smoked waiting for something... or someone.

Of those things, and the horrors I saw and heard in there, the pig farm was the worst by far, and it left vast psychic impressions on me. Not like tattoos... more like jagged deep scars that will never heal.

I sent up mental shields inside me to defend myself as he went to work on me, but he batted these aside with a flaming whip he'd created out of pure hateful malice and psionic energy.

At the moment he started to hit me with that, two things were happening in my mind at once. I was walking up a deserted country road, the stars and the night cold, hearing the pigs feeding. His pigs. His victims. I could see him standing there in the dark, watching, a shadow among deeper shadows he might not have realized were there, standing just like a human version of Shagbag... watching the pigs feed.

A cruel smile I could feel more than see.

I never wanted to believe such a cruel and evil person could exist. So I'd told myself such horrors were distant… and maybe not even really real.

But they are. And he was.

Shagbag's mind, as the psionic curling hissing mental cobra drove itself into my mind during our duel, which was really just a beating I was taking, connected us and showed me those horrors were real and what the Ruin revealing had done to him ten thousand years ago and all along the way.

It was… all too real. Far too real. Horrible in ways I can't describe.

When he created the mental flaming whip, I pointed the Glock at what remained of his explosive blast-devastated skull. But it was slide-locked, and I was out of rounds.

So it was useless.

Then he hit me with the psychic whip. Then again. And again and again. Each mental slash was like being flayed alive.

It left no marks you can see. I've looked. But they're there. Trust me. I can feel them.

Seriously.

I screamed. Or at least I think I did in that other place that was our battle and his mind. But who was there to hear? If a Talker screams in a psionic battle, can you hear it? The answer is… yes, I still do. In that other world where people like us fight with our minds, it's real.

It's our version of the dead world only Tanner can see.

That was when the mental cobra connected, and I could see… and hear him. Shagbag.

Lemoore the life-in-prison serial killer who never should've seen the light of day but smoked and waited as though he would. Eventually.

He was dying when the plague hit, the one we jumped through time to save the world from. When it hit, he was dying in a prison hospital from cancer. He was an old man and his cruelty and evil had never stopped throughout all the years of confinement and prison.

Even as he was dying, he still wanted nothing more than to murder the nurse who was easing his pain. The orderlies who cleaned and fed him too. I saw that. Sensed that.

He was totally, utterly, cruel.

He was evil.

He was hatred.

He struck me again with the mental flaming whip and began to lumber around me, cracking the whip and growling like a wild animal right there in the middle of the psychic battlefield and the remains of the blast-devastated X. He was probing my mind. I was down on one knee. Breathing heavy and trying to gin up some power for another psionic trick. But the blast had failed, and the other things Vandahar had taught me weren't exactly useful at the moment.

I could turn off my eyes, becoming effectively blind, and still see. Hey, cool trick when talking with medusae.

Useless here in Psionics Thunderdome.

I was drowning in a sea of horrors he called his memories, and it was like being lost in the ocean during a storm that had lost its mind and gone howling mad with murder and darkness. And cold.

It was so cold my teeth were chattering like they were going to break.

The nano-plague, ten thousand years ago, brought him back to life from the cancer. Made him powerful. More powerful than the prisoners who were transforming into orcs all around him, sealed within their cells, locked in and groaning, swearing, sweating, transforming on their bunks as the Ruin revealed. Tearing everything apart in rage and pain to make it stop even though it would not, and could not.

He was, even then, already more powerful than the others. He knew that. He was… something special as he reached out and ravaged their minds with his new powers of domination.

He could steal their life force just by pointing the claw his finger had become in the revealing. He could make slaves and call them his faithful. He could give them his powers of darkness-seeing. And life-stealing.

But he hated them too. And because they were lesser and broken and ruined, they… worshipped him for this. Though at the time they thought it was just the politics of the prison.

The alpha wolf and the pack.

On that strange mad sea that was his mind, a ship, like a ghost ship with ragged sails and broken masts, came over a wave I was being sucked down into the trough of, and within his mind as I knew it at the time, I could see that it was something to him. That ship. That ghost ship wandering the seas of his mind. It haunted and taunted him.

The prow—you know where on old sailing ships a mermaid or something would be? I don't know what that's called nautically—had a carved woman, beautiful, her torso human, her lower body that of a curling leggy black widow wrapping around the hull.

The ship almost came down into the trough of the wave I was sucked under and for a long moment everything was anger-green, sucking current, and hot salt like the sulfurs of hell more than the sea. I waited for that strange ghost ship to slam into me and knock me senseless and I would drown there in that terrible sea of insanity.

Forever.

His psionic power was incredible, and it had been foolish of me to even attack him. I knew that now. He was dumping incredible amounts of mental energy to enslave me with his own psionics.

It wasn't even a fight. It was a straight-up beating.

And it was at that moment, as I was sucked under and drowned, that I remembered a cautionary note from Vandahar regarding the usage of psionics.

"During the great mental battles of two such as yourself, Ranger, you must remember that any time you spend your powers in the broad usage, you chance attracting even greater foes than yourself. The invisible world of psionics is more like a vast windswept steppe where others just like you, and often not so nice, smell the winds of the mind and come looking for prey to feast upon. Psionic predators feed on mental energies. You must be careful in that, Talker. Very careful you do not become someone's mental meal."

So I'd always been careful to keep my usage and practices brief and to be on the lookout for any other psionic presence when doing so. That was the active and passive scanning Vandahar had taught me. He called it "Detection Hunting."

But now, with this massively powerful being dumping large amounts of psionic energy on me, the chances of us drawing something worse into the conflict were growing.

Meanwhile… I was drowning.

Above me I could see the surface of the ocean he was trying to drown me in. I kicked, fought, grabbed at the moon in the night-mad skies there with my own mind, and pulled myself to the surface of the cold waters of the surging seas of hatred that were Shagbag's mind.

I turned, coughing, and saw the ghost ship with the spider hot chick mermaid on the prow below the bow, and now it was being driven away by the winds of madness that were his mind. Sucked into the storm to disappear like the ghost ship it was.

Note: the wind didn't howl here. It moaned and screamed and wept and begged as it drove the burning salty water into my eyes and tried to push me under again. And… it was the sound of all his victims, Lemoore Shagbag the Orc Night Lord, the howl of the wind was the murdered of ten thousand years, weeping on an ocean of eternal sorrows and midnight cold.

The ghost ship faded into the night, and on the back of it, like some ancient and fancy pirate ship, I could see the name of the ship stamped in gold lettering.

The gold was the clearest thing in the storm.

The Spider Queen.

I knew that name… my mind thought distantly.

My shattered mind, flayed open by the flaming whip of Shagbag the Night Lord, a serial killer of epic proportions from ten thousand years ago, knew that name.

The Book of Skelos.

The lost girl who coded the plague…

Shagbag sought her everywhere here in the Ruin.

Every. Where.

In those first *becoming* days, as his powers grew and he murdered guards and orcs of the prison he'd been sent to die in, orcs that had once been the worst criminals of our time, Lemoore had wondered… why him?

Why were his powers so… *god-like*… compared to the others transforming, or, Lemoore's word, *becoming*, all around him?

For ten thousand years he had sought the answer. Chasing the lost pages of the *Book of Skelos*. And at the same time, becoming a cruel kind of god to the slavish orcs whom he hated but hated less than every other thing in the Ruin.

Then the dragons came to the Ruin, and he made ally with them. And the Nether Sorcerer too, serving his dark cause for Shagbag's own ends. And the other realms of reality were revealed to him…

I saw this, and it was stunning. I saw this…

… just before a massive fifty-caliber round fired from *Mjölnir* went straight through part of Shagbag's brain.

In an instant the stars folded back and I saw other planes of existence and dimensions that he, Shagbag the Night Lord, or whatever, where even he had a kind of… he called it Heavens of Suffering… but it was really a sort of hell… where he ruled a dimension, or a plane of existence, of endless tunnels and deep darknesses.

And cold.

Utter. Cold. Hatred. And cold. Unending… cold.

All this in an instant as the fifty-caliber round tore through his skull and destroyed the mental battle between us.

But he wasn't dead.

How could the Night Lord be?

He was a god, not like us at all anymore.

CHAPTER THIRTEEN

I was on my knees. Shoulders slumped. Empty Glock in my assault-gloved hand.

My assault glove is giving up the ghost.

That was the first thought I had as I looked at the tears and ragged edges of the gloves I'd been issued ten thousand years ago at Area 51.

Shagbag, ruined as he was, staggered above me. There was no flaming whip in his hand now. He howled. The round from *Mjölnir*, sent by Sergeant Thor no doubt.

I'd find this out later. During the after-action review.

At the time, all I'd seen was the giant round tearing across the storm and sea of his mind, shredding the psionic battle just as two giant demonic eyes peered at me and said in that graveyard hiss…

"Ahhhhhaaaaaa… the Spider Queen. What do you know of her, thrall… and where is the book?"

Then I was back in this real reality, on my knees, empty slide-locked gun in hand. Staring at my worn gloves and thinking they, too, like me, were disintegrating a little bit more with each passing day.

Above me, Shaargazz, remaining eye hanging from its socket, leered around at all of us with wicked intent.

That was… sick.

Tanner was coming in, I was aware of that, firing his carbine and walking one foot in front of the other, just as we'd been taught, advancing and engaging. Shaargazz's gray dead skin exploded inward as each round from the MK18 found center mass.

Tanner had run to the scouts and then run back to support the QRF. He'd been at the bottom of the debris pile that was once a bridge and stairs that climbed to the top of the Sûstagul wall and the Observatory, when the suicide ruck went off and devastated the *X*.

Thor must've fired again but the round caught Shagbag in the chest and blew out a desiccated lung.

None of this bothered the serial killer playing at being an orc god.

Not the five-five-six in high dose that Tanner was dispensing.

Or fifty-caliber rounds from an anti-materiel rifle at distance by one of the best shooters in the regiment.

The one remaining claw Shagbag had swept across all the dead there in the well. The exploded bats. The lifeless shadow panthers. The parts remaining of the orcs and legionnaires who'd already died by violence and destruction.

"Die already!" shouted Tanner as he closed and fired like it would do something. That was my friend. He'd fight, even if winning wasn't an option.

Have a friend like that if you can find one. If you can't, be one. That's my wisdom. Mark it down on whatever shallow grave I end up in. I'm cool with that.

Tanner was gonna fire until he brought the Night Lord down.

But that didn't happen. In some distant part of my mind, I knew there was no winning against this Shagbag. The Night Lord. Lemoore.

Tanner fired more anyway.

The dead, all the shattered dead, began to rise around the orc demon. Golems of both legionnaire and orc began to form as the torn-apart pieces and corpses of what they once were crawled toward each other to form something new and horrible out of former enemies and allies alike.

"Aw, hell no!" shouted Tanner, close now, standing over me. He popped a grenade and thrust it into Shagbag's chest where Thor had blown open a huge hole.

Oh, I remember thinking… *that's not good.*

Then Tanner grabbed me and hauled me away from the impending detonation, putting his undead body between me and the soon-to-be blast.

I could see Shagbag as I was dragged backward and away, my mind fried, that awful headache building like a snowstorm of iron in my skull. All of this happened in slow motion, or so it seemed. Shagbag just reached into himself, pulled out the love grenade, and casually held it in his fist as it exploded.

The dead were clutching at us as Tanner dragged me away from the blast and absorbed shrap.

He doesn't feel pain anymore.

My friend is slowly dying even though he is already, technically, dead.

There was nothing we could do to kill Shagbag. Nothing. We'd lost the *X* and now all the dead there were going to animate and retake the point under his control. And then the Guzzim would swarm the walls once more and own this piece of the pie.

I'd failed.

We'd failed. Because of me.

I raised the Glock, forgetting it was slide-locked once again and pointed it at Shagbag, telling myself I wasn't done. I still had my knife. I'd get free of Tanner and I'd cut that leering eyeball hanging from Shagbag's socket free. Maybe that would do something...

I don't know.

But I was willing to try.

Shagbag clutched the grave-shroud cloak of darkness and shook it hard as once more a winter storm began to form all around him and us.

He'd make it cold. He'd make it his. He'd make... death.

Kennedy told me later he was casting something called Cone of Cold, in the game of course, and that was bad.

Then Big Baby D came up through the broken stones of the wall, the actual wall and the floor of the Observatory atop the walls of Sûstagul, surfacing like a great white shark ready to attack, and in one instant it did what it does and tore Shagbag right in half with one bite.

I forgot to mention the Rangers acquired a "dog" in the Ruin. Let me tell you about that now.

It all starts with Specialist Thounsavath going to the Street of Cages in the deep alleys of Sûstagul where strange things are often found.

He had an MRE spoon.

CHAPTER FOURTEEN

LET me explain what a Big Baby D is. I probably should've explained this earlier in the account because it was something that happened during some down time in the city. But things have been a little... fantastic lately. As you've read so far.

In my defense, I'd gotten distracted. And no, it wasn't about coffee–although I could use a cup. Or ten. I was knee-deep in getting the whole suicide ruck thing going and making sure none of us cooked off in the explosion. Ya know, the NCO business of running the QRF and holding the wall. I thought that was the answer to settle the evil orc shaman and their god, but it turned out to be more than just that. Shagbag and all. Almost enslaving me.

NCO biz. Because apparently, I totally know what that means.

In the prior days, between fighting off slavering hordes of orcs smashing into one gate or another, while the truly terrifying Ranger-grade orcs hit us from another direction altogether, I was struck with two things that made me realize I had been truly ignoring certain parts of Ranger culture while I trudged from one side of the defense to another in search of orc scalps, and coffee, because let's be honest... me of course. The first thing was a battle-tested Joe-ism: "The only thing truly stopping you from doing something is yourself not thinking you can do it." Something he said often. Of course, being in the Joe cult now, I was applying that to myself in spades. Taking up this leadership role as the QRF leader like I was researching a cleverly evasive dialect of Chinese that had found its way to some quarter of a city where there shouldn't be Chinese.

Which is a thing here in Sûstagul. Seriously. Old Talker would've been fascinated.

For the record, I love when that happens. Take New York for example. Lots of places where you run into Chinese—mostly Mandarin and Cantonese. But what about Fuzhounese? Funny enough, that day when I was just roaming around and trying out my Mandarin on street vendors and cab drivers, there was this other guy asking if anyone spoke Fuzhounese. My hand goes up and I offer my services, using this newcomer like a whetstone to a blade.

I'm the blade, if you didn't catch what I was doing right there.

Back to the point. I was all over the Joe-ism when it came to myself and how I conducted myself as a junior combat leader, but I hadn't thought about how it applied to other Rangers. I hadn't considered what would happen, and the kind of truly awe-inspiring chaos it would create if we, as combat leaders, just got out of the junior Rangers' way and let them do their thing. Even now I shudder to think of the total bedlam that would cause.

Which, in the middle of a city-wide assault by seven-foot muscle-bound aggro freak-orcs hired by undead sorcerer lizards in the service of Sût the Undying to kill us, might not be a bad thing.

So, one morning after the first battle, when Specialist Kayson Thounsavath rolled out from duty on the walls to come find me, I took it as a mild surprise because here was a Ranger I really hadn't seen up until now. I know that because of the uniqueness of his name. Cambodian or Laotian if I had to guess, which was cool because of how great it would be to dip into those languages.

If I had the time in between orc raids and my friends dying and all.

But Ranger Thounsavath came bounding through one of the low walls during the lull that came after the battles every morning, searching me out with the enthusiasm of a bloodhound on a scent.

In the Army you learn to sense when someone is gonna want something from you. And right now... I was getting that, and it wasn't a bad thing. I needed something to do to get my mind off... stuff... and no doubt there would be coffee, either in trade or along the way. So that's a win.

"Good thing I found you, Talker! I thought my mission was tango uniform," Thounsavath said, a little jubilantly.

"We met?" I asked, not sure I remembered him.

"Oh, look at you, all famous courter of elf girls and confirmed disciple of the Church of Joe. How quickly they forget. Of course we met, bro. I got slagged on the beach when we crossed the black and the medusa hoochie tried to swamp us with her genie. Damn orcs shot me in the face with an arrow. Went through my cheek and cut my neck a bit. Still here though, brah, thanks to Chief Rapp," Thounsavath added with a punch to my shoulder.

Oh yeah, I remembered. You're the guy I saw get shot right through the cheek with an arrow. I think about that all the time, bro.

Seriously, I do not. I try to block out the bad. It's how I stay optimistic and open to the possibilities of coffee somewhere to be had.

You have to be honest about these things.

"What can I do for you, Specialist Thounsavath?" I said, secretly delighting in saying his name. Thinking I was gonna pick up some easy Cambodian, or even Laotian.

"Call me Kayson, Bro. Everyone else does."

"Can do. Whattaya need, Kayson? Hey, how do you say that in Cambodian?"

He made a face and told me. I ignored the face and scored some language gold.

There's a little of the Old Talker in me yet. And... it's good to see the young buck. Hey there, stranger. One day you'll be me. Let's grab a cup sometime and I won't tell you all about it. Trust me. It's best you don't know.

So the enthusiastic specialist planted himself against the battered stone wall I was leaning on. Ancient and as old as the Ruin itself. History is something you lean on here. And there's a part of me that wishes we knew more, and that stones could talk.

I can't speak for anyone else, but after a night of fighting, then working the next night's defense during the following day, bone-tired, I was running on fumes, and I'll be honest about that. Thankfully they were aroma-of-coffee fumes, but my doses were getting... extreme. Sometimes I could hear my heart thundering in my ears. I told myself that was nothing to be concerned about, I had corporal things to do. Ranger. RAH!

Close to empty with the occasional hit of cold brew to keep me going, I waited for what this Ranger wanted. Thounsavath had the enthusiasm of a kid waiting for Christmas morning.

So I was feeling pretty good about the impending MRE coffee packet score.

I know, a lot of the time you get the big-picture battle and officer stuff because I happen to be around that element of the command team. But this is pure lower-enlisted stuff. Shady and possibly dangerous. Like the mafia.

"I was wondering if I could pick your brain on something I heard," he began. "See if you spoke the lingo-local and can give me a basis to go on re something I'm working."

Languages you say, Specialist? Yes, I vaguely remember a time when all I was good for around here was languages. Translate this, Talker. Tell them that, Talker. Make sure you get it right, linguist. Get over there with Tanner and dig that latrine pit, Ranger. But, with corporal rank and all hands on the wall and fighting for lives… languages had taken a back seat for the moment. Besides, the average Ranger already knows a few and is generally pretty adept at picking them up fast. All they need is time with the indigs and they start sounding like them.

Now… it's like the good old days when we first arrived, and everyone was trying to kill us. The nostalgia was overwhelming as I was being asked to language at the expert level.

Stand back everyone, linguist on duty.

"Did you hear any of it?" I asked, rubbing the tired out of my eyes and pretending I wasn't giddy.

I'm a pro like that.

"*Sié no⊠h sū?*" Kayson responded. "Or something that sounded... kinda like that. I made the guy say it a few times so I could get the gist. Feel me."

Uh-oh... this guy's been hanging out with that other Ranger that got sent into the dungeons below the fortress with the dwarven Reaper team.

I ignored the tired slang and repeated the phrase. Correctly.

Thounsavath nodded excitedly. For a Ranger, Thounsavath is not very stoic. Rare. And... refreshing.

Still, his badly butchered attempt to regurgitate the bit of Fuzhounese he'd heard punched me right in the gut. It was like being the lady from the neighborhood outside the little food cart that sold noodles and tripe, hearing the non-Chinese guy dropping perfect Fuzhounese.

Since arriving we'd heard a host of languages. Some were familiar, dating all the way back to our time with almost no variance in how they sounded. Then there were the languages like here in Sûstagul. Pidgin scrawl that sounded like a bunch of rando phrases smashed together to mean the exact opposite of what was said. Cockney, anyone? But this... hearing Thounsavath get out the words close enough to have me recognize them... suddenly, and unexpectedly, made me laugh hard enough to almost fall off the wall we were sitting on.

For a moment I was me again. The Talker who'd first started out.

Hello, stranger.

"Did I say it wrong?" Kayson asked.

"Nah, man! Close enough that I need a little more. You said you talked to this guy?"

Kayson clapped his hands and thrust out a finger away from the part of the wall we'd spent the night defending. "Like right now? Solid! Follow me. Sar'nt Monroe! I'm stealing your team leader for a minute."

And just like that I was following the rail-thin Ranger who was leading me through the streets of Sûstagul. It was during this whirlwind expedition, while following Kayson to this apparent source of a rare dialect of Chinese, that I took in the full measure of what our fight with the Saur was costing everyone else. The locals. The Guzzim Hazadi shot gargantuan boulders, catapulted into the low quarter, where they smashed the mud brick houses to smithereens as if they were the merest of tissue paper. The people who had survived these strikes now sifted through the ruins, finding what had survived, and what had been broken forever.

To me, that image, that was as old as war itself.

The rising sun had already done its work, turning the streets normally smelling of sand and spices into a garbage heap of corpses turning ripe under the random debris fields of orc Bronze Age arty strikes. Robed citizens hugged the walls to keep away from the invaders, us, these new men who had come to their city to wrest control from the previous invaders. To them... we were just the flavor of the month.

I wanted to be different for them.

Like the family at the coffee house. I wanted to give them hope that things could be different this time. I wanted to feel the touch of Amira. I wanted to look into her eyes and see the belief she'd begun to place in me that I could help them.

When I was tired, on the wall after the night's fight, I thought of her cool hand, her brown eyes, and I kept improving the defenses and doing everything I could to give them a shot at seeing the other side of this.

"Talk-ir," she would say to me. "You are good. Even my whore sister makes offerings for you to be safe. And that is rare for her because she is such a filthy whore and even though I love her, she knows she must burn in hell for what she does."

Amira is the angel of coffee.

Her sister is the devil.

Both are praying for me, and all the Rangers and centurions on the wall. When you see the destruction of this city in daylight after the night's attack you are reminded how thin the line is.

And it is very thin.

Maybe that's why I ordered the suicide ruck deployed. I knew how thin it was, and that we could not lose one square inch of it without exposing those who are praying for us.

A man carrying a child in an arm wrapped in bandages dropped items from the other arm, which seemed in worse shape than the first. I knelt for the items before he could lunge for them, catching the pieces before the sand could claim and grit them. The old man, probably the kid's grandfather, backed to the wall, his chest heaving in heavy dry gasps as he looked at me in total fear while I clutched the items. A small bundle, looking like jerky of some kind, fell on top of an ornate carved comb with accents of red stone set into the top of the hairpiece. It was elegant and beautiful in how simple it was. I handed him both and stepped away, backing to the wall so as not to seem like a threat.

"*Salam*," I told him in Arabic. Peace. Typically used as an abbreviated greeting in certain parts of the city. I hoped he took it in the spirit it was given. I just didn't have the time to play the hearts-and-minds thing Tanner had warned me to stay out of.

But I would do what I could, knowing it would never be enough. Like I said… I'm an optimist.

Twists and turns through the city brought us to the Street of Cages, the place in the Sûstagul markets where all manner of animals were on display so they could be sold. We had the typical sights you'd sometimes see in those movies my parents used to watch. Remember the other Indiana Jones one… not the one with Mola Ram Not-Orc. The one with the shoulder monkey and the tomb full of snakes. *Lost Ark*, that's it. It was like that, only with the extreme weirdness the Ruin could provide.

And there were monkeys here, in fact. Rattling against rattan cages piled on top of each other, screeching as they reached between the bars of their confinement. Tiny simian hands groping toward us in hope we'd want to pet or hold them, for which the price was the contents of a sack near the cages. A bag full of nuts and small fruits. Dates, too, like in the movie.

While looking inside the little pouch, my eyes were drawn across the street to a pen I hadn't seen as we entered the market. Standing way taller than I was, ostriches chirped at passersby who got too close to the wooden rails keeping the birds in. They slammed against the boards in warning whenever anyone who wasn't their herder got close, nearly breaking the enclosure just to get their point across.

They weren't even the strangest of beasts, not by far, on display here in the cages of the market as we walked past enclosures holding all manner of creatures that walked, swam, or flew. And the deeper we got, the more exotic the animals became.

Man, I could have used Kennedy on this one. Some of the things had to have been in what he called the Monster Manual.

The younger Rangers were always asking him, "That one in your Monster Manual, Kennedy?"

When the Ranger wizard acknowledged it was, their next question would be, "How much experience do we get for killing it?"

I had no idea what this meant but it seemed important to a lot of them.

A small monkey with serpentine skin instead of hair lounged on one side of its cage on the outside of a shop full of curiosities. The vendor snapped his fingers at the browsers, as if getting their attention for just a moment held the promise of a sale. Catching our eyes staring at the monkey, the proprietor set down a four-foot worm swimming in a glass jar and went to stand next to the monkey cage, promising us in his pidgin dialect that owning the exotic animal would bring us luck. He reached for the lizard simian's arm, stretching it to demonstrate the flap of skin attached to its extremities, and assured us the creature could fly. His eyes suggested a sincere belief that we would consider this a feature not a bug.

I walked away, following Thounsavath who'd dragged me into this strange slice of city life with promises of his own. A pledge to introduce me to the man doling out the rare dialect of Chinese I would have thought extinct by now. We continued to step through the very impressive display of livestock, with only the temporary distraction of a four-foot dragon singing in its cage keeping us from our destination.

Hey, wouldn't you stop? A four-foot-dragon-looking thing with a tail ending in a scorpion barb. Whistling a tune sounding like "My Sharona." Who wouldn't want a My Sharona Singing Stinger Dragon?

Deeper and deeper we went into the market, and at times it was like walking into another world untouched by the battle along the walls. Kayson managed to drag me into a shop at the end of a quaint, twisting, and well-kept alley, prying me away from the curious sights and sounds of other exotic animals and small monsters threatening to overwhelm my senses. I could have walked down this street one hundred times, with a full night's sleep and a coffee in each hand, and probably still have missed the entrance to the shop.

The outside walls framing the doorway had legitimate Chinese characters tracing down the door.

Curiouser and curiouser, as some chick in a fairy tale once said.

The first line of characters spoke of curses for anyone who came into the shop to cause trouble or had bad wind. The other side simply said welcome.

So... shoes and shirt not required?

Walking into the shop, I felt the tiny hairs on the inside of my nose crinkle at the smell of jasmine and smoke wafting through the small space. The floors were clean and well-kept, and laden shelves lined the walls except for periodic breaks for some painting of a sultan, khan, king, or local god. Tiny cages sat on the shelves, set a few inches apart from each other. Behind the tiny-thatched bamboo bars, black birds with bright orange beaks and tufts of feathers over their eyes like horns chirped a hypnotic chorus of tweets that made me nostalgic for Sunday mornings in those ancient New York boroughs, where old men fed the birds and made similar sounds.

At the end of the shop, a bald man wrapped in the desert robes of a Bedouin leaned over an open book along his counter, a feather quill pen scratching out marks along the yellow and thick page. He looked up from his work, and I noticed two of the black birds sitting on either side of the binding. When he raised his chin to look at us, so did the birds. All the birds, in fact. The symphony of chirping halted as the keeper took note of us, clearly violating the sanctity of his shop.

Recognition dawned on the man's face, and as he came from the counter toward the encroaching sunlight threatening the atmospheric gloom in his shop, his gaunt smile suddenly became charming and warm.

Business was to be had.

He produced an object from within the robed sleeves, holding it toward Kayson as I stood there, me waiting to hear some sliver of Chinese in any dialect, so far from where it was originally spoken.

"*Siâ diâng,*" the shopkeeper said, holding out a plastic MRE spoon to the PFC.

"Any clue?" Kayson asked.

"Oh yeah. Lotta clue," I said, patting the kid on the back. Switching to the shopkeeper's particular dialect of Chinese, I asked, "How did you come by the kid's spoon?"

The man whirled on me, and I caught a plethora of details in that moment. First and foremost was the robe, or what was under it. The only Bedouin thing about this guy was the outer layer. Underneath, he wore a thick woven jacket that reminded me of the old karate gis you'd see in the kung fu movies, except this one was fully wrapped all the way to his throat. I don't really know if that's what it's called, but it was thick cotton and looked like armored paper towel, if the paper towel was a dark blue. The texture on the fabric gave me that kind of vibe. An ornate knife thrust up from the belt near his abdomen, carved in black wood wrapped in silver relief with an animal head marking the end of the pommel. Leading into his moccasin-style shoes he wore equally thick, woven pants that had sewn-in knee pads, like a Bronze Age version of the Crye Precision pants we all wore.

So that was interesting.

His smile never wavered as he faced me to speak. Pure businessman and not threatened in any way by strangers from a strange land. A waterfall of small symbols tattooed from under his eyes and down his cheeks appeared like an overflow of beautiful script, unlike the dire warnings they actually were to someone versed in the language like I was. Warnings of dismemberment and death at the hands of powerful spirits should the inheritor of the tattoos be harmed.

I remembered the Chinese sorcerer we'd smoked on my first Reaper. Where Kennedy got the staff and I got the ring that made me invisible.

"A pleasant surprise to be sure," he began. "How wonderful that you speak my language. To answer your question, this young one came into my shop and since he didn't speak as I do, he attempted negotiation with the universal language. Food. Your meals are very tasty. Are you this man's servant?"

I laughed because for once I outranked someone. "No, my friend. He is a soldier like me and I came to aid him in whatever negotiation he has with you. As I see you have his spoon, it appears you don't have need of me."

The old Chinese man smiled slyly.

"Ah, but we may, as he has seen what I have to offer and would like to purchase. Except, your soldier does not know the words for prices, and thus he hinted he would come back with someone who could speak to me of price and payment," the shopkeeper noted.

Peace and tranquility spread across his wrinkled old face.

"I'm Talker. And what may I call you, sir?" I asked, trying to be polite, matching his cheery disposition because we were playing at the pro level now.

"I am Haoxuan. A pleasure to meet you, soldier called Talker of the Rangers. Are you… Rangers… to be the new conquerors of the City of Pythons? I have much to offer adventuring soldiers looking for an edge over their most dangerous enemies, should they be willing to meet my considerable price for rare antiquities of such value and worth."

Sales talk.

"And what is… for deposit?" I said, gesturing to the shelves and seeming not sold.

Haoxuan corrected my use of the word "deposit" to the word "offer," for which I was grateful. I couldn't think of the right way to phrase it but wanted to get it close enough that he'd get my drift. After sleeping only a handful of hours in as many days, and getting the equivalent of a Coke and a smoke to sustain me through it all, I was surprised my brain was able to keep up even a little, never mind spitting out Fuzhounese like a champ.

But I liked him more because of the gentle correction. We smiled and the smile he gave was warm and in his eyes too. Which is a thing I look for.

Fake smiles never reach the eyes. That's the tell.

Translator gonna translate, amirite?

"The birds we have here are called Flight of Recall. You show them a message or something you want to send to someone, and then think of the someone you want to send it to," Haoxuan said. He picked up one of the loose birds from his desk, stroking the feathers at the top of its skull, for which the animal cooed its gratitude.

Haoxuan set it on the desk toward his ledger. The black, orange-tipped bird angled its head to the side as it stared at the page, then eventually peered up at his handler. Haoxuan blew out a three-note whistle and the bird vanished, appearing on my shoulder with a slight flap of its wings and the patience to sit where it landed until told to do otherwise.

"Bring it here," Haoxuan said.

I did so, and the shopkeeper flipped multiple pages in the ledger until he got to blanks. He took the bird from me, and set it at the front of the book where it was perfectly content to remain as long as it could see everyone surrounding the table. Another three-note whistle, and the animal began to sing. With each note that passed its beak, a portion of the blank pages took on the elegant strokes and symbols the man had penned on the previous ones. In a few short minutes, the entirety of the ledger pages had been faithfully recreated on the new sheets.

"Did this guy just invent the fax machine?" I asked, trying to sound less impressed than I already was.

But Thounsavath was impatient. He cleared his throat and interrupted the way things were going.

"That's not the half of it, Talk. Trust me, bro. Tell him we want to see the thing in the back. Tell him."

He looked at me eagerly. Bouncing on the balls of his feet. His boots making the floor creak.

"Something you want to tell me?" I asked him, sensing the guy was a little too jazzed up about whatever he was truly after.

He leaned in close, talking low like the old man couldn't hear us. Which he clearly could. Thounsavath is horrible at negotiation. I'm betting that ten thousand years ago there was a Camaro at twenty-three percent interest in the batt parking lot with his name all over it.

Sucks to be the shady car dealer holding the paper. We got hurtled ten thousand years into the future and that guy got turned into a soul-sucking wraith or some other horrible monster.

Which… really wasn't much of a Ruin reveals, was it?

"Well, bro… we lost Zamora on the first day," Thounsavath whispered. "Sar'nt Z was the regimental dog handler. Bro went missing after the first fight on the island when we landed back at the beginning of all this. Lost the dog too. I know it won't make much of a difference, but when I was rolling through the Street of Cages here, I was kind of wondering if they had something we could use to scare the orcs from breaking our line of defense and getting in the wire. The way the dog used to. And if they did manage to break through, we could have something to hunt the squirters with. I could be, like, I don't know… the new dog handler for the company. Like Joe says… see a job, find a job that needs to get done, Ranger. Feel me, Talk?"

I do.

"You have training for that?" I asked Thounsavath, confident it would have been a question Sar'nt Hardt would ask. Keep them Rangers honest, especially with themselves, seemed like a mantra he'd follow right next to PT them to death just because.

"No, I never made it to the Vohne Liche course. But this guy has a… dog… in the back, controlled by a whistle. Only it ain't no dog, Talk. It's better. Way better, bro."

Now I understood, and I turned back to the old shopkeeper who was still smiling warmly at me. I had the distinct impression he understood everything that had just been said between Thounsavath and myself.

"What do you have in the back, Haoxuan?" I asked.

Carefully he nodded, and then delicately returned the MRE spoon to the PFC, shaking the Ranger's hand and even adding a slight bow. "Your soldier, Talker of Rangers, is a good boy. He let me try some cake from your magic food. It was very tasty. This is my way to thank him for his hospitality. I showed him animals for some of our best clients. He used enough sign language to let me know he was going to bring you back. He has done so. We can proceed after the tasty cake."

Kayson produced an MRE packet with the aforementioned "tasty cake."

I had made serious arguments in the past that it was neither "cake" nor "tasty." But words… they're my thing. Or were.

He nodded excitedly and his ancient eyes glittered.

Cake was his coffee. This… I understand.

The shopkeeper motioned for us to follow him. We went through a curtain of beads separating the front half of the shop from the shadowy back, and entered a room the size of a volleyball court filled with soft white beach sand on a boxed floor. On what looked like cut-down telephone poles set above the makeshift sandbox were over a dozen hunting falcons. Their eyes sealed away by tiny little leather hoods, the falcons twitched this way and that, ready to be plucked from their perches and be brought outside to work the fields as, or so the shopkeeper explained, was their job. Fly and hunt for the man with the glove.

You could almost feel the falcons wanting to be helpful and get after it. Or maybe that was my psionics dialing in on their collective emotions.

I wondered if the falcons on the stands had some sort of magical property like the horned birds in the main shop. If we took off the falcon hoods, would they shoot lasers out of their eyes or be able to lift something as big as Sergeant Monroe off the ground, even though they're a quarter of his size? Whatever they were, it was an impressive sight to experience being that close to death on golden wings and getting the emotional vibe that they viewed hunting and killing as being... helpful.

Judging by the number and complexity of the portraits on the wall, Haoxuan and his crew had been at this for a long, long time, and had gained much popularity with the locals by doing it. The shop felt as ancient as the city itself. And hadn't the old man called it the City of Pythons, its ancient name, as opposed to Sûstagul?

Also, the thing that worried me about the painted client list on the wall, was there were more than a few Saur pictures breaking up the stately chins and robust noses of the human eastern princes who had previously controlled Sûstagul.

We exited the building into a back-alley yard, hemmed in by the leaning structures adjacent to the shop. Another man dressed in similar fashion to the shopkeeper rested on a back deck, smoking a reed pipe serenely. Aromatic tendrils of smoke wafted from the man's nostrils, filling the back-alley patch of earth with the smell of rum and cinnamon. He nodded to the shopkeeper, and seeing us, stood almost to attention and leveled a very curt but distinct bow in total silence.

Haoxuan turned to regard us, holding out his hands to keep us from exiting the deck onto the dirt lot beyond. "My people have been the best beast masters for war animals to forgotten khans and long-dead sultans from lands the maps do not even remember... for generations. We happened upon a very rare find, Talker of Rangers... and judging its value and its age as a newborn, we brought it up beside our other working animals knowing a great price was to be had. Then it ate the other animals and that was very bad."

He laughed at this, and his bony shoulders shook as he did so.

"Those first few outings can be forgiven," Haoxuan said to the smoking man. "There was no protocol for taming such a... rare... animal."

More excited tittering as though some knowing joke had just been shared.

"True enough," Haoxuan agreed with himself when the smoking man remained silent and serene in his haze of scented smoke. "A member of the Saur nobility heard of our acquisition," he announced proudly, "and made a move to acquire it from us at great price. We trained it and got it ready for sale, expecting much profit. Yet we have not heard back from the Saur commander who commissioned it, and we think you Rangers have killed him."

He made a *tsk-tsk* sound with his lips and teeth.

"It's still young and has some growing to do, but we are hoping to sell it before it reaches... ah... maturity. This training yard will be too small then, and it would kill all of us."

Okay.

"What is it?" I asked, feeling like I was going to need to explain to Thounsavath why Dad and Mom couldn't let him keep his puppy.

"Hey, Corporal. Don't forget to translate for those of us that only speak English," Thounsavath reminded me. His white teeth beamed against his soft brown skin, and I felt... bad.

Haoxuan waited for my side conversation with the PFC to fizzle out before continuing. "These creatures, Talker of Rangers, are known to us. Where we come from, they are the great... ambush predators... of the steppe. They devour men..." His eyes glittered, and he smiled broadly. "... horses..." If possible, he beamed even more broadly. "... and even the mighty saber-fangs roaming the endless sea of golden grass beyond the edges of the known. Nothing, Rangers... nothing is safe from a tremor-maw bursting from the ground."

Tremor-Maw.

Earthquake Teeth was the exact translation of what he said.

Uh... Thounsavath, hard pass on the "dog."

When Haoxuan started talking, we'd been just standing there on a wooden deck staring at an empty dirt lot. This place seemed... tranquil, peaceful, some inner secret garden, immune to the war raging along the distant walls we could just see the tops of in the afternoon sun. Walls turning bloody red by a trick of stone and the light.

There were no Rangers looking to bug me. No translations. No asking what I was responsible for or if I could cover down on a guy. It was just quiet here. As the other man who'd been smoking tapped my arm to hand me a cup of something, the whiff of rich, salted coffee, strong and hot in the ceramic container, woke my senses and made me want to stay here forever.

"*Qahawa*," he said.

Coffee.

I almost said... screamed really, *I know!* With the sudden enthusiasm of a child on Christmas getting the gift they thought impossible and beyond their parents. Almost. But I was cool and played it like a pro who wasn't a werewolf or something. *Oh, is this coffee, I've heard great things. How interesting. I'm totally not a drug addict. Human just like you. How about another cup, or six.*

"Thank you," I said hurriedly, letting the man go back to his pipe. "Haoxuan, did you say burst from the ground? Did I get that right?"

Thounsavath happily accepted his own cup from the smoker. "What did he say?"

"Something... I'm not sure I have the right words for," I noted.

"Yes, yes, Ranger. You did say it true. Shall I show you now... what you came to purchase? While you enjoy sipping your cup of *qahawa*," Haoxuan asked.

I'd already pounded it.

My cup was refilled from a copper pot that was beautiful and made me want to weep. But maybe that's just me. Your mileage may vary. Don't @ me.

Then Haoxuan produced a pan flute. Seriously. Three reeds strung together with silver wire and wrapped in silver accents. Silver script lined the reeds in tiny relief, and it amazed me that without the aid of high-powered lenses and things like vise clamps, someone was able to carve such amazing detail into something so small. Haoxuan chirped two quick whistles from the flute suddenly, the musical notes hanging oily and slick in the courtyard.

They were almost… disconcerting. Like… something terrible is about to happen in a movie.

The notes tripped the psionics I'd been working to keep under wraps as they, or by extension, me, grew in power and experience. The oily notes held the promise of power in a magical spectrum I'd been able to pick up on. Unlike the hungry, ravenous power held in *Coldfire* or the indomitable will infused into *Mjölnir* to keep it from breaking down, this magic was old, and demanding. A domination that broke will and forced… subjugation. For all intents and purposes, it was the musical equivalent of… a leash.

Instantly a rocky jut pushed up from the soft tilled ground, and then moved slightly at the delicate notes. In a flash and rumble, the spike sank into the earth, as if a sinkhole had swallowed the entire rock.

Whole.

"Yeah, boy!" whooped Thounsavath knowingly. "Here come the dog!"

"What the..." I stammered. The thoughts I was getting, the musical thoughts attached to the leash, were primal.

Seeking.

Hunting.

Sensing.

Like those falcons. But worse. Much, much... worse.

Then I felt it all at once. Sudden exhilaration as the rock and earth moved against my face. Not *my* face, but the face of whatever beast they'd just woken up. I was in its thoughts and hearing it down there. Feeling it. I felt my fingers strain as talons the length of human arms sheared into rock below and forced it aside so it could continue on its course.

Hunting.

Feeding.

Dragging under.

Haoxuan knocked on the railing to the porch, sending a brilliantly shimmering vibration through the ground. The thing's mind flared and I felt the thrum of electricity course through it, or more to the point, four thrums in the men standing over the ravenous beast moving beneath the sand below us.

Psionics is very weird to explain. But it's not unlike translating languages between speakers in real-time. Advocating and answering. All at once.

"Excuse me, please," said Haoxuan, and gestured at the serene smoker.

I snapped back into my own mind, staring at a goat bleating at my side.

Serene Smoker slapped its rump, sending the terrified animal scampering into the back yard. It pounced and jumped, somehow sensing the vicious presence beneath the earth. I watched in abject fascination, almost forgetting the steaming cup in my hand.

C'mon. As if. Would you honestly think I'd forget about a nice Turkish coffee cut with orange peel? Or any coffee? Me Talker. Nice to meet you. I have a problem, but we don't have to overcome that.

The ground in front of us erupted in a volcano of dirt and rock. Only it wasn't rock. Shaped like a giant, stone-colored bullet, the monster's ever-expanding maw caught the front half of the poor goat as the thing breached the ground in one eight-foot leap, breaking the goat in half in the space of a heartbeat. The limp, shattered back half of the goat's body flopped against the side of the armored mouth as four titanic limbs slammed onto the dry ground of the yard, bearing the monster's weight. A second snap waved the high dorsal fin on the creature's back, giving the horse-sized predator the appearance of being even taller than it was.

For the record... I did not drop my coffee.

Thounsavath spilled his and started screaming like he was rooting for his favorite football team now that they'd just scored a touchdown.

"Tremor-maw," Haoxuan repeated proudly. "We are happy to sell it to you, if you are willing to meet our... considerable... price, Rangers. As you can see... we cannot keep it here much longer as it is still growing."

I nodded absently as the tremor-maw stomped about the yard in a circle, huffed, and dove back into the earth once again like it was some pond or pool or even the ocean. In a few short strokes it tunneled to the spot it had been occupying to begin with, letting the sun warm its armored dorsal fin.

This thing was a damned shark!

Meanwhile, Thounsavath wanted his puppy now that we were standing at the mall window for the Ruin's version of a pet shop.

"Talk, if we got the gold for this, we should pay it. Those things outside wouldn't stand a chance against a full-on landshark," Thounsavath said. "You know… orcs and all, bro. That thing would chew them up faster than a two-forty going high cycle. Hey, and no barrel change, man! Feel me?"

Haoxuan held up a finger in protest, halting whatever thoughts hovered behind my eyes. Lucky for me, he didn't know my only thoughts were the surprise at seeing what I had just seen and the contents of my cup. But also, the horror of what I had just witnessed.

I had no idea the Ruin had landsharks.

I'd like to opt out of this game now, I thought distantly and killed the coffee, eyes clearly telegraphing a refill from the beautiful copper pot.

"Before you agree to take this animal," Haoxuan began, "I must warn you… Rangers. There are three rules for governing such a terrible beast. Betraying these rules will result in ruin for your kin, even as the animal hunts your enemies. Rule one. This is not a pet. It is a powerful predator. It does not want your… scraps. It wants prey. You must feed it at least once per week, or, when you are not paying attention, it will hunt anything it can detect. Even you yourselves."

Okay. For the third time. Seriously. This is a very bad idea. I made a dad face at Thounsavath. Sorry to crush your dreams, son, but your pet will murder us in our sleep, or when we just go for a walk.

Haoxuan held up the little black silver-accented pan flute. "Rule two. You must call it to you daily or it will roam far and away, seeking prey. The flute is not hampered by range, so it will come if you call, but if it is leagues away from you, it will take time for it to arrive.

"And the final rule. Never. Ever. Lose the flute. Whoever controls this key and can play the notes I will teach you, controls the animal. The same rituals carved into this instrument line the armor of the creature. They are linked. Be wary that you control this always, Rangers."

"Can this landshark be taught not to hurt our people?" I asked prudently.

I did not want to explain this to the sergeant major. This was a sure way to get cut off from the blue percolator. And that... I did not need. Sorry, Thounsavath.

Haoxuan nodded even as he and his associate laughed. "I like that. Landshark. Funny, Talker of Rangers. To answer your very wise question, it has the same intellect as a... wolf... and it carries a similar outlook. Everything is prey until it isn't. But it can be trained to recognize your kin."

The merchant stepped from the porch, unwisely I thought, walking into the yard toward the partially submerged dorsal fin. He held out his hand, and the monster worked its way loose from the earth to rub its snout into the shopkeeper's outstretched palm. He roughly patted the animal, no doubt to send vibration through the dense, armored skin.

"But make no mistake. This is not a pet. And if you lose the magic flute, something you never intended to kill… will pay for your careless mistake."

I translated all this to Thounsavath, who nodded like a teenager ready to take hold of his first gun. "What do you think, Talk? Knife Hand go for this, bro?"

It was like we weren't even speaking the same language. My translation had been clearly coded with… this is a very bad idea.

Thounsavath's read was: *Great, let's do it!*

But… facts were facts.

"Oh yeah, the captain will," I said. "This thing and him aren't far apart. But something tells me if you replace Zamora as the new detachment dog, Smaj is gonna want to make sure you're the right man for the job. And the smaj… he's the devil in the forest at night, Thounsavath. He'll take your soul if anything goes wrong. You feel that, Specialist? This could end real bad for you."

"Hey. I was responsible enough to come and get you for translation and a second set of eyes. Brought this all forward after my own vetting and initiative," Thounsavath said. "I got this. My fam had pits back on the block, and the block was… rough, Talker. Real rough."

Seriously?

I tried one last defense if just for the Article Fifteen hearing that would eventually come of this. And… I'd just made corporal. Getting busted back to private again was gonna suck if this thing ate one of us because we missed feeding time.

"All negotiated at the end of a spoon," I pointed out.

"Right? You hear about the guy getting that MRE spoon kill, but what about the guy that bought a weaponized MRE *using* his spoon? That's me, bro. This is Ranger Legend Hall of Fame stuff. It's gonna kill!"

Literally.

"Yeah. You're going to have to unpack that last one for me," I admitted. "MRE?"

"Oh, you know. MRE. Monster ready to eat, bro. Feel me? I'm gonna call it Big Baby. D too, to make it sound gangsta. That's legit, Talk. Legit."

The second he said it, I realized I had forgotten to pay attention to another segment of Ranger culture.

Never leave a private unattended.

People once thought robots were going to take over the world. They stood no chance against guys like Thounsavath. Looking for work, he'd found a job. And that job happened to be running an actual Great White Landshark that could come and just bite you in half.

Which is exactly what it did to Shagbag just when things looked grimmest.

CHAPTER FIFTEEN

THE aftermath of the death of the god of the orcs, or the serial killer from ten thousand years ago that had stayed too long and made himself their god, was like someone had set up a slaughterhouse on the cracked rocks, broken stones, and drifting sand of the desert Observatory on the walls of Sûstagul. Big Baby D had his pound of Shagbag's flesh and began to waddle-wander across the X, chewing up and swallowing in great disgusting gulps what remained of the dead orc god.

You've probably already guessed this... but the Rangers love that part. Of course they would. A giant eight-foot-long landshark they'd made their dog, waddling around on its stubby legs and snapping up more pieces of Shagbag the Now Torn in Half that they tossed to it.

Tanner lit a smoke and stood back to watch the pageantry... as it were.

At the last of the battle, Shagbag had tried to animate the recent dead to take the objective, but now those corpses of shadow panther and shredded dire bat had just gone back to being dead. And in some cases, where chimeric corpses had formed golems of the flesh of orc and legionnaire... they had simply stopped moving and were now dead again.

That was probably for the best.

"Hey… why Nunzio got a orc arm now!" shouted one of the legionnaires as their formations moved in to secure the area. Other Rangers were arriving on scene and had come in to assist what was clearly a very bad situation just minutes ago.

I was too tired, and working a new problem, to make a crack like, "See this mess… this is my mess. I made this all by myself. Pro-level leadership work here, folks."

So I didn't.

At that point my bell had seriously been rung, and I was convinced Sergeant Monroe was dead. I even asked Tanner if that was the case and he ran off to check, after handing me one of the thermite grenades I asked for.

When he came back, I didn't even hear the answer that, "Sergeant Monroe made it, Talk. He's great, man. All good to go and ready to roll. Ain't nothin' gonna stop that stud."

I didn't hear that.

Instead, I watched the popped thermite grenade flare brightly in the dark and begin to immolate what remained of Shagbag, mumbling to myself, "That's for the best," as it melted what remained of Lemoore's Ruin-revealed fractured head and twisted face and the upper torso. Or what remained. What Big Baby hadn't torn in half and swallowed.

The smell was awful. But here in Sûstagul… that's just Tuesday.

Tanner handed me a smoke and muttered, "Only way to be sure, man."

Like it was a line from a movie and I should know it, or something pop culture. I didn't know the line. I had something else on my mind and I was trying to see if I could pull it off. If I could "carpe diem that stuff," as Sergeant

Chris says, and get it done. Long shot. Dangerous. Ask for permission and I'd lose a window. I was sure of that. Maybe. But I'd seen something in Shagbag's mind between the storms on the sea of madness and the moment Sergeant Thor's round blew off one hemisphere of Lemoore's brain.

Don't even get me started on how that didn't even stop Shagbag. Fifty-cal to the head. There was just… too much to deal with for me to consider that part. Not right now. Maybe later. Right now… there was a window if I had the balls.

The question was…

I'd seen something. Something very important. Something that needed to be acted on right now or be lost. But no one was really in charge right now. The legionnaires and their noncoms were securing what remained of the Observatory—spoiler, not much. Other Rangers were coming in, making sure the defenses were still there, and setting up new ones to react to the new terrain and possible threats from other points along the wall. There was that feeling we were waiting for a senior NCO to show up.

Not that we were leaderless. Rangers are never leaderless. They are, right down to every private… leaders and trained to be so.

But right now, there was some hang time where an NCO was expected and that would determine what happened next regarding the defense of this portion of the wall. We'd be told to hold this position. Others to return to our primary and secondary positions to meet the next attack. The night was young, and there was usually more fighting and attacks to react to and flip the script on.

The Rangers had all kinds of blind alleys to lure raids of orcs who thought they'd broken through our defenses.

Too bad for the orcs, there were fifty-gallon drums, rigged with fougasse, ready to be set off in order to cover the orcs in burning napalm.

Or other nasty surprises. The Rangers might've been low on ammo, but they were downright chock full of dirty tricks and then some.

So I listened to the battle out there, usually raging at other points along the walls. It was clear tonight it was already dying down, and again I'll mention it was still early in the evening. The battles usually went past midnight with orc and goblin probes, raids, and major assaults and counter-counter-assaults well into the darkest hours.

The orcs loved the night.

But things were dying down.

Even now the guns weren't talking at the Gates of Eternity. Soprano and Jabba showed up humping the two-forty Lima. They'd been retasked by Sergeant Rico to support whatever was going on here and to shut down any enemy breach in progress with high cyclic fire.

Instead, the Ranger's newest dog, Big Baby D, had seen to that. Now the massive thing was waddling around, snorting and huffing as Rangers threw it more scraps of what remained of the enemy and laughed as the giant bullete snapped at the tossed parts and swallowed them whole.

That's what Big Baby D is. It's called a bullete. Pronounced *boo-lay*. In Kennedy's game it's basically a landshark that swims through rock and sand and bites you in half when it gets hungry and you're not expecting to get bitten in half by an underground shark that swims through dirt and rock. Because why would you be?

The Rangers made a dog out of it, of course they did, and Shagbag messed around, and as they say... found out.

The Rangers were throwing Big Baby scraps despite Nunzio's friend shouting at them in Italian not to feed it any of their dead comrades, which the Rangers didn't.

They were getting pretty good at identifying rando orc parts due to the amount of stacking they'd done since day one in the Ruin.

The orcs found out. As they say.

The Rangers were feeding Big Baby scraps despite Haoxuan's warning.

Thounsavath stood by, his silver pipes tucked in and dummy-corded to his chest rig. Laughing and smiling. Proud of his dog.

The captain, to my surprise, had been downright giddy, in Knife Hand's own stoic permanent look of indigestion way, meaning he smiled briefly for half a second between problems when apprised of Thounsavath's dog acquisition for the detachment.

Side note: I could tell the captain was actually proud of his Ranger going out and finding such a perfect killing machine as a tamed bullete.

But I had other fish to fry, or rather, one fish in particular. And if I was gonna do it, then I needed to do it.

Sergeant Joe was expected on scene at any moment.

So I had to move now. Before that happened.

Tanner had grabbed my assault ruck on the way back into the Observatory, or what remained of it, and now I picked it up, fished through it for my spare cold brew reload because of course I did, me, I then drained it in one go, and finally and unceremoniously... dumped everything out of the pack.

"Jabba!" I hissed at the nearby goblin AG delighting in the antics of Big Baby D begging for scraps from the Rangers. Jabba gave me a surprised look and pointed comically to himself, tapping the ragged chest rig he'd acquired from somewhere along the Rangers' travels. He's put all kinds of wacky voodoo stuff all over it and everything he's managed to steal or coax from the Rangers along the way.

I have a feeling Jabba's kit makes the sergeant major's eye twitch. But he is a valuable asset. And a pretty good AG. He can carry impossible amounts of ammo. And if you give him a Moon God Potion he can carry twice as much.

It was at this particular moment, regarding my forming plan and need to act fast, right now in fact, that I first wondered how much Jabba weighed. A hundred pounds, maybe, soaking wet. No problem. That's combat jump weight, I've done that.

Tanner watched me dump my assault pack.

"Uh… Talk… whatcha doin', man?"

I pointed for Jabba to come to me, hissing, "*Didi mao*," which he understands to mean get a move on.

"Talk, I ain't super smart but… you're up to somethin' crazy again, ain't you?"

In my defense, I thought Sergeant Monroe was dead. Smoked by Mola Ram Orc. And yeah… I was a little crazy. In hindsight, after what happened next… probably a lot crazy.

Nonstop battle does that to you.

And… Brumm. Kurtz. And the others.

I held the mouth of the assault ruck wide and told Jabba to get in.

The look the goblin gave me said it all, but he did it anyway.

"Bro…" continued Tanner.

I held up my hand, a knife hand I might add, and ignored the slight tremor in it I saw there.

"I gotta go out there and do something tonight, right now, Tanner. We got one shot to smoke the one guy that's uniting the orcs out there. I... saw it. Know what I mean?" I pointed toward what little remained of the dead orc god.

Tanner thought about that. He knew. Or at least he understood both of us saw things others didn't with respect to our own Ruin-revealed powers.

"I'll go with you, man."

"You can't, Tanner. You don't fit in the bag. They'll see you. Jabba can get in the ruck and the ring will cover us both. Hopefully." I held up the ring that made me invisible. "I'm goin' Reaper and takin' the gob with me because he might be able to help me navigate what's out there among the tribes and war camps. Right now, after being inside that..." I pointed again toward the horror-show remains of melting Shagbag, ignoring my tremoring finger, "... that thing's mind... I have a small psychic trail to find his... his high priest. The guy that..."

I couldn't say Sergeant Monroe's name. I couldn't say any of their names. Not Kurtz. Not Brumm. Not any of them.

Remember, I thought Sergeant Monroe was dead.

If I had said his name maybe Tanner could've got to me and made me see I didn't need to go out there. Explained again that the chief was already on Sergeant Monroe and the big Ranger minotaur was going to be okay. He'd just been hit by some kind of Mola Ram whammy knockout ray from the High Priest of Shagbag. Who was now, if I was understanding the impressions I was getting, becoming...

what Shagbag had been, after starting out a long time ago in a high desert prison, becoming.

I could sense him out there. And if I concentrated real hard I could see how he'd escaped. Down the ropes, surrounded by his guards, heading off into the dunes. If I closed my eyes, I could see him using his staff, shouting raggedly, pulling himself through the wind and the sand as his elite guards, shining knives out, watched the shadows and readied themselves to spend their lives protecting him. Mola Ram Orc. He was the uniter of all the tribes. They were here because of him. He'd been Shagbag's high priest and used their religious fervor to unite a horde to break the walls.

And now he would... become their god.

I had to shut that down or more Rangers, my friends, my brothers, the guys I worshipped, don't tell them that part, were gonna die.

Warts and all.

Tanner nodded.

He's my friend. He's a Ranger. He understands this.

"Okay... whatta I tell Sar'nt Joe?" he said.

I looked at Tanner as I shouldered the goblin-loaded ruck. I fingered the ring for a second, not sure it would work for the both of us.

If it didn't, the plan was canked.

If it did... then I'd go right into the middle of the enemy, their beating dark heart of purest evil, and I'd tear it out and smoke Mola Ram Orc good and proper.

"Got a spare mag for the Glock?" I asked, hearing my breathing starting to get fast and ragged. I told myself that was because the desert is dry. The air. And not the fear.

Because I wasn't afraid. I was something else. Something worse.

Tanner gave me his last mag. I looked at him and tried to say "Thank you," but my voice was gone. The air was dry.

"What do I tell Joe, Talk?"

"Burritos, Tanner," I whispered. "Tell him… burritos."

Then I was gone into the night and the wind… and the darkness beyond the walls.

CHAPTER SIXTEEN

WHEN I snuck back through the gaping crack in the outer wall, climbing up the ropes the orcs had left behind when they'd stormed the walls of the Observatory, I found Sergeant Joe waiting for me at just before dawn. Tanner too.

"Burritos, huh?" asked Joe calmly.

At first I thought he wasn't as mad as he should be. That was probably something NCOs master. Luring you into a false sense of surviving their wrath. Then I realized the look on his face was pure wrath of God, like some giant dark storm cloud tornado that was going to jack up your trailer park dreams of a better tomorrow and possibly a medal of some sort.

It was at that point... I had no illusions.

I had done... well, messed up, as they say. And regarding a medal... it was never about that for me, now. Lately. Maybe the guy I used to be. He was a collector of sorts.

An achievement hound.

But I'm not that guy anymore. Last night, going Reaper all on my own with Jabba, that was about something else.

I dropped my ruck.

My heels were instantly locked, and I was read the entirety of the riot act. In full. There're a lot of words I can't repeat. Waste of ink. But... you can fill in the blanks.

Basically… who did I think I was because I certainly wasn't a Ranger going off all Lone Ranger like that? Apparently, Captain Knife Hand, in the absence of hard information, withheld by Tanner and omitted by Joe, had listed me as DUSTWUN (Duty Status Whereabouts Unknown), and as possibly either killed in the explosion or taken captive by the orcs.

This was… bad.

Sergeant Joe, who knew the truth, said nothing, and got more and more pissed by the second as the lie of what I'd gone right off to do took on a life of its own. Officially dead made things worse. NCOs hate when stuff has to go down legitimately, for the record and all.

I didn't understand the nuances, but it looked like Sar'nt Joe was going to blow a gasket and I worried for his health. Not as much as I worried for mine, but in my defense, I *was* concerned.

He was literally… apoplectic.

A state of intense and almost uncontrollable anger.

Again, in my defense, and I had a feeling I was about to start using that phrase a lot… I had no idea he would lose it this bad. The degree to which his anger achieved… new heights… was stunning, and I was honestly not prepared for it.

I stared forward, took it, and hoped one day it would be over, though at that very moment I was pretty sure it was never going to end.

Tanner was left to watch over the legionnaires who were still guarding this spot on the wall, and Joe literally marched me off toward the CP.

Joe was seething and ranting so hard, at one point I felt the distinct possibility that he was just going to kill and bury me in the sand or one of the open graves and let my officially dead status continue. By the time we reached the CP the sun was full up, I was smoked, and aware I was about to get seriously smoked on levels I had never even contemplated.

It was at that point I realized how much I had to lose. And that was when I felt cold water run up my spine and the bottom drop out all at once.

If you would have told me, going into the command post, that I was about to get reduced in rank, for sure, goodbye corporal, have my Ranger tab yanked by Joe himself, and get my scroll pulled and sent off to hang with the Air Force guys and gals, I would have given you one hundred percent chances that was going to happen within the next thirty minutes regardless of the horde of monsters just beyond the walls ready and willing to kill us later tonight.

The Army will shoot soldiers for crimes right in the middle of a battle. They've done it before, I'd read about it, and I realized now… it was a possibility I had not considered.

Maybe you're reading this and thinking I'm being overdramatic. I assure you, if you could have seen and heard Joe, you would've felt the same way.

The feeling… you want to throw up. You want to be anyone but who you are.

I had this plan. I'd said nothing on the way to the CP while Joe ranted and raged, epically, sticking his thick finger in my face to make points about what being a Ranger means, and what it means in practice, and that it doesn't mean going off all half-cocked on a suicide mission without at least inviting a few of your closest Ranger buddies to go along with you for fun, games, and survival.

Don't even get me started on how awful he made me feel when he started talking mission and pointing out all the ways I could have gotten everyone killed.

He was right.

Torture and interrogation and I could've given up the whole defense. And me... if the orcs had coffee I probably would've talked. I mean... who're we kidding. I'm sick. I have a problem. I'm the real monster here in the Ruin.

"Never go alone!" Joe practically exploded titanically as we got close, and I could see the team leaders, NCOs, and other command team personnel gathering for the morning meeting and noting my dressing-down.

Meanwhile... surprise everyone, I'm not dead.

I had a plan...

They could rip the rank, and even the tab. But I'd put my hand over the scroll and ask them not to take that from me. No. Not that. Anything... but that.

Yeah. That was my stupid plan.

It wasn't even a very good plan. It wasn't even grounded in reality. But as Joe pushed aside the thin tattered red curtains to the blasted-out mud brick house that was the captain's command commandeered post, it was the only plan I had and I realized... the scroll, being here with them, was the only thing that mattered to me. They could take my rank. They could take anything else.

Just leave me that.

Please.

I have said it before. I'll say it again. Sometimes you pray even when you don't believe.

Then I saw the captain and knew my plan was nothing more than pure fantasy and I was going to die. Or worse, get tossed from the Rangers right here in the middle of a battle when all hands were needed on deck. My hands would no longer be needed because I'd failed to meet standards. I realized that now.

That… is how badly I messed up.

When you're guilty, you're guilty.

You don't Ranger the right way, they'll go on without you if you don't meet standards. They'll fight outnumbered rather than take a chance on a loose cannon they gotta rely on to complete the mission.

Everything Kurtz had beaten into me seemed to be clear and make sense in the daylight of another day.

Things had seemed different last night. Like… I don't know… that I could get away with it. That the risks were worth it.

I don't know if I was wrong, or right, I just knew I was in big trouble and that… I'd let them down.

On the way over, Sergeant Joe was in the middle of a rhetorical tirade on what the Ranger creed meant, specifically *N*, as in *Never shall I fail my comrades*. I will always keep myself mentally alert, physically strong, and morally straight, and I will shoulder more than my share of the task whatever it may be, one hundred percent and then some. Right in the middle of that, he'd asked a question and I'd actually been dumb enough to answer it regarding why I'd done what I'd done.

"They killed Sar'nt Monroe, Sar'nt. I—"

Joe exploded again and not for the last time.

"Monroe's not dead, you half-baked pineapple! If you'd stuck around, you would have known that!"

So after that… I really had no excuse.

As I was sayin', when Joe pushed aside the curtains at the CP, I saw the captain and felt fairly certain he was just going to murder me right there.

He was full were-tiger. Great.

His claws and the striped fur along his arms were stained with orc blood. Yeah. That's just perfect for my impending disciplinary action. As was his battle rattle. Also stained with dried blood. He was, in were-tiger form… the actual spirit animal of each and every one of his Rangers. His fatigues were cut and shredded and there was blood on his fangs.

If they all could have been changed into were-tigers, they would have.

All of you who have been called into the company commander's office to get non-judicial punishment understand the gravitas of this moment I found myself in. Now imagine that moment with an apex predator killing machine that's actual half tiger.

Ya feel me?

Damn you, Thounsavath. Damn you straight to hell forever.

The captain was briefing the team on the latest developments regarding the battle and the scout raid into enemy lines last night.

I stood there and listened… and as I did, I realized this meeting had nothing to do with me at all.

This was the command brief.

And it was pretty clear the captain didn't know what had happened, or rather was not yet apprised of my heinous transgressions. As he began the brief on the incoming Saur legions marching up through the desert to land just outside our walls, and how bad that was for us, he paused, drank some coffee, and acknowledged my presence, and that I was still alive.

"Good to see you're not dead, Corporal. I had a feeling you'd turn up. Sergeant Major, adjust his status."

At this point Joe took his thumb and drove it into the small of my back, my kidney specifically, before I could open my mouth and ruin things.

It was like being shanked. In prison.

I said nothing.

Then I saw the sergeant major look up from his notes and stare me right in the eyes like the stone-cold killer he was.

He knew what was up.

He knew the whole story.

And they knew I knew Judgment Day was a-comin'.

CHAPTER SEVENTEEN

THE captain's situation briefing regarding the overall on-going battle focused on the impending arrival of Sût's premier Imperial Saur Legions on the march. This was the enemy game-changer, and it was clear we were facing a very tough fight. Tougher than so far, once they arrived.

"We are going to have to get very creative in dealing with this problem sooner than later, Rangers." The captain paused, and it was clear that what he was indicating was serious by orders of magnitude. "Once this new force is at our gates, it will be... without better resupply from the Air Force Forge aboard the C-5 Galaxy... beyond our current capacity to conduct meaningful operations. The option being calculated at this moment, should that happen, is for the Air Force to bring in a MOAB, we pull back from the city, let the enemy take it, and detonate. But in that case there will be nothing left, and a large civilian population will be displaced. We will also lose our base of operations to prosecute Mummy in the Valley of the Kings."

That gave rise to the other problem...

And that other problem was the airfield.

"Before we go over the latest drone update regarding the Imperial Army coming up from the south," continued the captain, "we have to discuss the airfield. Wulfhard and his people indicate it's ready to go now. Air Force contingent is going to load up from their current destination and head toward us. Twelve hours later, once we give the green light, the C-5 will attempt to land after the field is cleared by the attack helicopter element forward of the transport and the onsite Air Force commander has determined the field is a go. The C-5 will only get one attempt. If she misses, or the pilot says it's a no-go, they'll head back to their last mobile field and wait until we can make further improvements to the field to get the bird on the ground.

"To win this battle, Rangers, we must get their Forge in close proximity to our elements forward at the line of battle. We can't fight at this level much longer. I am aware of that, and as your commander… I am in awe of what you've done with so little. But I cannot continue to expose you to this level of…" He paused for a long moment. Then, "You'll get killed trying to make it happen. That's the math. We need better resupply, or we're pulling out. I won't waste your lives that way. That would be wrong. And I won't do that here."

The captain paused and gave a low purring growl that radiated nothing but pure menace. I think he can't help doing this. It's just the predator side of him taking over. He was aware that he did it and turned toward the sergeant major as if to change the subject or distract us from what he could not control.

"Sergeant Major, what's the status on the security of the field?"

The sergeant major cleared his throat, remained sitting, and spoke slowly as he delivered his report.

"Sir, field is as secure as it's gonna get. Having the Air Force bird come in after first light cuts down on the enemy opportunity for action because we know they're night fighters. Generally. But that cav element they've got out there in the hills and greater desert is crazy enough to go for it if they see the bird come in, and I've got to think they've, on some level, sir, figured out that whatever we're doing out there at the STA—clearing, scrapping, leveling, and getting a defensive taxi area with high dirt berms to fight from and hold once the bird's on the ground... sir, they've got to know that's important to us. That's when they'll go for it as sure as buttered grits for breakfast back at the Benning chow hall."

But the sergeant major wasn't finished. He took a sip of his coffee from his canteen cup and coughed, clearing his throat.

Then he continued.

"I got two scouts operating out in those cracked hills west of our position, sir. They got one radio that's barely working on a good day. Last report twelve hours ago indicates the Guzzim cav element is getting ready for a major push at any time now. If we can get the drone overhead and indicate somehow it needs to go out there and take out as much of that element as it can, that would go a long way toward getting that bird inside the secure taxi area. We do that, mission accomplished, sir. We secure that Forge here on site, and we can start getting a lot of much-needed ammunition and comm gear pushed out to our guys on the line.

"But as you know, Captain, we can't comm with the Air Force back at the FOB because something is interfering with that globally. So, short o' something like making a big arrow outta rocks and white paint that tells her to go and strike them camel jockeys out in the sand and broken hills... I have yet to think of a way to effect drone support for the defense. One thing I can say… the orcs attacking the walls, they ain't the same ones attacking the airfield. They don't work together like a combined arms unit should."

He paused and took another drink of coffee.

"Right now, I got two mortar teams ranged on the sands to knock 'em down before they reach the field with antipersonnel munitions. That'll do fine on large orcs with scimitars and lances and the camels just the same. Archers on the back too. The two-forty team and one squad of Rangers hold the secure taxi area once it starts up, but that will shift them off the walls. I'm fairly confident we can hold there, especially during the day. Worst-case scenario, and this is already in the planning, once she's down, we clear the bird during the day, Forge being the top priority to offload, and get everything inside the city walls. I also have one sniper team set up on overwatch at tower three. They can contribute meaningfully or I'm a Navy SEAL on leave in San Francisco, sir.

"In short, sir, that is everything we can do on our end to make sure the bird can come in and get to the secure taxi area. I've walked the entire airfield and it's… good enough, sir. Air Force can't work with that, then they ain't aimin' high enough, sir. Good pilots, and I've worked with those boys, they can get that bird on the ground.

"Oh, and I've also got that Otoro fella. That monkey is one killing machine. Problem is he don't follow orders. Tells me he senses a guy he's got blood debt on is out there in the hills and he's a-waitin' for him to make his try on us. Then the samurai's gonna do one-on-one combat for honor or somethin'. I'd factor him into the plans, but… probably best I don't and just appreciate the fact that he cuts two or three of the enemy down at a time with those long ninja swords of his."

It almost seemed at that moment the sergeant major was done. But then he cleared his throat again and added one other thing.

"Sir... I hesitate to add this, but... we gotta consider all aspects of the situation."

He paused, and it was clear he didn't want to say what he had to say next. The sergeant major suddenly had that same look of permanent indigestion the captain has. Often. As though the chow hall just served them a big old glass of expired milk and it's already not agreeing with them. More and more I see many of the NCOs constantly wearing the same look.

And even I know... that's not good.

Tanner explained it to me this way when I mentioned it to him. "Nah, Talk. They all get that way eventually. They all get that look. Burden of command. Leadership is tough. Bein' in charge sucks, but someone's gotta do it. Hats off to them boys, but it ain't for me. Lifetime PFC, bona fide member of the Sham Mafia, that's the best and don't let anyone tell you different. You can always find out who's in charge by who looks the sickest about it."

The sergeant major picked up his canteen cup with his remaining hand and rubbed the side of his chin with the stump of the other.

"I don't want this to be a Cisterna situation, sir. So I'm going to be as cautious as that commander was and not hope it doesn't get us killed because hope ain't a Ranger value. But here's how it is to this old boot, sir...

"There's something out there waitin' to jump us on this one. I can feel it, sir. Right down to my OD green socks.

Been here right in this exact same situation before and suddenly gunfire on all sides before you know it. Normally we'd get off the *X*. But we gotta hold the *X* this time and I don't like it as much as you don't."

He looked around at everyone. Letting them know he knew what they were thinking. And that he was thinking it too.

"There's something out there that knows what we're trying to do with the airfield and that it's mission-critical to us. Critical not just to mission, but to our very survival. That's why they're stacking all the savage barbarian camel cav out in them wadis and arroyos. They know we're going to go for it soon and bring that big ol' resupply bird in, and they got somethin' planned for that when it goes down."

Silence hovered over the whole brief, and I was reminded that somehow I'd survived. Next, I began to think about hitting the coffee the smaj had after the meeting broke up. Then I remembered the look he gave me and that I wasn't out of the frying pan yet. Not by a long shot.

Still… Hey, coffee! Talker FTW!

"Any ideas, Sergeant Major, what they might be planning?" asked the captain quietly.

The sergeant major said nothing for a long moment and made no face. He was like a statue.

To me, that said a lot.

Then, after a deep long exhale, he floated his concerns.

"Sir, there is somethin', or some*things*, moving around in those late afternoon clouds that stack up to the west. Up in the sky, sir. I ain't no Specialist Kennedy with all his monster mumbo-jumbo, but I got a feeling there's a kind of air cav out, the Ruin kind if you know what I mean, or something significant, waiting for the right signal to come from their commander, and then they'll go for the airfield at the same time the ground war starts... which should be at about the same moment the Air Force bird is wheels down and heading for the secure taxi area we've established and fortified."

The captain thought about this for a long moment. Then shook his head, or tiger's mane really, and ran his bloody paw through his hair, or fur, I don't know... this is getting weird... growled slightly, and yeah, that's not creepy, and then finally spoke.

"We have two Carls left, Sergeant Major. Fifteen rounds of air defense munitions. Reposition them and their teams to the secure taxi area. Tell the Air Force to stand by to send the C-5 in. We're as ready as we're going to be. We'll make our move soon, and we will be ready for whatever they decide to throw at us, Rangers. If they wanna make that mistake, then we will make them pay for it. Dearly."

CHAPTER EIGHTEEN

THE captain picked up with the rest of the brief, and the impending addition of more veteran forces to the enemy numbers was the elephant in the room we knew we were all facing.

Even for Rangers... this was getting a bit much. We were thin and at the end of ourselves and the real knockout blow still had yet to hit the field.

Before I relate all that and what he informed us of during the morning brief at the CP, with drying blood on his claws, fur, and fangs, I need a few paragraphs to explain what we were facing so far. Then you can see that what he was apprising us of was... a lot.

It was gut check time.

But it felt like Get Out of Dodgeistan time, really.

Right now, our enemy was two separate groups of enemies. We were facing two massive armies of orcs out there in the desert. One to the west facing the Gates of Death. The other to the east throwing themselves against the Gates of Eternity and the Gates of Mystery on the eastern side of the city.

To the west was the desert camel cav which was basically a vast "wild Mongol horde" of mounted orc riders, archers, and lancers. They were effective at raiding and their schtick basically seemed to be attack, then please come chase us out into the desert where we will surround and murder you.

The Rangers were totally like, *Hey, we'd do that too!* So they didn't fall for that.

Instead, the Rangers opted not to die surrounded in the desert flats and full of orcish arrows, and were content to let the mounted, wild, robe-flapping, scimitar and gaudy lance-lowering charge of the strange horde come sweeping out of the sandstorms in the deep desert and die en masse within effective fire kill zones of the two-forty Lima gun teams, snipers, and lots of mortar rounds.

Believe it or not... it took a while for the orcs to figure this out, and once they got tired of leaving huge piles of their dead scattered and rotting across the sands near the walls of the city...

The buzzards were so thick that the sky seemed filled with darkness some days.

... the orcs then tried a new plan which was basically direct assault and attempt to create breaches in the walls.

They were not skilled at this. At all. But, due to sheer numbers, they were able to push on the western gate on occasion, the aptly named Gates of Death, and then die en masse closer to the wall than they had with *Come and Get Us.*

They fired a lot of arrows, though. Really fast. And some of our dead were because of this, as were a lot of visits to the medics and Chief Rapp for extraction surgery.

Thankfully they weren't big on poison.

Still, the Rangers there got a close-up view of the buzzards feeding even closer to the walls the next day. And the smell.

As the gun team there said: "Brings back memories. Just like the island."

They didn't seem to mind this as much as I did. Seriously, ever try to drink a cold brew after smelling a slaughterhouse? A slaughterhouse that's been rotting in the desert sun, that is? Coffee is very aromatically empathetic. It's delicate that way. Keep it near your old socks, and the beans, and the brew, will start to smell like feet. Not good.

Coffee should be kept in a bank. Guarded by Rangers. It's the only way to be sure, as Tanner likes to say a lot lately.

The dwarves near the airfield outside the western gate hardened the defenses by reinforcing the battered old walls of Sûstagul, building defensive and supporting ramps with amazing speed, and making brief forays outside the walls to dig pits and trenches that broke camel legs and weren't so obvious if you were on a speeding camel, until the last second that is.

Then down you go, and Rangers shoot you to death.

Sometimes it was knives out on the sandstorm days when the air resupply couldn't get in.

When the dwarves weren't improving the defense, they were building the airfield. No easy task. Especially since it took several attempts to explain to them that all we really wanted was a big flat space for a giant bird to land within.

For some reason they could not understand why you wouldn't want walls, pits, trenches, murder towers, and spiked berms. And many other defenses they were dying to build for us.

Eventually, they finally got it.

And as a consolation prize we let them run wild with the secure taxi area which they turned into a small desert fortress that, honestly, in the trips I'd made over to that side of the battle, not taking my coffee with me because I'd learned dead-orc-rotting-in-the-sun coffee was awful, and yeah I drank it anyway, it was clear it rivaled the defenses of old Sûstagul itself.

Seriously, I was impressed with what they could do.

High dirt walls. Spiked berms. Pits. False entrances where cave-ins and rockslides could be released to destroy enemy pushes that had gotten too close and too effective on the secure taxi area, made it a place to be respected. The Rangers were practically dying, in their stoic dip-spitting-stream way, to try out the defense and fight from there.

And there were "murder towers."

Murder towers are a big thing for the dwarves.

I asked Max, aka Max the Hammer, their weapon master and Wulfhard's personal champion, why they found murder towers so... effective.

"Vell..." he began, bewildered that I could not see the obviousness of their brilliance. "Ve climb up. Then ve shoot down on zhem vis der crossbows."

I told him, "I get that. Why's that... different than what we do with our gun teams and the towers?"

"Ah." Max slapped his bald head. "Nozhing. For you. But for us... when ve are in ze murder towers ve are tall like ze giants of ze Dire Frost. Vhen ve are in our murder towers. Der Mordensturm makes us giants, Talker!"

I think I got it. Being tall was a big thing for them even though they were so effective at being small. And very dangerous. And deadly.

They have lots of knives. Among the five weapons each of them seems to carry all the time.

"Don't get me wrong, Talker. Ve like ze vork ve do. But sometimes it's nice to kill ze enemy anozher vay. Like how you have you kaffee sometimes kalt, sometimes kochen."

Sometimes cold.

Sometimes hot.

"Do you see, Talker? It's gut to vork both vays."

Work in Dwarven means killing.

I understood and he saw that I did.

He did that German speaker thing of looking at you when you get the translation and smile because you know what they know now. They smile expectantly and nod.

Some things survive ten thousand years of Ruin.

Amazing.

So, against the Orcs of the Wide Desert, as the Mongol horde orcs were known, we'd learned this through capture and interrogations, as long as the Rangers could get ammo resupply from the daily Black Hawks, we were good to go. The Wide Desert Orcs didn't have the skills, or technology, to breach the walls.

All they could do was get close and die.

And further perplexing, it didn't seem they wanted to coordinate with the other orc army to the south and east of the walls in any meaningful way.

We estimated Wide Desert Orc strength at somewhere around twenty thousand. We got this from drone recon and we couldn't tell how many were warriors and how many were just camp followers, which they seemed to have an abundance of. On drone recon they look like an entire nation scattered out across the sands and glowing on thermal.

It must be madness out there. Alien to anything we've ever known.

They had huge pens of camels, handlers, and weapon-smiths out there. Chief Rapp guessed each mounted warrior had at least seven to eight camels and four archers who were slaves of a sort. As were the many wives, smiths, and stable keepers.

Drone strikes on this bunch, and also gun runs by the Little Birds, were useless when they were in the deep desert. The horde was so spread out across the sands, it was almost impossible to hit them before they massed, suddenly out of nowhere and for no reason at all, and then wildly attacked us with total and complete abandon.

They had no signals we could detect like horns or drums. We theorized they either organized using some magical means, perhaps shamans in a kind of trance who communicated and coordinated, or they had lesser messenger orcs who ran between all masses, tent to tent, spreading their plans.

Or maybe it was some arcane tradition that had them attacking whenever and however only they knew.

We know they had a khan.

A lesser khan, as did the other orc army south and east of our position.

Apparently, orcs use a multi-khanate system for loose tribal governance.

They do have a grand khan who rules them all out of Umnoth, but it seems, from what we've gathered, the orcs don't get along well or much, rarely work together, and might, over several lifetimes, never even have an audience with the Grand Orcish Khan of Umnoth.

So, who knows? Orcs are nuts.

As I said, the Rangers under the leadership of the sergeant major can hold the western gate as long as they're resupplied daily. Two or three days without ammo resupply and things get iffy over there. Due to weather, sandstorms, there have been days the choppers couldn't get through. The day that follows this failure to resupply is all hands on deck to hold the western gate.

The Gates of Death.

Now, here's the tactical problem, as outlined by the smaj, facing Ranger elements at the western gate.

The C-5 Galaxy Air Force large transport aircraft.

The airfield the dwarves have made needs to be clear of any enemy when that bird comes in. Orc strike on the engines, or landing gear, could be catastrophic. The Galaxy needs to land, then taxi back down the airfield to reach the secure taxi area. Yes, in a perfect world it would just land and hit the taxi area with a minimum of exposure, but in this case the winds off the coast and some other factors have forced the STA to be set up the way it is in relation to the direction of landing.

Which means land to the west and taxi to the secure area near the Gates of Death and beneath the walls of the city.

This means the C-5 will be out there and exposed while it taxis. And… the wild raiding desert orcs seem to have a penchant for showing up at the wrong time, covering a lot of ground fast, and swarming everywhere all at once while shooting arrows like it's a bodily function.

We have Otoro. Every day the samurai goes out there, into the sands alone, and faces them with both his massive ninja swords, cutting down dozens if not hundreds of them in battle.

The whole time he calls for them to send Axe Grinder so his foe may come and die like a warrior.

Now, the raider orcs might not be able to take the walls of the city, but the STA has yet to be truly defended, and once the bird is on the runway, effective fire, without hitting the taxiing Galaxy and her air crew will be… a little more difficult.

The Little Birds are going to perform gun runs to keep the horde back once they sweep out of the desert, but they don't have all the ammo in the world. The Black Hawks are bringing in the air crews and maintenance personnel so they can help get the C-5 secure behind the defensive walls of the secure taxi area.

But the Rangers are going to have to hold the walls while the big plane is offloaded of the most crucial piece of equipment to our survival.

The Forge.

Once that's inside the walls, up and running, the game changes for us.

But when the landing happens, it's not going to be an easy day for anyone. Everyone knows it, and for some reason… we can feel it.

The Rangers' quiet bravado… just gets quiet when we talk about the defense of the airfield. Even they know it's gonna be the real deal that day. And I can tell they're, all of them, plotting to high score that day. It's the quiet before the storm.

And it feels ominous.

Long day, lotsa death.

Whenever isn't it that way here?

Amirite?

Shoutout to coffee though. Me Talker.

Now let's talk about the massive force to the south and east of Sûstagul. We do not know the numbers. We just know there are more of these orcs than the other raider orcs and they never seem to run out of orcs to throw against the walls we're holding.

It's not a matter of if they're going to get through the walls, only a matter of when. We simply don't have the numbers to keep them off, even supported by two half-strength legions of the Accadions. So when they do breach, that's when the Rangers do what they do and ambush, set traps, and lure the unlucky breakout orcs into dens of total murder they never emerge from.

Most of the Rangers are now organized into these killing squads whose job is to not hold the wall, but to destroy anyone who breaches the wall. They are often staged behind the lines of Accadion legionnaires. Back in the streets and districts of the city.

Unsurprisingly… they're really good at this. Rangers love to mollywhomp, and these ambushes are the very definition of Surprise, Ranger Smash! And also, many of the citizens of Sûstagul, whose very lives depend on the Rangers holding the wall, and the city, pitch in on the work of making traps, water supply, feeding the Rangers, and even at times, cleaning Ranger weapons so the teams can get some rest.

The port kids, the mer-urchins, have taken this responsibility and have gotten so good at it that the armorers can't gig them on unclean weapons. It's not uncommon to see them, littles and older children in ragged clusters, kneeling on patched pants, squatting in the shadows, biting their pink little tongues, as they concentrate scrubbing and oiling weapons, rodding barrels, and all the while being wet-sponged by the women of the city to keep them working so far from the waters of the port which they must return to.

At night they go back to the dark sea and patrol the waters, reporting to Gill.

Sergeant Monroe's friendship has paid dividends beyond our expectations.

If we lose the city, then they could just slip into the waters and swim away to the safety of the deep-sea forests of azure that is the ocean to them.

But they don't.

They're as in it to win it as we are.

Gill says they always ask after "The Good Bull" and if he's okay and not hurt. Every three days Sergeant Monroe goes to visit them and sits with them as they clean weapons in the afternoon.

War is so much more than what you ever thought it was. There are things I never expected to find when at first I started out on this journey. Amazing things. Beautiful things. Noble things.

I need to see those things more.

The Guzzim Hazadi are the elite orcs, and they seem to be our biggest problem, as you've read in my account. They're us out there in the night and sand. And they want in real bad.

But, after what happened last night, I think that's no longer going to be a problem.

The rest of the orcs attacking the city from the south and east, augmented by the Guzzim, are known as the Black Claw Orcs, and they come from farther south, beyond what we would have called the Sahara.

Maybe.

Wherever they're from, it's clear they're not from around here. They're definitely in the employ of Sût the Undying and the Saur, and they seem to be being used as cannon fodder. Basically they're just wasting our time and resources, and our lives, until the real battle gets here.

I asked one of the prisoners we captured why they were fighting against us. We'd done nothing to them.

He indicated their khan had been told by the Priests of Sût that if they took the city, it was theirs to plunder. He also said it was generally accepted among the orcs that the Saurian temples had no illusions, and it was expected that the orcs would die by the dozens and probably never take the city.

The orcs had suspected that the Priests of Sût had exaggerated in telling them the streets of Sûstagul were, basically, "paved with gold." But they had come for plunder anyway, even knowing they were little more than cannon fodder, or the orc equivalent of that term. So far there are no cannons in the Ruin.

Catapult fodder I guess.

Early in the battle, when survivors who'd breached the city returned to the massing desert tribes with the truth that treasure and hoard were not "overflowing through the streets," the orcs had a minor revolt and slew their khan in a moment of madness.

It was clear all the orcish generals were going to go their own ways after that, some heading south, returning to their jungles to fight the cat men, others heading into the Eastern Waystes to raid and plunder the ancient cities of fable and legend like their forefathers had done so long ago.

Then Mola Ram Orc appeared one dark and stormy night, and the bloody sacrifice that occurred over the subsequent few nights terrified and cowed the tribes into continuing the fight against the city. A sudden religious fervor swept through the orc hordes and soon the generals were dead, and a dark salvation was promised once Sûstagul burned, and the orcs embraced their new destiny in the darkness and the cold as promised by Shaargazz the Night Lord.

I have a suspicion about all of this.

I have no idea if I'm right or wrong here—maybe some of it is coming from the psychic bridge I had with the serial killer ten-thousand-year-old pig farmer orc god, or demon, whatever—but I think the orcs got played and that Sût, if he really is that powerful, called in some favor on that level of things and got the orcs ready to destroy themselves and waste our time, resources, and lives… so the Saurian Imperial Legions under the command of the medusa general could show up and hit us with the two punch and make it a right cross.

The orcs were the rope-a-dope. The third medusa and her legions were gonna be the kitchen sink.

In other words…

The orcs were just the jab, and we'd lost twelve Rangers and a lot of legionnaires just dealing with that. Now we were about to get right-crossed straight out of the desert by a legendary Saurian general and close to sixteen thousand crack Saurian troops.

These were the best of the best the Saur had to offer. And they were bringing siege engines and powerful priests and sorcerers.

We now return to the captain's briefing on the straight-up *mollywhomping* we were about to get.

CHAPTER NINETEEN

"RANGERS... we are facing a combined force of over sixteen thousand," continued the captain. "These are, according to Vandahar, elite troops stationed in the south, operating out of the Ethiopian Rift, where the Saur have been fighting a war for some time."

Vandahar, who was there under what little shade could be found at the bombed-out CP, lit his long-stemmed pipe and murmured that this was indeed true.

"We won't be able to hit them with any of our ranged assets like the drones or the Air Force," noted Knife Hand. "Their commander is quite savvy, and apparently she separates her army into platoon-sized elements to move over long distances."

Vandahar sent a smoke ring out and supported this. "She is quite clever indeed, and perhaps... one of the most dangerous enemies you will ever face, Rangers," he commented, as if simply letting everyone know we were collectively out of milk and someone should pick some up at the store.

"This means," continued the captain after Vandahar's aside, "that this force won't come together until they're right at the gates and ready to launch their attack—if they operate according to past behavior.

"A week ago, the drone operator hit their siege engines that were being brought up out of the valleys to the south, and those are now off the board. But again, Vandahar assures me the siege engines are not necessary to breach the walls for this force. Their... asymmetrical operations... may prove more than sufficient at creating a necessary breach in the walls that will allow their fortress to maintain a hold once created... and then break out into the city at large."

There was no overhead, no PowerPoint, nothing fancy like what we'd been used to when being briefed. There was a crude catch-as-catch-can sand table of the city, but even that wasn't being used now.

The words of the captain were enough. His tone was serious. His demeanor intense. It was clear we couldn't face this approaching force without a Forge to keep us supplied. And right now the Air Force Forge could only send as many replacement weapons, ammunition, launchers, mortar rounds, and C4 as could fit on one Black Hawk for the air resupply.

If it were closer at hand, the Forge could arm us to the gills, sorry Gill, and then we could face the Saurian Imperial Legions closing in on us from all points of the compass to the south.

"It would be at this moment that normally we would make the decision that this battle is no longer worth fighting, Rangers. We disappear and fight another one somewhere they don't want us to be. But we can't do that today. For the obvious reason that without this city we can't stage our hit on Mummy. Further, the people of Sûstagul will not survive if we abandon them now to the Saur. We brought this war to them, and I feel obligated to make sure they see the other side of this."

The captain cleared his throat, which sounded more like the low growl of a predator in the jungle and no convenient zoo cages between you and it. And it was feeding time.

Still creepy if you ask me.

"Chief Rapp and I are developing a plan to strike at the inbound force's command and control structure when the time comes. We are down to less than one hundred of us. Augmented by a Legion force under the command of Captain Tyrus, we have a very good chance of going for a decap and shutting this fight down. Everything we've learned about the enemy force we're facing breaks down to its commander. She's a monster. Yes. She's also a brilliant tactician and she has yet to lose a war, and according to Vandahar, she's fought more than her fair share of rough fights against some foes that... that I would have serious concerns about. The Saur troops surrounding her, we're not particularly impressed with them. Line troops, better armor and gear. The accompanying asymmetrical elements on the other hand, they're magic users and..."

The captain clearly looked uncomfortable with this part and reached down to pick up his notebook and read out of it as though that were somehow putting some distance between him and the incredibly geeky stuff he was about to say.

"... and... cat ninjas. Those, next to their commander... are going to be the problems we think we need to give the most serious consideration to. We have no hard intel, but we expect the Katari—those are the... cat ninjas... according to..."

Look of indigestion.

"… Specialist Kennedy. They should be operating in the city well in advance of the main body. Their goal will be to counter, and secure access to the city via some of the gates we've blocked off. They are known to identify and murder small unit leaders in order to create chaos. Watch your back, team leaders. Sergeant Kang, I want you to boo-by-trap these gates with our remaining explosives. If they monkey with them, I want them dead. The… ah… magic users… will come with the main body when they arrive, but the plan we are developing may be able to mitigate their contribution to some extent once we attack."

Captain Knife Hand put his notebook down.

"I'll give it to you straight, Rangers. What we're planning on executing is going to be a rough fight… maybe one of the toughest you've ever been in. Until it goes down, and I expect by the end of the week sooner than later, I want max rest, foot care, and gear prep for mobile operations. We are going to move fast, mobile, and carrying as much as we can hump right into the enemy. Those of you familiar with your military history will understand the concept of a hatchet force and you can consider this your WARNO to begin planning and execution."

Warning order. WARNO.

"The op order will come with minimum time in advance and expect to deploy within two hours once that happens. All Rangers. We will leave the defense of the city to the Accadions in order to go out there and take their commander's head."

Uh, sir, I didn't say. *A medusa's head can turn you to stone.* Again, I didn't say that.

Remember, I think I'd just survived my own decap. So Talker is good Ranger.

"For now, I'd like to ask Vandahar to brief you on the enemy commander's disposition, so you know what you're facing and what to expect. Should we face heavy casualties... I want her dead, Rangers. That is my intent."

Readily will I display the intestinal fortitude required to fight on to the Ranger objective and complete the mission though I be the lone survivor.

Chills. I knew the creed. The last paragraphs. That line.

I be the lone survivor.

I wanted to be worthy of that.

I didn't want it to happen.

No more Kurtzes. No More Brumms.

Without standing, Vandahar turned to face us all on the stool he was sitting on, took off his hat, and smoothed his long beard as he sent another smoke ring into the air, drifting off and out through the gaping cracks and holes in the CP.

"Your captain is right, Rangers. She is... very... dangerous indeed. As a medusa... yes. But as a foe, very much more so."

He watched us and sent another smoke ring into the air. Then he smiled wanly.

"But... she is a special kind of medusa, Rangers. Not like her two sisters you have faced at all. A thrice-birth among the medusae is rare. And all three are given different gifts, or so it is said. Her two sisters could, just by meeting your gaze, or the gaze of anyone for that matter, turn you to stone with their eyes alone. That would be how most medusae wield their powers. But this young medusa is different from others in so many ways. She is both beautiful and… deadly, though not in the way her kind is wont to be. Her power is in the snakes themselves. It is the venom of the snakes that causes the stone-turning. Among her kind she is considered… a runt. Imperfect and lesser. Hence why her sister, the queen, traded her as a prisoner of sorts to have ally with the Undying Pharoah himself."

Vandahar laughed at this as though thinking of a joke he had neither the time nor inclination to explain to us.

"Well, she got the wrong end of the stick with that move, eh, Rangers? If she'd had her younger, lesser sister in command of her armies, then perhaps the events at the citadel might have been much different. For you Rangers… even deadlier."

He stared around at all of us. Even Captain Tyrus, who loomed, by his very presence, nearby in his armor, silently watching everything like the commander he was. It was clear Vandahar was attempting to make a point and ensure we got it. How serious he was regarding this new legendary and impossible enemy.

"She is crafty, brilliant, and a capable soldier, Rangers. She has fought the jungle wars of the Southern Rift to a standstill using her skills as a commander, and a warrior without peer. This was a blow to the plans of the council, as we'd hoped the Aslani could have put pressure on the Lich Pharoah from the south and delayed any assistance to the Nether Sorcerer and his forces in Umnoth. She spoiled that plan—and the Aslani are not incapable warriors, especially in their jungles—by defeating the tribes and scattering them to the deeps of the Emerald Sea."

Silence.

All around me the Rangers were busy writing in their notebooks, making sure they had everything down.

"In battle, one on one, she has never lost. The snakes of course can do the work her swift sword does not accomplish, and that is why she leads from the front of her armies. But at the same time, she often seems to be everywhere within the force, and we suspect magic of great power of some kind. I will not... as your commander says... not tell it to you... straight... is that right? No... I will tell you... straight... yes. That seems how you say it. But you Rangers... and I have journeyed with you long now and I fear our time is coming to an end, but you must know you are facing great powers perhaps beyond your ability to meet at this current time. She is worse than the powerful and cruel dragon you faced, and any other foe... by far.

"But you have two things, Rangers, two gifts from the Hidden King himself, that may... just *may*... defeat her in the end. One is your speed. You move fast, Rangers. She moves faster. Again I cannot deceive you in this. If you can hit her before her armies form around her and her powerful sorcerers cover their advance into the city with deep ancient magics even I can not stand against... then perhaps you can stop the attack before it starts."

Vandahar stopped. His ancient washed-out blue eyes were old, his face more lined and tired than I'd ever seen it, and in that moment I wondered how old he really was as the morning sun fell full upon him.

"Still... I will go out with you to do battle against her, Rangers. And perhaps... an old wizard may be of some aid. Even though I feel that if there is to be catastrophic failure... then it will be by her hand, and lightning-bright sword."

The Rangers, silent, continued to write this all down. If the odds were against them, the news dire, and the situation as dark as it could get, you wouldn't have known it by their demeanor. It was Tuesday to them, and they were going to kill anything that stood in their way. Even a hero, or mythical monster, straight out of Greek legends.

The captain cleared his throat and stepped forward.

"What would be the second aspect that may help us defeat her forces, Vandahar?"

The wizard seemed surprised at this and wiped some sweat away from his forehead, smoothing his hair as he did so. Smiling once again after he'd become so serious with the telling.

He took his pipe and held it out, pointing with it at all of us.

"Oh, yes... that. Well, she is a prisoner, Rangers. A valuable slave to the Lich Pharaoh himself. She is forced to do what she is excellent at. Like a tool. But you must understand, and I think you do: no one wants to be a slave, and perhaps in that, there is something for you to work with... though I would not counsel you against doing what you do so well, which is kill like the lightning moves in the night. Swift and sudden, Rangers. Swift and sudden."

He paused, studying the Rangers before him.

"And without remorse."

CHAPTER TWENTY

SO, we got that going for us.

Two orc armies ready and willing to expend our ammo and lives at costs of a thousand to one to kill us and take the walls. No air support. Limited resupply. An airfield defense coming soon that's going to be one very bad day.

And...

Four incoming legions on the march of veteran troops augmented by Ruin-equivalent Green Beret cat ninjas... and lizard wizards... led by the Ruin's version of Alexander the Great.

Who happens to be the medusa.

I thought about this as I was practically frog-marched off to the sergeant major's campsite, away from the CP, where a small smoldering fire and the blue percolator waited. Like some kind of heaven no one ever made a religion about but that I would join immediately no questions asked.

Because you know... coffee.

So, things weren't all bad.

"You're benched, Ranger."

Those were Joe's last words to me before he stormed off to fix another in an endless list of problems he had to get solved before the next fight. Along the way to the smaj he'd told me why.

"It ain't because of last night, man. And it ain't because you did wrong, Talker. You showed initiative. Good units, and a Ranger company would be the model of a good unit... encourage junior leaders and soldiers to show initiative, especially in crisis situations where momentum in the battle space can be achieved if it's acted on... instead of flying up the chain for a decision. You see a problem, don't ask permission, get it done, Ranger. Positive leadership environment leads to Rangers doing what needs to be done without being told.

"Bottom line, if you would have given Tanner a GOTWA before going out there on your little hunting trip for one, then the chain of command would have respected that decision. Straight up. If the chain of command didn't, then that reflects negatively on the judgment of said chain of command. They don't trust that soldier, then they should have never put him in a position of leadership in the first place. I'll fight to the death on that one and I'm built like a whiskey barrel with anger management issues. So try me. It's that simple, Talker. I always told my guys that loyalty goes right down the chain just as fast as it do up it. I'd fight the captain, in his current state, for my guys. And they know it, Ranger. *You* should have known that. If, and big if here, but if command had punished you for taking initiative and hitting a time-sensitive target then that meant they shouldn't have made you a corporal in the first place. When you make someone a leader, Talker, you place your utmost trust in them. You place your life... in their hands. You trust them to take advantage of an opportunity on the battlefield. Yeah, what you did was impetuous, but it was time-sensitive and there was no way to get permission in time to hunt. I get that. That ain't why I'm benching you."

Warts and all.

I didn't cry. But I wanted to at that moment.

Why?

Because I felt like I'd let Joe down. The guy who'd made me a Ranger. Everything he said was like a gut punch and it knocked the wind right out of me in ways I never expected.

I know... I can be a bit glib. Flippant even.

"I'm benching you here with the sergeant major, Talker, because you need to come down off the freight train of grief you've been riding since..."

He didn't say their names.

And I could see for a moment that he couldn't. But Tanner, and others, had noticed how out of control I was getting so that... it... never happened again to another Ranger.

"You gotta ruck that, Talker. Later. Another day maybe if you live. But right now we ain't got time for that. They knew. They were cool with it. Deal with it and get back on the line because it's thin, man. Real thin. Always was. Anyone telling you different... is a damn liar."

Then he turned and walked away.

My mouth was hanging open and I was fighting hard not to show any emotion. Any weakness.

"You get him, Ranger?" said Joe, turning back to me. "The guy you went out there for last night?"

I swallowed hard and nodded.

Then...

"Yes, Sar'nt. Burritos."

Joe nodded to himself and muttered, "Good." Then he stalked off into the late morning heat.

CHAPTER TWENTY-ONE

THE sergeant major returned later and put me to work.

"Boys are gonna need a new latrine pit. Over near the mortars. Grab an entrenching tool and get to work."

Then he told me the dimensions he wanted.

So I went and dug.

I didn't get any coffee.

CHAPTER TWENTY-TWO

I think, over the course of the next three days of unofficial extra duty, everyone in the Ranger detachment, and the legionnaires who came by to see if Al Haraq and the succubi were around, figured I'd done something really bad to end up digging the pit, cleaning weapons, and at night following the sergeant major around, acting as a messenger.

No one said anything, but it was clear they knew I was… being disciplined. I said little regarding what had happened out there, I don't know why, and kept working.

No fighting.

I carried water.

Rations.

Ammo.

I ran messages and got close to the fights, but never in them.

In the mornings I slept like a dead man for a few hours. Then I worked on the latrine pit. Next I followed the smaj as he checked on all elements across the besieged city and along the walls. While the smaj was checking and meeting with the NCOs I was there too. I cleaned weapons for guys who needed rest. I ran for water. I ran for rations.

They were grateful.

They were beat up.

They were going to do it again that night.

There was coffee. Some. Sometimes Amira found me, saying nothing, pressing a ceramic pot full of the greatest magic potion ever into my hands, then running back to her shop.

Don't ever tell me there aren't miracles. Don't ever tell me there's no good in the world. No matter how horrible it gets… there is good. And don't be surprised if it smells like a medium roast Arabica.

I worked, I lived, I tried to understand… what I had done, where I had gone wrong.

There were… stages… to my… I don't know… whatever I was working through. Grief.

What are the stages of grief?

Denial.

I'd been through that. Just after… at the beginning. And there were times I'd tell you I was done with that because the anger, the second stage, had come in pretty quick on its heels.

But when I thought about the djinn, and the two wishes he owed me… Aren't wishes, real wishes, a kind of denial? A chance to make things… not? A chance to make things… right?

I dug the pit and had a lot of arguments with myself about this. About the nature of wishes. Because it wasn't really denial, not if… not if I made the right wish, said the words right, then… couldn't I fix all this? Couldn't things be made right?

Then it wouldn't be denial now, would it? It would be just like it never happened.

I dug and worked on the wish, day by day becoming more sure that I was gonna attempt the impossible. That I was going to outsmart fate… and bring them back. Apparently I had to get it just right, according to Kennedy, or I might tear the entire universe apart.

"How so?" I asked him as I shoveled.

Kennedy sighed and pushed his RPGs up his nose as he watched me dig in the late afternoon heat. I remembered I had not helped him dig when it had been his turn as all this first began.

I remember thinking it was very noble of me just to come and watch him dig, like I was his friend or something.

Now it was hot, and I wouldn't have minded if he'd dug some.

"Listen, Talker. The wish… it's almost malevolent. It will seek the worst possible answer to your request. So, let's say you just wish… like… 'I wish Kurtz and Brumm were alive.' Well, here's a few things that could happen. Kurtz and Brumm are alive, just not here, but in some other dimension, maybe. Hell, even. Or yes, they're alive, *pop*, except with all their life-threatening, basically fatal injuries, and they die almost immediately because you didn't wish for them to be healthy and whole. Variations of this could be terrible. Or they're alive, but the wish uses what's called future perfect cognition and picks the multiverse closest to your wish, in which the rest of us die and they live. Then shifts reality over to that. Or… it resets the entire timeline back to when they were alive."

"Why is that bad? What happens then?" I asked.

"Who knows, Talker? But here's the second-worst thing that happens: your wish resets everything to normal, I mean even before we came to the Ruin. Except that you, the wish-maker, have the knowledge of what happened. Everything bad. Everything… in fact. And then you are forced to live through it again *Groundhog Day* style, and again and again and again, over and over… make the wish… and again, relive it all again including making the wish. For a hundred thousand times… or an infinite number of times. You, basically, by using the wish trying to save someone… set the universe into a recursive loop. That's a special kind of hell, Talker."

I put down my shovel and wiped dirt from my face.

"This wish thing sucks!"

Kennedy agreed and sat down on his helmet. It was late afternoon. He'd be getting ready to go out on the line again.

Since *Burritos*… the orcs hadn't been doing well. Their attacks were halfhearted now. I knew why. I went out there, found Mola Ram Orc with the help of Jabba, and smoked him once in the skull and twice in the chest. Then I got the hell outta there.

It was like a vision of hell, out there among the orc tents and tribes. It wasn't just medieval… it was… savage in ways people can't understand. It was barbaric. I still have nightmares about it.

Before I came back into the Observatory, I told Jabba to go in another way so if I got caught, he wouldn't be able to add or subtract any information from the lie I was determined to tell.

He made it back to the gun team and no one really much noticed what the little gob had gotten up to because Soprano is supposed to keep an eye on him.

The battle was still going on along the wall at night, but the orc pushes and breaches weren't effective anymore. And it seemed, to some of the spotters and snipers, that mass sections of the orcs were beginning to desert. They were running out of steam without a cult to believe in. I'd left Mola Ram Orc just as dead as Deep State.

My guess… is that shook them. And now they were rethinking the situation.

Still, the Saurian legions were inbound. Just days away now. Our drones were getting taken out by something, so who knew when they'd really get here. Everything was a best guess now.

"What the worst thing, Kennedy? The worst thing that could happen if I don't say the wish… exactly right?"

He corrected me. "Phrase it, Talk. When I ran my campaign, I was so litigious about wish usage, my players started writing three-page documents of contingencies just to cover all possibilities. Some of those guys were headed to law school. I could usually tear apart their request in under an hour and find a way to make it as bad as possible on them."

"Why?"

"Because I'm the Dungeon Master, Talk. That's my job. That's what I do. Throw every horrible thing I can at them, according to the rules, run those rules, and once they've overcome the obstacles, or I've killed their characters… that happens more often than not… then they win. They get treasure and experience. That's all. It's fun. Very satisfying when it's played at that level of difficulty. Anything else is just navel-gazing and that's as boring as social media used to be."

"So then… what's the worst thing, Kennedy, if I jack it all up… what's the worst possible outcome to a wish?"

He looked at me. Then unconsciously pushed his thick glasses up the bridge of his nose.

"That's easy, Talk. Worst-case scenario… you rip the very fabric of reality apart, and we all die."

CHAPTER TWENTY-THREE

THE next morning, in the dark, the C-5 Galaxy departed her last LZ and arrived over Sûstagul mid-morning.

The enemy immediately made an all-out attack against the airfield, the secure taxi area, and the Gates of Death on the western side of the city.

What followed was a disaster that barely got salvaged by the Rangers... and the Air Force. Everyone did their job, lives were lost, but we are able to fight again tomorrow.

In the sergeant major's book, as he put it to me later in the dark, when the fire was nothing but coals, "That's a win, Talker. If you can get up in the morning and still punch the enemy in the face... that's a win in my book."

That morning, the Rangers were already on the defense, and I was busy running messages as our comms were bad with all elements, even the Air Force.

Almost immediately, as soon as the Galaxy was overhead and still in the air, the desert orc tribes swarmed out of the sands and made for the airfield the dwarves had carved out of the landscape west of the gates. The Ranger gun teams opened fire after the mortars section began to make it rain beyond the field. Huge dirt blossoms of sand exploded, devastating the enemy advance. But the orcs seemed determined and came on anyway, throwing everything they had at us. On cue, even as the Galaxy was lining up for approach to the airfield, engines straining, being attacked by the enemy's air assets, griffins and a roc, mythical beasts, the Nightstalker Little Birds charged out from their temporary LZs inside the city and started making gun runs across the surging orc cav, swarming for the field to intercept the Galaxy once it was down.

The orcs died in waves out there as the Little Birds raced overhead and poured down death on the archers and camel riders… and still, the orcs kept coming as spent brass rained from the sky.

The Air Force Galaxy crashed into the strip a short while later.

If it weren't for the Air Force personnel on board… we'd all be dead within the next few days due to lack of resupply. The Rangers wouldn't have abandoned the city and its people to its fate, and so they would have fought with pickups and tomahawks even as the Saurian legions climbed and overcame the walls and cut us down amid piles of spent brass and their stacked dead.

I have no illusions about this.

Thanks to the Air Force, that didn't happen that day.

Like I said, I was running here and there and didn't contribute to the fighting. Later, in the evening with the smell of burning jet fuel still hanging over the city, I cornered one of the Air Force tech sergeants and asked him to tell me what happened. Blow by blow. For the record.

I'm at least good for that.

What follows is what happened that day at the airfield west of the city. Near the Gates of Death.

In the moonlight, the orc dead litter the near and far horizon. It looks like the end of the world out there.

I am simply amazed.

The Air Force got it done despite the apocalypse of a major air disaster right in the middle of an enemy attack.

They lived up to their motto.

What follows, is what happened that day.

For the record.

CHAPTER TWENTY-FOUR

AIR Force Tech Sergeant Gunter sat in front of me, bouncing his knee while he downed the cup of coffee I'd handed him like it was the best thing on the planet.

To be fair, it was the second-best thing on the planet, because it was my coffee and he drank it. The first best thing would have been if *I* drank it.

Because it was mine.

Warts and all. I am honest about what a horrible person I am.

We were at the sergeant major's little camp, away from the CP, but near enough. The blue percolator is here and that's all that matters.

It's been a long day.

To be fair, when I offered Sergeant Gunter the cup, I never thought he'd drain the whole thing. You know, just take a sip and give it back to me. After all, wouldn't he have known by now I was the coffee guy in this unit? I mean, I was trying to be nice and this chungo goes and drains the whole thing like it's easy to brew up a satisfying cold brew out here among battlefields full of dead orcs and blasted-out ruins of the city.

Like there's an endless supply.

Philistine. Some people just don't get it.

He handed me back the cup—the empty cup—and brushed his heavily muscled arm across the front of his mouth. You can tell this guy had hands-on heavy work, all day, every day, in whatever he did for the Air Force.

Despite the fact that the Air Force guy looked more like Sergeant Monroe before the change, he was clearly shaken by what had happened out there today. His people... had been through it.

As they say.

I wanted to get it all down for the record because I had seen bits of what happened... and even I knew things were off the rail and getting worse. A disaster had started to snowball into total defeat for us. What happened out there today... what happened when the Galaxy tried to make the field while being attacked by flying... Kennedy calls them griffins... basically flying lions with eagles' heads. Giant. Huge wingspans. They attacked the incoming Air Force transports like enemy fighter aircraft swarming a fat and slow target.

It had to crash-land on the runway.

What happened almost killed us all.

"Tech Sergeant Gunter," I started. "Really appreciate you helping me with this so I can get all this down for the official record of our time here. Helps us AAR this stuff so we can hit our enemies harder the next time..."

I just sorta stopped. He had this... thousand-yard stare on his face. Like he wasn't listening to me. Like... he was back in that Galaxy right now, AARing everything from there... to here.

Then he seemed to remember me and came back to the interview.

"Yeah, Corporal. And it's Robert, or Rob. Unless there's a big stack of brass hanging around, we don't really yell out ranks, serial numbers, and all that Ranger jazz. That's mostly Army and Marine stuff. In the Air Force we just kinda know who's in charge of what, and then we do our thing. Cool?"

"I can dig it," I said. "So… what happened out there, Sar'nt?"

It's just that way in the Rangers.

Sergeant Gunter held up his hands, opening and closing his fingers in an attempt to get them to stop shaking. He was just… working through it.

They'd been in the thick before, but with attack aircraft at their disposal and a host of combat controllers on the trigger. He told me that. Again, the Ruin makes everything weird. So why not get attacked by giant flying lion birds on approach to the LZ? Part of what he was experiencing was just… dealing with it. The Ruin. We'd all been there. The other part… was an actual real live aircraft crash, air disaster, or what they call… a major incident. According to Sergeant Gunter, he and his people hadn't done as much fist and fury as the Rangers had since day one in the Ruin. The abandoned, continent-spanning city with the lion people had been the biggest dustup they'd had so far. And when it got heavy, the CCTs held the line until the entire flight was wheels up again, then off into the wild blue yonder.

Sergeant Gunter began his account of what happened. Haltingly at first.

"So, we deployed the combat controllers when you all took the city. They jumped in to set up operations and security. Wilson didn't make it on that one, don't know if you heard? Chute literally came apart when he tried to deploy it. Burnt in. We know it all tracks back to what you told us about calling this place the Ruin. How it eats up tech after a bit, but we thought that was only modern electronics. iPhones, cameras... stuff like that. You know? Having a full-on parachute completely disintegrate on a guy was... terrible."

But I didn't say anything. Didn't want to interrupt the flow now that he was starting to talk.

"Did we find him?" I asked over my shoulder. Tanner was there and hanging out with me. He confirmed the fate of the combat controller with a shake of his head.

It was dark now and we had just the light of the smaj's fire. The fight, despite the airfield that day, was starting up all along the walls again as we began to talk.

I was benched and Tanner was here waiting for something from the smaj.

Or keeping me company. Or just one of his eyes on me. I'm that guy in the company right now. No use fighting it.

Tanner's coming apart, physically. Rock solid in his role as a Ranger slash undead bounty hunter. As we talked, he had this little skin tag about the size of my thumb that had been threatening to fall off his face for the last hour. When he shook his head that the Air Force security guy hadn't made it, it creeped me out that it waggled back and forth and refused to give up the ghost.

It's the little things that make the Ruin... the Ruin.

My friend. The undead terminator. No judgment. He's here. That's all that matters. People tell me lately it looks like I don't sleep much. I don't. Sometimes I just lie there and think about the wish. Sometimes I do sleep, but nightmares. Or just... lights out.

I don't wake up... rested. And I miss that.

Confession… if I could just put my head down on Last of Autumn's lap, and sleep for a moment… just one minute… I bet I'd be okay. But… she's not here. And that will never happen again.

Still… I bet every soldier has had that moment.

Sergeant Gunter had that faraway look on his face, like he was replaying the whole thing, everything that had happened out there on the airfield, on some TV only he could see right now. But it was playing out right in front of him… and it never would not.

But he continued talking.

"The CCT guys had already worked with the dwarven contingent to clear a runway to the west side of the city, south of the port. I mean, the combat controllers are no joke, but those dwarves can build. Know what I mean?"

I did. We'd seen it. King Wulfhard and his dwarves were hardcore. Like some Ruin god had really wanted to play a joke on all the evil in the world and smashed Ranger-level aggression into whiskey-barrel-sized combat engineers who never slept and worked constantly. Oh, and he made them short, just to add insult to injury.

I have never seen them sleep.

Dwarves are busy all night, late into the night.

"So, these dwarves got after it," continued Sergeant Gunter. "I mean, like epic-level digging and clearing land for that strip out there. No power tools. No C-machines. Just brute strength and the occasional bull they found from somewhere, or someone, to pull a road grater they built themselves. You know them, right? One minute they're running bingo on everything and the next they have all the kit and plenty of grit to use it. In short order we had our runway. I came out on one of the birds to inspect progress and it looked good to go to me a week ago."

He looked at me, seeing me and Tanner for the first time in recounting. He smiled wanly and laughed a little. Coughing.

He has a nice smile. A real smile.

"So, once they're done," he continues, "we have an airfield overlooking the water where if something goes wrong… then we have free access to the surf for fire prevention. Let me tell you what, Talker. Can I call you that? I know how you Army guys are about rank and whatnot."

"All good, Tech Sar'nt," Tanner interrupted. "You outrank us anyway, Sar'nt."

"No worries, bro," Gunter shot back. "Okay, so, the Rotor Joes, that's your Army aviators, the Nightstalkers flying your Little Birds and the two Black Hawks, them and our guys started making regular runs on the C-5M, the Galaxy, using the Black Hawks to bring in resupply. Mostly stuff like Class One and Four. Food and ammo. Things were humming right along, even with the linebackers chucking rocks over the city at the choppers trying to land and resupply you guys."

"Linebackers being the orcs, Sar'nt?" I asked. Had to be sure, what with this being the official record and all. And since this guy clearly couldn't be trusted after drinking my cold brew, I had to be sure Air Force translated to Ranger.

It did. Same language, small differences that make them dialects. That's all.

"Yeah, that's it. Linebackers are orcs. One of our loaders, Burns, he liked to remind everyone he was a linebacker back in high school. He ended up what you boys called getting Ruined, and it turned him into an orc."

The Ruin reveals…

"He was kind of a jerk before, but now, that kid has a temper six ways to Sunday. Had… actually."

Sergeant Gunter went far away for a moment.

"Anyway, we got our loader line established and we're running flight load in addition to LOGPACs to and from our staging base at the Galaxy. We were getting it done."

Writing all this down, our story since arriving at Bag o' Death Island, had me pretty clued in to how most people told a story. I'd have to get official accounts from a host of people across the company—or what we have left of it—to keep the record straight. You learn to know when the fork in the story is coming. Take this fork, the things are just status quo with not much to recount other than just giving a report. But this other fork usually started with a long pause so the storyteller could collect his thoughts about how they remembered it all going down when it did go down. What was real, and what was perceived as real because of the chaos of the moment.

It usually starts with something like…

"I coulda sworn…"

"I mean, it all happened so fast, Talker…"

"What else could it have been?"

Up to this point, Sergeant Gunter had been recounting his tale with more than a sense of quiet pride in his organization. According to the army crew chief that brought him in to see me, Gunter and his crew had almost singlehandedly loaded every flight mission since arriving in Sûstagul. They were a tightly tuned machine, strapping and rigging various loads to fly at a moment's notice. Under cover of the Air Force combat controllers, Gunter's team of loaders and maintainers had shown themselves to be a group of highly motivated workers who got the job done, day in and day out.

No matter what.

I add… that made the difference out on the wall each night for us. Trust me. Without these guys we would have been a lot of dead Rangers.

Including me.

I resume…

There were the phrases you heard over and over again as the fork in the story lead to all hell breaking loose. And that was what Tech Sergeant Gunter was doing now, and I could almost smell why he was doing it. Between the smoky barbecue scent on his clothing and the faraway look dominating each pause, I could tell he'd watched someone burn out there in the wreckage.

Tanner and I both knew that look. Well.

Remember Tanner just a few days ago, asking Kennedy when we were gonna meet something good? Something like a unicorn, or something.

I remember Kennedy just shrugging.

"So, we finally get the word from your brass," Gunter continued, "that they need the C-5 to make for the strip the dwarves built outside the city—still weird saying that out loud, by the way—and we get to work doing final checks before touching off to bring the fat lady up and down. I used to be a weapons maintainer for fighter aircraft before I got this gig, so the culture stuck with me. We got airborne early this morning and we had everything locked down on our side. Next up came the word from combat control that the fat lady, our C-5, was clear for touchdown. So we locked ourselves in and got ready for the epic level of stupid you get coming into hot fuzz."

Tanner leaned in and offered the guy a cigarette, but Sergeant Gunter declined.

"Sounds like you guys had everything popping. Uh, what's hot fuzz, Sar'nt?" I asked.

Side note, or observation...

A lot of guys would have fallen over if a freakshow face full of zombie offered them a smoke, as Tanner had just done with Gunter. They certainly wouldn't have just continued talking like it was no big deal. We Rangers all knew Tanner and what he was going through, and still it freaked most everyone out. But Gunter not only waved off the smoke, he unapologetically reached over and plucked the dangling flap of skin that had been bothering me, hanging off my friend's face, right off.

Total chill.

"Sorry about that," Tanner said.

Gunter shrugged. "We had a guy from our team, Maldonado... he got stung by this scorpion thing the first week we were wheels down here. He turned out... similar to you, except he didn't stay as cool as you, Ranger. We might not have been here as long as you Rangers, but we've seen some real dead stuff. But... in answer to your question, Talker, hot fuzz is our buzz word for an HFZ, a hostile fire zone."

Tanner lit the turned-down cigarette. It was only middle to lower enlisted here at the smaj's pit, so he didn't catch a smoking for smoking. Seriously though, by this point the Ranger NCOs were starting to give up on trying to discipline Tanner using normal methods. Seeing as his unusual physiology kept him from feeling any pain, there wasn't much they could do to him now.

"So we're in the bird," Sergeant Gunter began again, "and I got to keep my junior airmen from flipping their lid now that we're descending into arrow fire and potential strikes from flying boulders from the ground. I'm quizzing our new guy, Reedy, on next steps. And he tells me he knows the deal and all. While I run the forklift to pull off the full weapon carts from the bird, he gets loaned out to the Fifteens because we brought the jammer. That's our MJ-1 bomb lift truck."

Now that was a new one to me. Gunter's lingo was almost a language unto itself, loaded with Air Force mission-specific talk, honed over years of plying his trade as much as we had. "Can you clue me into that last bit, Rob?"

"I don't know if your brass gave you the situation from our brass, but the long and short of it is, we went through the QST a lot like you guys. Air Force taxi running an Army unit. In this case, a crew out of Task Force One-Sixty. Judging from the nods, you guys know what the Nightstalkers Special Operations Aviation Regiment is, so I'll continue. Our group out of the AFSOC was tasked with hauling the big kit and flying around the short-range gun rotors for the multi-purpose company out of regiment. They brought their own MOS-Q'd guys, which all start with the number fifteen. Know those guys?"

Tanner did. I was still new in that I'd only ever been with the Rangers and not even back in the world. Here in the Ruin was pretty much all of my experience.

Talking to Gunter, or Rob, was a lot like using a Rosetta stone. As long as you had a little piece of the language, you could use it to figure out the rest. Since I didn't have a lot of experience with the Air Force, a lot of what he was saying was going straight over my head until he unpacked that little bit for me.

In a way… for me, he was completely mesmerizing. It was like he'd lived everything we'd lived… and that somehow made it real… for us. Sometimes, in the Ruin, you can't even believe you're there, running into the next weird monster. But this guy, for me, was such a rock of straight-up matter-of-fact truth… about the whole thing… it made you feel like it was actually real, and you weren't a liar.

Or losing your mind.

I really liked him. I bet he's a good hang. Even back in the world. That one we left ten thousand years ago that ain't anymore.

But then the part of me that had been thinking—obsessing really—over wishes wondered how much could be done with one, perfectly phrased wish.

The words had to be just right.

But words were my thing, right?

Isn't that at least the one thing I'm really good at?

I heard Kennedy telling me I could tear apart the fabric of the universe.

I felt like some Greek hero in a tragedy, convinced he could get it all right by his own… skill… only in the end to get it wrong and end up blind, or chained to a bench in Tartarus, having gotten it all soooo very wrong.

Or… the fabric of the universe. Ripped.

"So I was backfilling the kid, Reedy," continued Sergeant Gunter, "on being handed over to the Fifteens because he drove our jammer, when the pilot starts freaking out over the aircraft comm. Crew chief barks into our radios, we got bogies drafting us from the clouds and we need to hang on. We're in the sauce, on deck, and things are about to get spicy."

On that last bit, he dropped a pro-level Ranger move sure to come from someone like Sar'nt Hardt and took the cigarette from Tanner's cold dead hands, pulled a long drag, and handed it back to my buddy.

"You good?" I asked the Air Force NCO.

"Yeah. I don't smoke," Sergeant Gunter affirmed more for himself than us when I took a look. "Okay, now. I couldn't, at first, believe what I was seein'. It's just, I couldn't believe what I saw out... The Ruin gets... more real... every day. Every time it shows you something like that. Something... fantastic. You know what I mean?"

I do.

"So, we hear we need to lock it down and brace for whatever was coming at us on approach to final, but I never thought to, I mean who could have... What I'm trying to say is, there was never a time when I was going to look out a port window and see... dark black griffins... flying right at us like incoming enemy fighters."

Wings. Lion body. Eagle head. All black.

Pure nightmare fuel.

Tanner leaned forward as if he couldn't get enough of what he was hearing, taking the time to light another cigarette he'd bribed the Forge tech to produce for him. "Griffin. That's like a bird monster, right, Sar'nt Gunter?"

Gunter nodded furiously, taking another drag from Tanner's smoke to calm his nerves, muttering again that he didn't smoke. "Yeah. When we first got here, we all used to run LAN parties on off hours. Gaming, on our off time. Of course, that was before our laptops disintegrated. But for that first little bit, we were running one of those co-op RPGs where you get to pick your class and run around grinding for loot and easy kills until you level up. So, in the game, and keep in mind, it might not reflect this place, griffins were lions with the heads of eagles, and giant bird wings. In the game, you had to be careful when using them around other PCs because they had a taste for horses. One minute you fly in after reconning a raid position in the game, the next you're apologizing to your bro because your mount ate his mount. That ever happen to you guys?"

We were too busy picking our mouths up off the floor. He'd used the same clarification Kennedy had about events in the game not necessarily matching reality.

"Yeah, that never happened to us," Tanner said. "Our, um, laptops got slagged the moment we dropped in. Rough landing, Sar'nt."

"I feel that," Sergeant Gunter muttered, having just lived through the crash of a C-5M Galaxy.

The Air Force NCO reached over and lifted the cup of my coffee so formerly filled with life-giving, energy-restoring magic, and finding it empty, set it down absently next to me.

I felt that.

The moment taunted me with the cold dark caffeine-deficient void. Despite the calamity this man had been through today, the Ruin was clearly revealing him as a vampire who would drink all my coffee.

I am not a good person. I get that about me.

"So yeah, as we were coming in for a landing, our engines, or something about the plane, must have attracted the griffins towards us. Only they weren't like the ones in the game we played. First, these were real live monsters. Jet-black and they were so fast, I mean really fast like a falcon in a dive, the bird... not the old jet. But the F-16 is fast too. They were tearing down through the sky to catch up to us. The first one hit us from above. You guys ever see that picture of an eagle stretching out its claws for a fish to haul in? Well, it was just like that, only it didn't expect the air frame to be as sturdy as it was. It struck the back of the aircraft like a bird hitting a clear window. We heard it hit hard. Then came the sound of its claws scrabbling across the hull as the thing scrambled to stay on top after being stunned by the impact of its own attack. The wind just swept it off the bird, sending it to God knows where."

An itch traced along my finger, an electrical impulse bopping the nerve, nearly triggering my reflex to refill the cup. I mean, after all, it was empty, and what better way was there to pass the time listening to the story than with a nice Turkish coffee cooked in a rubric over hot sand, and then doled out all steaming hot and filling the air with that earthy, salted aroma?

Coffee!

Not that I was thinking that or anything as I was totally focused on getting the airman's story for the official record. Totally.

"At this point, we were still a couple of miles out," continued Sergeant Gunter. "Charita called down that they were talking up the CCTs on the ground and if we could make it a few more minutes, they had an asset to clear us a path."

"Charita, huh?" Tanner said. "What's she like?"

"Taken," said Gunter.

"So, the asset?" I asked, already looking to throw off whatever scent Tanner had in the part of his rotting nose that still resembled a nostril.

"One of your snipers," Sergeant Gunter said, finishing the thought. "They said if we got within sight of the airstrip, he could provide cover fire for us on the way in. And with six more of those high-speed low-drag jet-black falcon-griffins chasing us through the sky, we were going to need every bit of help we could to get it down on the ground and clear the loads. By the time Charita called it in, we had two of the monsters on the back of the bird starting to cause serious trouble. One slashing through the fuselage, the other going after the wing just like the episode of *The Twilight Zone* with Captain Kirk. Fuselage dude got his claws in right away and was seriously slashing up the joint. The second guy pounced on the wing, but the wind immediately carried him off after some light damage. Not to worry though, he caught some air and flew away to come back at us again."

"You said there were six of them?" I asked. "What happened to the other four?"

Sergeant Gunter pointed at me, then tapped his temple. "They followed their buddies' tricks for making the plane. They caught up with us by screaming for the clouds, then dive-bombing us. Unlike the first cat that thought he was slick and got knocked senseless against the hull, the rest of them knew now to slow down just before impact. They're clever."

I snatched up the empty cold brew bottle, waving it around like a prop. "When did it go from bad... to busted, Sergeant Gunter?"

He sighed, shaking off the tension of the moment trying to come back on him.

"We were on approach when Charita called back that we had a hitchhiker on the side of the aircraft. Remember that other guy the wind swept off the wing? Well, there must have been something on the part of the aircraft he was convinced was his because he'd landed near the wing and dug in his claws like he was climbing a tree. Ya know, like if he was climbing it sideways.

"So, Master Sergeant Sandoval, who was the NCOIC of the loader crew, steps to the side door and he's got the Sig drawn from his chest rig. We knew we were in for a street fight, right there, when the load boss yeets his hand cannon in flight and gets ready to go Gunfight at the OK Corral to protect his bird."

At this point, Rob is holding his hands like he has his mitts about the sidearm, holding it just in front of his chest as he stares toward the nonexistent pistol.

I immediately knew that look.

I remember the feeling across my face when I made it myself. I looked to Tanner, and even though the man was slowly becoming an unnatural being neither alive nor dead, he still remained my friend. He gave me his own, reassuring nod, to let me know he never once blamed me for what happened to him. Never cursed me because it hadn't been me out there. If anything, he'd owned his condition every day because it meant his brothers, his Rangers, never had to feel what it meant to be what he was becoming. No one from his crew, the family he'd been selected for by passing RASP and paying the daily rent demanded by a patch on his shoulder, would ever have to feel the pull of the grave with every step of walking death.

In that moment, I felt that expression stretch across my face again because I think, after all this time, I understood why Tanner was so keen to accept his condition. Because in that moment, tied to the pain Tech Sergeant Gunter was feeling in staring through empty hands he wished had a pistol, I wished I could have changed places with my friend.

Tanner knew, or felt, things in ways we did not. Even though he was technically dead.

Holding the make-believe pistol, Sergeant Gunter raised his grip slightly, and started pulling the imaginary trigger. "So Sergeant Sandoval, or Sandi—we called him Sandi—starts blowing rounds through the bulkhead, into what he hoped was the black-feathered griffin out there. Not rage-dumping the mag by any stretch. Not screaming because he knew what he was doing was futile. My man Sandi surgically shot through the skin of the aircraft, tagging the griffin crawling on the outside while avoiding all the good stuff. Because he loved his bird, and he was responsible for us. Luckily the avionics were all in the ceiling or under the deck, so a couple of rounds through the bulkhead was no big whoop. Load crew doesn't get a lot of time to shoot so a lot of us go on our own, for those… just-in-case times. Close encounters. I'm sure Sandi never thought his time would include a winged lion with the head of an eagle, but there he was, and he owned it like a boss when it came his turn to defend the bird."

Sergeant Gunter looked around like he wanted to make sure we were following him so far. He could have cared less whether we believed him. He was there. He'd seen the elephant, as the smaj says.

So had we. We understood.

"He planted four shots through the skin of the aircraft and must've caught just the right spot because the griffin curled up and fell away. Spiraling off into the desert. So right there, Sandi assessed and adjudicated the threat to his aircraft and his airmen. He holstered the weapon, throwing out his best knife hand to pull us out of our surprise and put us on mission. 'I need all of you to lock and load.

You're on pest control now!' he shouted above the scream-ing engines."

Sergeant Gunter pounded his fist into his other hand, as if each hit struck the truth of what had happened to the C-5 up there. "And we were on it, Ranger, with a quick-ness. He didn't want to have us putting any more holes in his aircraft, so we pulled the aft doors, locking them against the frame. I floated the high sign to Sandi while he was plugged into the comms system, talking with the pilots and the flight engineers. I was also really glad for our ear pro, because the wind off the skin of our plane running toward the airstrip at a hundred and forty knots was near deafening."

He made a face that indicated we knew what he was talking about. After all, we do jump out of these things.

"These black griffins are all but trying their best to bite and tear at the aircraft skin and doing a good job of it, so... we start blasting. We're blowing rounds outside the plane. Almost as one, the creatures take flight in the wind, and we thought the rifle rounds were enough to scare them off. We're thinking it's all good when one of them blows into the open troop door in a hot second, landing near Lautner. He'd seen it coming and put two shots into that thing, but if the griffin was affected by it, it didn't act like it was. It had to pull its bulk in through the door because its frame was wider than the hatch. And I'll tell you... that's a sight you never expect to see. So, my guy on the opposite troop door reversed direction and helped us all dump a bunch of rounds into it, dropping it to the deck."

Sergeant Gunter balled his fists up at this point in the story, feeling the rage and loss my brothers in the Rangers felt too often on the ground.

"Dammit… we were so distracted by the one we'd seen come in the door after Lautner, we missed the other one sneaking in from the other side. It pounced on Sandi, and we just stood there… or rather… I stood there while the thing batted him to the deck of the aircraft with its lion claws and snapped its beak around his neck and shoulder. I thought it would have pecked him, but that eagle's beak just broke his shoulder, tearing at his flesh.

"Sandi didn't just sit there. He dumped a full mag into it, point blank, as the thing tried to rip the flesh right from him. Round after round of his nine-mil hit that beast but it kept coming at him like it didn't care, making this weird sound as it did. I haven't been able to get Sandi's screams out of my mind. Or the sounds that thing made. He wasn't crying… in pain. He was yelling for us to get back. Get away from him!"

Silence.

Sergeant Gunter ran his arm across his eyes, clearing the tears from his face, forming at the recounting of his friend's combat action to protect his aircraft. His crew. When he stopped talking and dipped his head to clean himself up, my friend Tanner, despite his hellish appearance, placed a withered hand on Gunter's shoulder. He turned just enough so Rob could see the part of his face that was still human, showing the airman he was still just a man, despite being the walking coffin he was becoming.

Tanner's voice became ethereal, stemming from that other place he went to sometimes when he tapped into the hereafter. "It's pretty wild that I see death in everything, Sar'nt. And a lot of people might think that sucks and all, I get that, but I also get to see the beauty… in some deaths too. The beauty of a soul who would give up its struggle so others can continue the march, man. I didn't know your NCO, but I can see that part of himself he gave... to you. It's there like a glow on you. Time, training, and talent, all given freely to a guy whose potential as an NCO was plain for your master sergeant to see, so... he invested heavily in you, Sar'nt Gunter. I can see that... all about you."

Sergeant Gunter looked at my friend in wonder. "Is he really... here... right now?"

Tanner nodded. "The part that you carry with you, it's there plain as the moon on a full night."

Sergeant Gunter laughed, his shoulders straighter now.

The mantle had fallen on him. All the good, all the rough, he wore the mantle of his mentor now. I think that too, among soldiers as far as time goes back... has been true.

"Yeah, he went out like a boss," murmured Sergeant Gunter. "But I wasn't the only one who felt it. Remember the kid I said was a linebacker? There was a lot of talk from the CCTs about smoking that dude when he got Ruined after he got here. Sandi convinced everyone it was still Burns in there, somewhere, and that even though Burns looked like an enemy, to us, he was still part of our team. That damn lion bird never stood a chance against a guy like that who takes a stand for one of his when guys with guns want to do him like our CCTs did just because he'd started to look like an enemy."

Tanner and I did the best thing you can do when someone is grieving. Telling the good, the bad, the memories. No platitudes, or trite bumper sticker sayings. We just listened. We just let it come and be told aloud.

That too... is old.

I thought about Brumm. And Kurtz. As I listened. All the other Rangers too along the way. Ones I didn't know. Ones I did and various snapshots of my interactions with them, somewhere in a pocket close to my heart. There were times something happened, and I wanted to talk about them. To someone. To anyone. Wanted to remember them and mark down there in the mud of time that they had existed. But then I remembered others were grieving too. And that we were on mission. And I thought I was supposed to just... be quiet.

I have learned... to listen. Just listen and let the survivor talk when it comes. Because... it must.

"Burns body-tackled the griffin on Sandi into the bulkhead, slamming huge hooking punches right into its ribs," Gunter continued. "Straight-up Ruin linebacker. My dude pounded on this thing like he was a drummer looking to drum solo hard for what it was worth. Every time that creature tried to turn on Burns, he hoisted all of it above his head and just slammed it right back onto the deck. It eventually got its beak around and bit his arm, but that just pissed Linebacker Burns off. Burns took hold of the bottom part of its beak with his off hand... and just ripped its mouth wide open. And then, with a good grip on the feathered parts of its head, Burns roared like a monster himself and snapped its neck before throwing it straight out the door of the aircraft."

Tanner tapped me on the arm. "Bro. We needs to hire us some linebackers. Real Ruin monsters."

"Don't need to. We're already here, man. Look at you. You're stone-cold death walking, Tans. Monsters are gonna think you're the big hereafter come for their monster souls."

Rob joined us in the laughter, grateful for something to wipe away the pain of losing his mentor. I only enjoyed the moment insomuch as I looked at the tiniest bit of coffee swill at the bottom of my cold brew, visible through the transparent, hard plastic lid. It felt like an allegory for our lives right now. We were almost spent, and though there was a little of us left at the bottom of the reserve, we were running dangerously close to empty. This guy had lost his friend and could laugh about how cool the guy had been, while I couldn't rinse the sour taste out of my mouth from Brumm and Kurtz going down.

Sergeant Joe had told me to ruck it. Here was a guy rucking it like a pro. And me... I was willing to rip the universe in two to bring them back.

Was I?

I felt the sides of my eyes go a little moist just then. I could taste the sadness for two men who'd taught me the brutality of this life under the scroll, while also showing me the camaraderie and perseverance of a tribe of relentless brothers that remained invested in installing Talker two-point-oh. Ranger Talker. They could have given up on me, but as Joe liked to say, "You get your best shape against the fire and the anvil, Rangers." That's what those two brothers were to me. Had been to me. Hot fire to mold me, and an anvil to beat me into shape. I had to be grateful for that now, even if I didn't realize the worth of it at the time. Now... now I knew.

And then I heard Al Haraq's bass laughter, soft and almost taunting, reminding me... things could be different. Things... could change. "The words must be just right, Master. Say them, and I will grant your wish. For better, or for worse. It will be granted... Master."

And then he would smile, watching my face, waiting for me to make the biggest mistake of all time.

I wonder how many times he's done that. Seen that mistake made. I imagine… a lot.

Sergeant Major Stone drifted into the blue percolator stronghold, three cups of steaming, glorious bean water held in a single hand. He expertly negotiated the space and hit me with a disapproving stare as my head nearly went full Pez dispenser the second my nostrils caught wind of the fresh brew from the old blue percolator.

"You Tech Sergeant Gunter?" Stone rumbled. He handed each of us a cup and sat down on the little camp stool he seemed to prefer while in the presence of the percolator.

"I am, Sergeant Major," Rob said, rising and snapping to parade rest.

"Sit down, bud. We're just jaw-jacking right now and it's hella difficult to drink coffee with your hands behind your back." The smaj settled against the remains of a cracked wall like some old Texas gunfighter, firing up the percolator to launch into another brew. "Why don't you finish this story so I can get my boy here on to something other than trying to pen the first-ever best-seller in the Ruin. Ain't no bookstores I can find."

"Roger that, Sergeant Major," Rob said, careful to enunciate every syllable in the man's rank. "And thank you for the coffee, Sergeant Major."

"You're welcome, Airman. Now let's get to it," Stone reiterated as he settled back to listen, his stump rubbing his jaw, his dark eyes watching us.

"So… we thought we were in the clear just then because we couldn't hear any more lion claws over the hull of the Galaxy. And with Burns launching the flying lion out the bird to clear the deck, I knew I had to take over because Sandi was gone. I plugged my mic into the comms socket and nearly had my eardrums blown out as our comms specialist and our engineer took turns trying to get Sandi to respond. 'Lock it down! Lock it all down right now!' Charita shouted through the mic."

"Now, which one's Charita?" the smaj murmured.

"She's taken, Sergeant Major," Tanner noted.

Stone flashed his best *Did I ask you* look at the undead corporal and nearly put the Ranger on his heels. In that momentarily frozen second, Rob responded, "She's our communications NCO, Sergeant Major. But at the time, she was warning us the reason we didn't have a problem with black-feathered griffins anymore was because we had other problems right at that moment. I shouted over the engine to get my guys to hold on to anything they could. We were going down. Or so I thought. I was guessing the pilot had to crash the bird onto the deck. Instead, the impact from the attack was the most epic hit I've ever felt in an aircraft… in my entire life. It literally felt like a car crash where both sets of wheels were doing fifty. It was a real bell-ringer, Sergeant Major."

Sergeant Gunter held up his arm, displaying the bandaging that went around a series of lacerations and road rashes from straps cutting into his flesh when the aircraft impact occurred. Most likely from threading his arm into a cargo net right before they hit.

"We weren't down, we were still in the air, and I risked a run to a window and could see entire shreds of fuselage just falling all over the landscape below as the biggest bird I ever saw flew right across our flight path. It looked like a giant eagle, and if I had to guess at a wingspan, I'd say it was easily sixty or more feet across. This thing reminded me of the giant eagle from Helheim in that game we played where you're a god hiding out in the wrong pantheon and you adopt that kid that turns out to be a god too. You guys ever played that one? No? Well, this was definitely not like it was in the game because this one was... well, it was attacking us. Attacking our aircraft to be specific."

The smaj raised his hand. "You related to a kid named Kennedy, son?"

"No, Sergeant Major," Sergeant Gunter responded. When the sergeant major waved off the implied question, the Air Force sergeant continued. "So anyway, this thing swept right by us, slashing at the dorsal side of the plane, and I can see pinholes of light where its claws went right through the fuselage, which is bad, because unlike smaller aircraft, there's a whole other deck above our heads. I'm staring out the window and I know we're in a load of trouble because we have no weapons to take on something that big. This thing was almost as big as a C-130 and it was engaged in air-to-air combat with us like we were playing football or something.

"Now at this point, I'm shouting at my guys to get ready to fire out the open troop doors in case we can get a shot off on it. Charita calls back distance and direction this thing is tracking from. In typical predator bird fashion, it's diving right at us. The pilots, well, they took the plane off course a bit, banking across the mountains to give us room to get offline from the attack. And it worked, too, because the giant eagle thing swept away to gain altitude for another run at us. I seriously thought we weren't going to make the runway. The giant bird did a real number on the Fat Lady—that's our name for the C-5M, Sergeant Major—

and the whole frame was shaking like I'd just put quarters in a seedy motel with that magic fingers bed thing. Know what I mean?"

The smaj nodded he did.

"Now, I wasn't able to get a bead on the bird diving at us to finish us off, but the pilots could see it. They said, one minute it was diving at them and blocking out the sun the closer it got, and the next it looked like something hit it so hard it couldn't stay in the air."

"That would be our guy Thor," the smaj said offhandedly. "Got word from your boys in the CCT sighting you in. He stepped up to the plate and took the shot from the STA. Nailed it dead center. Boy's a shooter like I ain't never seen… and I seen some."

"You know it, Sergeant Major," Gunter said. "I saw that thing plummet right past us and hit the desert like a wet bag of laundry. Splat… all over the sand. But we weren't out of the woods then, yet. Our plane was seriously jacked up by that giant bird and it was going to be a miracle if we didn't come in so hard we blew through the runway and ended up in the drink."

The smaj turned to Tanner and me, adopting the face normally worn by his boss. "I spoke to Kennedy about the whole thing. He says the attack on the C-5 reeked of dark magic, whatever that is, possibly controlling the animals sent in to attack the Air Force comin' in. Especially the roc, which is that giant eagle thing. According to Kennedy. Apparently if you get them early enough, they can be trained like any bird of prey. In his game, of course."

We said nothing.

The smaj had been infected by the private who used to dig latrines and who the senior NCO swore he'd kill or make a Ranger out of.

"Lot of that going around lately," I said to the sergeant major.

"Yeah. Don't remind me about the private you helped land that dog shark thing that ate the Shagbag."

"Isn't he a specialist, Sergeant Major?" I asked.

"Not the way he's going. Thing's a menace," the smaj retorted. It seems I wasn't the only one to think giving Big Baby D to Specialist Thounsavath had been a bad idea. "Please continue, Sar'nt Gunter."

Rob exhaled, clearly still processing the entire landing of the C-5M aircraft. He downed the last of the smaj-brewed coffee and continued. "So, we had the combat controllers on the ground, and those guys are real pro. Talking to the pilots, guiding us in, and dropping all the weaponized math they use to vector in aircraft for landing in a hostile fire zone. If you get a pilot and controller really in sync with each other, we can work some serious magic. If you look at places like Iraq and Afghanistan, combat control set up some serious flight protocols in and out of the air bases there to give our pilots the best chances to avoid enemy fire."

"I've been on a few of those rides," Stone commented from the shadows.

"Roger that, Sergeant Major," Rob agreed. "So I get my guys locked down and Burns, that's our orc, he holds on to Sandi because he ain't letting the guy that covered down on him going green and all... get splattered all over the airstrip. We lock in, and the pilots guide us to the ground with the aircraft doing its level best to shake itself apart during the trip. Our pilots were hardcore all the way, keeping us mostly straight and on track for the run."

He was back there again. Flying in a rattling aircraft screaming for the ground and there was nothing to do but hang on.

Balls.

"We hit hard, and I felt the landing gear in the back of the plane crack, or just fail, or do anything but their job when we made contact with the ground. Something in the controls must have been gacked by that roc thing, because we immediately started skidding sideways across the airstrip once we were down. Bits of the plane came apart and I watched through the window port as the wing on my side just snapped and splashed into the dirt. The whole impact was a crazy mad minute of earthquakes and fear that the load we rigged was going to snap free of the rigging and just crush us in our seats. It finally stopped, and except for the echo of the impact still working across the bay, we were down, and the plane was mostly in one piece.

"I jumped up from my seat," Sergeant Gunter said, making a double knife hand motion to signal him breaking free of the restraints and getting his boots to the deck. "I ran through the cargo deck to check on my guys. Mostly everyone was intact except Burns. I found him wheezing in his seat, breathing hard through those tusks he'd grown when he became an orc. One of the ammo pallets had broken loose, snapping the wooden boards that held multiple crates in place, and just impaled him in the chest. When I got to him, he reached out and took my hand, just saying, 'I got him. I got him.' He was talking about Master Sergeant Sandoval. Through the whole crash, Burns kept

Sandi's body from being crushed. He paid with his life to do it."

Sergeant Gunter opened his mouth to say something… but nothing came out.

There was a long pause. Then he picked up the rest of the story.

"We all got our act together because we didn't have time to sit around feeling sorry for what just happened. We were the load crew and maintainers for this aircraft. That's our job. We had people to locate and gear to secure for offload.

"Once I knew what was going on, my radio lit up like a Christmas tree. It was the Rotor Joes close by. Your Night-stalkers. They'd been running ops out of the constructed airfields and were running re-loader ops on the gun copters all throughout the defense. They came hauling tail across the runway and got into the bird in short order. Sar'nt First Class Montoya, who's in charge of the Fifteens, was screaming for his guys to rip us out of the aircraft before we even knew they were there. It was chaos, but we knew what to do."

Tuesday, I thought to myself.

"So, the primary concern was to get everyone out of the plane and clear in case any of the ordnance went up. As the now-senior member of the loading team, it was my responsibility to get everyone away from that aircraft. I was directing my guys when Montoya grabbed me and pulled me aside. He told us word came down from his brass that the gunships, the MH-6s, had dry tubes and hoses that needed to get very wet with ammo if we were gonna hold the field. Ammo which we needed to offload. There was also the very real matter of the Forge, sitting under stacks of pallets broken open on top of it. To make matters worse, combat control calls us in the middle of my argument with a senior NCO from another branch and tells us the top of the plane is smoking."

Talker's side note here. While Sergeant Gunter is recounting this entire tale, the smaj is very diligently one-handedly creating culinary masterpieces in the form of his perfect ratio of hot water to ground beans. I don't know how he does it, but Sergeant Major Stone works the blue percolator as if his hand hadn't been cut off by a cranky Navy SEAL vampire with a Napoleon complex. Talker has hot bean water. Talker happy.

We now return you to your regularly scheduled side quest by another branch.

Rob presses his fingers to his chest, showing he was willing to take Sandi's job and be the NCO his boss had always hoped he would be. "So I tell Tonka—Montoya's boys call him Tonka for some reason—I tell Tonka I'm going after the flight crew. I don't care what he does with his Fifteens, but I'm telling my guys to get clear. I sprint outside to find the nose of the aircraft is about twenty yards from the rest of the plane. I can see the broken wing almost a football field away from us, and I can smell all the fuel from the six internal tanks in that wing, saturating the ground outside. I manage to negotiate over some debris and make it to the crew compartment of the plane. Charita is the only one conscious, seeing as she was tucked into the commo station and pretty much covered from the amount of debris flying around.

"Now let me tell you what, there was a moment I really thought I was dead and buried by the latest turn of events when Charita screams at something behind me. Staring right at us both was the most giant silverback gorilla I'd ever seen. And by seen, I mean like on a video or anything. This thing gently takes hold of my wrist after I screamed—but only just a little—and go for my sidearm, and then it calmly moves past me to get at the trapped pilots. To add to the strangeness, Sergeant Major, this guy is wearing samurai armor."

I waved my hand at Sergeant Gunter, letting him know I had something to add. "That's Otoro, Sergeant Gunter. We found him embedded with the Accadion legionnaires when the Little Bird pilots rescued us."

"Oh… so that's where he came from," said the airman. "Well, he just rips the pilots and the flight engineers free from their seats and carefully passes their unconscious bodies to a bunch of my guys below us who are gathering to start a rescue chain. With that handled, I'm about to have the E-7 I was very interested in, aka Charita, climb down and beat feet for the city walls when she stops me. She says she's been listening to the comms traffic back and forth between the Fifteens and our chain of command, and we have to get as much offloaded as we can. Without the Forge and the supplies we're carrying, our forces, all of the Rangers and the Nightstalkers, won't last another day. I tried to argue about the sparks spitting off the top of the aircraft possibly igniting the fuel and cooking us all to hell, but she wouldn't have it. She used the motto of one of the squadrons where I used to work, against me. She said *Seek, attack, destroy*, and then asked me where in that motto did it say we should run away."

"Pro NCO move right there," said the smaj. "Ask our undead friend here how that kind of stuff worked out on him."

"No comment," Tanner said, presenting his barely touched coffee cup in salute.

I've covered Tanner's backstory in previous volumes of our exploits in the Ruin. No need to recount them here. Needless to say, he had a lot more in common with Sar'nt Gunter than I did, although if my taste in women continued here in the Ruin, I was destined for just as much trouble as either of them.

"Well, Sergeant Major, it worked," Sergeant Gunter agreed. "I got my crew together and declared what I needed from my guys to get your guys what you needed so we all didn't die. I put some people on clearing out the Forge, my new guy Reedy got the duty for digging out the jammer to help the Fifteens, and I gathered up what was left to try and work some firefighting. We were still sitting on some pretty volatile stuff soaked into about a hundred yards of terrain, and the back of the bird was smoking. We either worked the problem or burned up trying to save everything.

"It could have taken us hours to get everything unscrewed and worked into the city like you wanted, Sergeant Major, but luckily, we had Charita on board. Our commo-savvy master sergeant ran off the flight line while we were on top of the bird dousing it in Halon 1301. We killed all the sparking and complaining that ruined aircraft had for us, and as we were climbing down, we saw a crowd of people running across the airstrip. I snapped up the hand mic hanging from my gear and called Tonka. Luckily, that Fifteen NCO didn't like surprises either, and ran out to meet the people running in. As it turned out, Charita had gone and found a Portugonian merchant who spoke something close to Spanish, and through his translations did a load of convincing to some of the locals. A good NCO would have gotten a few bodies to help us out. She apparently made a case strong enough for roughly fifty dockworkers to come out and give us a hand. I'm guessing most of them just wanted to see the magic metal bird that had killed the giant bird in the sky, or some such. Either way, we had a daisy chain of people working to offload ammo and run them onto blank pallets my load crew were reassembling away from the plane."

What Sergeant Gunter doesn't tell us in this account, and what I find out later is... heroic. And they've already been there, and done that, protecting the bird in the air from flying lion monkeys.

Or whatever those things the enemy aimed at the Galaxy are.

The orcs are sweeping across the airfield and the Rangers are shooting them down. Out over the desert the mortars go dry and then suddenly there's more orc cav massing to come in.

Gunfighter Two, one of the Little Birds, is dry on minigun ammo. She needs a reload immediately. No easy task.

Sergeant Gunter organizes a team, goes into the burning wreckage of the aircraft with a firefighting team, gets the ammo, and supervises the reload of Gunfighter Two while the pilot keeps it on the ground.

The orcs are pushing, the Little Bird literally lifts off, pivots, lowers her nose, and streaks right into the oncoming horde, dumping rounds everywhere.

The orcs that survive get freaked, as do the camels, and scatter, clearing the airfield.

Meanwhile the next Little Bird is coming in for a kill pill drink.

Take a moment to appreciate that scene.

Chaos. An enemy attack. A burning downed aircraft. Air Force personnel just running into the flames to reload while offloading and rescuing the wounded.

They got it done.

Seek, attack, destroy.

He didn't tell us that part. He's that kinda guy.

"So, at what point does the gorilla disappear?" the smaj asked.

When dealing with an NCO of the smaj's caliber, there comes a point where he's gotten enough context and wants to get to the heart of the matter. Leave the details for the troopers whose job it is to take them down, or to interested parties looking for that little nugget of intel that might give them an edge during their next run-in with the enemy. After all, the Rangers are primarily a tactical reconnaissance force who sometimes just like to jump up, yell *Surprise, Losers!* then punch everyone in the face before they disappear again.

Ranger gonna Ranger, amirite? Can I get a *whoop whoop*?

But the sergeant major had apparently heard his fill of how wonderful the Air Force was and how well they worked with the Nightstalkers. Either that or he wanted this little powwow session good and done so he didn't have to share his coffee for too much longer. I'm betting it's the second... but of course I would.

Me. Coffee.

Sergeant Gunter muttered to himself for a minute, going over the details of the events, collecting his thoughts amid the stream of stark memories running through his mind. "We had the smoke out, and we'd doused the area in all sorts of fire retardant. I wasn't really worried about us going up in a giant fireball by that time. We'd been unloading for the better part of fifteen minutes… and the gorilla samurai—we found out his name was Otoro then—he rigs the Forge with chains, hands a bunch of straps to the other air crew on the deck, and with a little help, he just drags the Forge off the makeshift ramp we'd put together for offloading. Reedy does a little magic with the jammer to get the Forge off safely, but most of the heave-ho was thanks to your gorilla. His strength is just… incredible, Sergeant Major."

The smaj says nothing.

"A bunch of us are outside the aircraft rigging the Forge for sling load so the Black Hawk can bring it into the city. We have pallets of ammunition for both your Rangers and the gunships stacked and ready to be palletized for a similar ride. The most dangerous in all this is the fuel bladder we use for refueling the aircraft. If it goes, it could still ignite the jet fuel still spilling into the ground from the damaged wing and then we all go up like game over. Otoro is watching us rope up the Forge, when he gets up and moves to the back side of the aircraft."

I swirled the last of my coffee and wondered when there would be more.

Not soon enough was the answer.

"I don't think anything of it," Rob confesses. "At the time I'm way too busy getting it done when Otoro knocks one of the Army guys out of the way, letting a bunch of arrows hit the hardpack where the guy was just standing. I mean like… lightning fast. And in typical jaw-jack fashion, I turn to face another batch of *aw c'mon*, on behalf of the Ruin. Running up from the surf side of the airfield is a giant ugly dude, dressed a lot like your gorilla samurai. Except like a bigger, uglier, more jacked orc."

"Those are usually ogres," Tanner interjected. "Sar'nt."

Sergeant Gunter nodded at the clarification and continued. "So he's sprinting in just huge steps, I mean just crushing it... eating the distance up between us while carrying a long-handled axe with a black head covered in red Asian script. He looks like hot death coming for ya. The details are real clear at this point because that thing was a murder machine. Straight up. Pure and simple. Hot on the guy's heels are a group of ninjas. But they're... cats. This is the Ruin after all. Cat ninjas... why not. Cat men with samurai breastplates. Even in the day it was super hard to see them as their clothing was dyed to perfectly mimic the environment of the desert shoreline."

"Oh yeah, those guys," Tanner commented, waving his rotting gloved hand. He'd moved some distance away to avoid annoying the smaj while he smoked. "Lizard king. When we smoked that guy, he had a bunch of those guys skulking around. They tried to hit us back at the FOB. They tried, they died. Talker here went *whomp whomp* on them with the grenade launcher. Straight up. He's got a gift, Sergeant Major. I'm surprised word about us hasn't reached these guys yet."

Sergeant Gunter pointed to my friend, a quick acknowledgment so he could get back to the story. "They storm up the beach after this guy, ogre with the nice axe, swinging slings as they run. I yell out to keep them away from the aircraft and we're all aiming weapons to get to work on 'em. Meanwhile Otoro sprints right at the big one. So now we can't shoot because he's in our line of fire. I mean, we can defend ourselves, but we don't have the trigger time you guys do to be able to shoot around a friendly.

"Two of the cat ninjas break off and start hoofing it for the plane. Pawing it. Whatever. They're still swinging those slings and we can't let them reach us. I know we can't. Me and Jamilla, she's one of my crew, we dump rounds into the first cat ninja, and he goes down. The thing he was about to launch was a tiny glass bottle at us, and when it broke on the tarmac, all I could smell was a combination of smoke and lighter fluid. If they got one of those on target, it would've set off the entire plane and cooked us all, and your resupply. The last cat ninja coming at us recognizes that if he launches his bottle, he's getting a hot lead injection, so instead he throws one of those eggshell bombs like you see in the movies. You ever see one of those? Anyway, my blood freezes at that moment because I can just picture the smoke bomb sparking the fuel and sending us all to kingdom come."

Tanner snaps his fingers. "Is this the part where he disappears and shows up somewhere else? I used to love those movies. Sho Kosugi was the man back in those days. What about that one where the aerobics instructor gets possessed by the spirit of an undead ninja and no one thinks she's the killer because she's all hot and innocent. I inherited those movies from my dad when he passed on."

"Dude, those sound awesome," Sergeant Gunter says. "You guys got any of those with you?"

Forget cat ninjas. Want to come close to death? Start small talk about ninja movies from the 1980s when you should be giving a report to a sergeant major. The smaj coughed over his hovering canteen cup, and the rest of us left dreams of black-clad, reluctant heroes fighting shadowy assassins, and instead focused on multi-cam-clad heroes fighting shadowy assassins with the possibility of an ignited apocalypse.

"Right, Sergeant Major," Sergeant Gunter apologetically. "So yeah, this guy just disappears and reappears behind Jamilla... and pushes his knife into her belly from behind all of a sudden. This knife. Ninja stuff. Sorry, Sergeant Major. But this knife. Here..."

The tech sergeant pulls the weapon from his bag, and I immediately think his sense of scale is broken. I think of Rangers' combat knives or their folding ones when I think of a knife. The blade on this was easily a foot long with a six-inch handle wrapped in silk cord that shimmered purple by the light of the fire. The blade had a pattern along the edge, reminding me of spilling something on the floor. But in the chaos of how it was applied, there was a beauty and strange symmetry to it. It was gorgeous and dangerous all at once. It was... fascinating to look at as the airman held it out for us to see.

Rob sheathed the blade and tossed it back into his assault pack as though it were a random screwdriver. "He pushed this through her back, and then slipped away from her toward the plane. He thought I would go to her. Try and do the manly thing and guard the woman lying bleeding at my feet. Instead I put four rounds into his back for GP. General purpose. Best way to take care of Jamilla was to take care of him first. Only thing I wasn't able to stop was him shattering one of those lighter fluid bottles on the plane. Only... I didn't give him the time to light it once it was done."

"Did Jamilla make it?" I asked.

"Chief Rapp and our senior medical officer have her now. He said the wound was through and through, and only meant to cause her pain," Rob said. "But at that point, I didn't have time to worry about that. The Black Hawk arrived overhead, dropping its hook for the sling load on the Forge. On the beach, your guy Otoro was slaughtering the rest of the cat ninjas while the big guy with the axe just watched. The cats were keeping the gorilla busy, dancing around him and occasionally getting in a stab he had to worry about. But the guy with the axe, he just let them play with the samurai while he walked past them all. He was like a really tall orc with more human features, and he was *ripped*. He practically busted out of the samurai armor he wore, and he approached us like we didn't figure into this at all."

I almost—*almost*, I emphasize—spit my coffee out when he told what happened next.

"That's when we shot him. At this point, we have the crowd backing away from such an obvious boss-level guy, which gave our Fifteens plenty of room to start shooting."

Another Talker interjection here. Don't mind me. If you already have this loaded into your hard drive, just drive around and get to what you need to get to. So the Fifteens, as Rob calls them, are the critical-skill MOS guys working directly for the Nightstalker pilots. They rig, load, maintain, and fuel the aircraft flying the missions over Sûstagul. As the premier combat support flight outfit in the Army, the 160th SOAR requires all their people to go through a rigorous selection process, just like the Rangers. Once selected, these guys get dedicated training on how to shoot, move, and communicate, all while learning to assess and address issues with the aircraft. They can even do their jobs in complete darkness.

Ever drop a tiny little screw while trying to get to a difficult part of an engine? Try doing that with night vision on. So when Rob starts talking about how they shot the guy we were supposing was Axe Grinder, those helicopter air crew got online with readied weapons and shot like they were a broom sweeping dirt off the porch.

Also, I still have half a cup left, for those of you keeping track. Carry on. None was spilled.

"So, old boy gets hit more than once and is not hip to the experience. He pulls back because he figures we're not going to shoot him while our pal the gorilla samurai— coolest thing ever—is in the way. And he's right. Rather than give our plane the personal touch, the super orc, ogre I mean, traces a line in the air, and the oil on the skin of the aircraft ignites."

Okay, even Talker who knows only languages and coffee, and not in that order, knows that's bad.

"The Fifteens went into action, immediately grabbing extinguisher bottles and chasing the flames. I was on Jamilla, dragging her away while keeping an eye on the ogre. Meanwhile the aggro samurai ape slaughtered the last cat ninja in a swipe that separated the top half from its legs. With a flick of his wrist, bone and gore fly away from the blade which materializes back in the scabbard so fast we couldn't see just how he did it. As I was dragging Jamilla toward the water just in case the plane went supernova, I watched as the two warriors, super orc or super ogre, or whatever it was, and Otoro, circle each other for what would be a dance of death that will be burned into my brain until the day I die. For all time, man.

"Overhead, the Black Hawk blasted us with its rotor wash as our crew connected the last cable, freeing the chopper to buffet us with heavy winds as it powered up for the heavy lift. With the cables tight, it hoisted all twenty-one thousand pounds of the Forge and raced for the safety of the walls in the city. Another bird slipped in behind it, swinging its tail so we could load whatever we could, including the people here, and get them away from the bird before it blew. And all the while, on the beach, Otoro and the uber-jacked mutant were going straight savage on each other, working their weapons with neither one of them really coming out on top."

Sergeant Gunter shook his head, looking away to that spot in the room where he'd pointed his imaginary pistol only a few moments ago. "No quarter was given between those two, none was asked. Bad boy kicked sand right in Otoro's face, blinding the big gorilla, and I thought this noble creature who had not only saved our pilots, but was saving us too, I thought he was done for right then. He jogged back a few steps, bringing that massive ninja sword over his shoulder to aim at where he felt the threat was, even though he couldn't see, his massive nostrils flaring, those deep dark eyes watering. Plane full of ammunition and fuel behind him on fire and all of us had some level of attention on this fight where their battle for revenge was really the battle for the city too. Or at least it felt that way, watching it.

"Axe Guy comes in swinging, and even from across the landing strip I felt the hairs on the back of my neck stand up. Not out of fear, but from something coming off Otoro right at that particular moment. It wasn't magic. I know that much. It was something deeper, far more connected to everything... around him. Connected to us too. Later, I asked around about it. We all felt it. Straight up. In that moment, he'd made a connection to all of us and our struggle for the city. Our fight to tell the monsters we weren't going to back down today... or any day. They couldn't have this place and its people because we were done being prey. In that moment, we were all Otoro."

Sergeant Gunter stopped and looked at us, seeing if we were actually believing what he was trying to download on us.

"He used our eyes to see past the sand and grit in his own eyes. He batted the axe away with his sword and then... then... he went into gorilla-powered jiu-jitsu mode. Ever watch those UFC guys do their thing? I'm here to tell you they had nothing on our guy Otoro. You going to go hand-to-hand with a gorilla that can use its feet just as well as its hands? You might as well just give up and hand him the title.

"Otoro slipped around big bad boy axe guy, using momentum to sling around his waist and hoist him into a suplex. That dude hit the beach and the gorilla was all over him. In a blur of motion, Otoro snapped an arm, breaking both bones just above his wrist. And that's where the UFC display ended. Then he just beat his enemy into the beach until he looked sufficiently rocked, leaving nothing to stop the samurai from roaring to display the full horror that was his bared fangs before he bit down with a savage rip and just tore that ugly sucker's arm right out of the socket with his teeth, pulling the clavicle and several ribs along with it."

Sergeant Gunter shrugged and ran his hands through his hair, as if trying to believe what he'd seen there on the beach in a battle without honor or humility.

Total, straight-up, combat.

"You know," I told him, utterly fascinated by the entire account, beginning to end, "if this Air Force loadmaster slash bomb tech thing doesn't work out, you could take a shot at being the Ruin's second-best storyteller."

"Just might do that after what happened next," Sergeant Gunter declared. "Otoro points to more of the fire seeping across the fuselage as my guys are getting it done. Reedy shouts that the jammer won't start, and I have to run over and pull an old loader trick. Sometimes the fuses blow out and you don't have time to run the spares. I pull a multi-tool from my kit and use the screwdriver to bridge the gap on the ignition fuse. The machine coughs and then purrs like a kitten under direction from one of my junior airmen. We're offloading everything as fast as we can, but that airframe fire is spreading too quickly for my liking. Otoro starts making these hand gestures while saying words I remember from those old ninja movies. I even remember what they were called. The kuji-kiri. The nine ways cutting. He finishes the last sound and gesture, and the wind starts blasting us. No rotors in sight, just straight breeze coming off the water and turning into a tornado right in front of us. It hovers over the burning fuselage like this crazy dust devil and just starts sucking up the flames like a cat licks cream off the floor."

Okay... so Otoro has magic superpowers. We just thought he was a Ginsu all-in-one killing machine with the sharp knives and gorilla swole. Now... wizard too?

"That gorilla samurai starts yelling '*Hayaku*' and motioning for us to finish our work fast as we can. One of the Fifteens goes for a box and burns his hands on the metal. We strap some gloves on him and we all work together to get the crate off and away from the burning bird. Even with the wind, the fuel pooling onto the ground is burning and we don't have long before this whole thing goes up. It's just a matter of time now.

"Otoro grabs me from directing the organized chaos and points. More enemy troops are screaming out of the desert once more, running and riding in a bid to take whatever it is their eagle god knocked out of the sky. You Rangers are firing your Carls at them. Area defense munitions from the sound of it. Just as I thought we were finished, Otoro pulls me around and stares into me. His eyes are human, more human than any I've ever looked into. That's funny now I think about it. At the time… chills right down through me. He's got old soul eyes. He nods at me once, then says, 'Go.' No explanation. I shake my head that I can't leave him there to die alone. Ain't gonna do that. Not on my shift. I don't know why, but even though I just met the guy, it felt wrong to let him fight our battles all alone. He nodded to Jamilla being loaded into the next Black Hawk touching down and pushed me toward the bird. 'Go,' he rumbled."

Tears from the airman.

It's part of the process and in dealing with a day like today.

Sergeant Gunter had rivers of guilt and regret pouring out of his eyes and not one of us judged him for it. We knew. We were already part of that club, scars and the badges to prove it. This holy space, where the blue percolator was an altar and the deacon of caffeinated communion sat presiding over the service, was a place warriors came to to cry for all those times they didn't have time to do so when it had to get done, and the line… the line was so thin you couldn't even see it sometimes.

"He…" Gunter began, trying to form the words between the tears. "Otoro dragged the axe guy to the front of the aircraft where pockets of fuel were catching fire despite the wind he'd called. He waited until our bird was well over the city and Reedy was driving the jammer back through the gate. Then Otoro, the gorilla samurai, turned to bow to us. As the first of the forces got to him, big orc warriors bristling with weapons and riding hard, looking to tear him apart, our samurai made those same signs again and his body shimmered. I don't know if it was the heat from the fire or what, but he was wavering out there in the heat and flames, like a candle about to go out. He held up the axe guy's head, because apparently he wasn't completely dead, and let him watch what should have been bad boy's rescue running in to get him outta the fight he'd just lost. Then Otoro raises his other fist into the sky, roaring in that way a gorilla does that makes you think you stepped in it real deep, and pounds his fist onto the beach. The fire-eating tornado changes direction, slamming into the plane, and ignites everything at once."

Gunter stared at nothing, mouth working, voice going down to a dry whisper. Nothing came out. But I could tell he was saying… *I screamed "No."*

We waited for him to finish. Silence for a few moments. I watched the stars.

"I saw the fireball from the other side of the berm at the STA," I said softly. "Shock wave went through everything. Scouts and your guys from combat control said it was like a MOAB went off and cleaned the board of the enemy rushing in to take the plane and anyone they could get their hands on."

"And the samurai?" the smaj asked quietly.

"Don't know, Sergeant Major," Sergeant Gunter admitted, his voice still halfway between here and there. "In that time we were connected, I could feel his presence in this… world. I know that must sound max hippy to a guy like you, but we were all connected to each other in that moment. I think we still might be on some level. I watched that flame go up around him, but I don't know if he's gone, or not… gone. I can only tell you what my eyes and my experience with JP-rated fuels can tell you. Nothing survives."

Quiet. And in it I wondered how much, if I just said the right words… could I make right again.

I wondered what the right words were… that make everything all better.

"Fair enough," the smaj said finally. "Talker, if you can distill all of this down to a report for the captain, I'd appreciate it. Extra blue percolator privileges if you can get it done by COB tonight."

"I'm on it, Sergeant Major," I said. Because of course I would agree to that. Coffee. And… in that one instant, the sergeant major had placed trust in me, and I'll be honest, I felt like I'd messed up so bad that the Rangers never would again.

And…

That felt worse… than… not coffee.

I'm sorry, coffee. Some things are just true.

"And you, Tech Sergeant Gunter…" Stone stood, and Gunter did so as well. The two men shook hands. "If we press on and succeed past this point, it is because you and yours," said the sergeant major looking Sergeant Gunter right in the eye, "met and exceeded the standard above and beyond the call of duty, and under direct, and very personal risk to your lives. Rangers are honored to call you brothers."

That felt like something carved on a mountain. So it had been spoken, so it was. I note that for the record because I think the record... I think it will survive me, even become like that *Book of Skelos* everyone seems to think is so valuable and the clue to all things.

This is what happened to us here. We lived.

"Sergeant Major..." Rob began. "I'm... uh... one request... Do you think when we take care of... Master Sergeant Sandoval's body... you would be there? Say something like that, Sergeant Major?" Rob asked. "He would have loved... what you just said."

The sergeant major nodded and turned toward his gear.

"After what you boys pulled off today... you call, and I'll come. Rangers lead the way, Sergeant."

CHAPTER TWENTY-FIVE

BY midnight that night, with burning jet fuel and toasted aircraft smell still floating over the war-torn city, as the temples rang their last bells and the singers called the faithful to final prayers, the decision was made to attack the massing Imperial Saurian Legions now entering the battlefield that afternoon while we were fighting over on the west.

Another Accadion legion had landed in the port to support us.

The Saur had used the cover of the battle on the west side to march forward in small units and now they were nearing our front gates and forming into large armies.

The captain's plan was simple. We couldn't fade, so we'd throat punch and go for the decap on their medusa general in one small-unit attack from the flank while the Accadions marched out from the gates and formed outside the southern wall.

It was a bold plan.

We're Rangers, and that's what we do. Of course we would. Even with three legions of support, two of those were at half strength and the city could not fight any longer. We had to assassinate their general and throw their forces into chaos.

Maybe that was the win...

But this was the only card we had to play.

The sergeant major told me, after I finished the report, to then report to Sergeant Hardt and get ready to go forward as a rifleman in the morning. The scouts had taken casualties in the last day or two. They needed warm bodies.

Tanner too.

I got my gear together, said goodbye, and left the sergeant major alone and staring into the fire.

He said, as I went, "See you on the other side, Talker. You boys watch out for each other. You're good Rangers."

Then we were gone, Tanner and I.

On the way to Hardt's scouts we said nothing. The city was sleeping and only the dogs were out. It had been a long day.

The only thing Tanner said was, "You seen White's girl, Talk? Local. Way too fine for him."

I had not.

But I was amazed that despite being unable to hear, White had managed some game.

Ranger gonna Ranger.

"She's like… a stone-cold fox, man," continued Tanner. "Nice smile too. Dark, exotic beauty. Skin is real… creamy. Need to find her sister. Hope she's cool with zombie dudes and all."

I laughed.

Tanner chuckled dryly as we passed along dark streets and lost alleys.

"You're thinkin' about that wish, aren't you, man?"

I was.

"Someone needs to talk to you… before you do it, Talk."

But I didn't hear him. Was going over the words and hoping… hoping I could get them right.

We reached Hardt's scouts, but he was away at another sand table walk with the captain. The team leader told us to rack out and we'd get a final brief just before dawn.

As he understood it, we were just doing a movement to contact. But there was gonna be some tunnel work. Then... Ranger Smash!

Of course, Ranger Smash!

I fell over and slept like a dead man.

But I had a dream. A good dream

Dreams... who can figure them out. But... it was a good one, even though there was trouble.

Last of Autumn was in this great throne room, and there was trouble. Something bad had happened and there was chaos all around her. I know, doesn't sound like a good dream. It wasn't life-threatening, but I could tell she had her hands full, and everyone was pulling at her. She turned and saw me and smiled.

And then we were holding each other. In the dream.

I was just so... so glad to see her. Even with all the trouble.

And she was glad to see me. Even with all the trouble.

I woke up just before dawn. There were tears in my eyes. It was quiet out, and the sky was red in the east.

CHAPTER TWENTY-SIX

IMAGINE you know nothing of ancient history. Bronze Age warfare. Why? Because there is no past so ancient that the technology of the time makes the present look like some fantastic age of wonder and magic.

It is the same as it ever was, and war… war never changes, the young Rangers like to say for some reason.

Imagine you are… let's call it a *Bronze Age Warrior*. But in this case, you are either an Accadion legionnaire, or a Saurian legionnaire.

Human versus lizard man.

You face each other in the morning light. You and a thousand to your left and right, ready to spill blood, count coup, and see the other side of this battle maybe someone will tell of in the years to come.

To be fair, I don't think the Saurians call themselves legionnaires. But we have yet to penetrate down to that level of their society and for purposes of tactical planning we just use the Accadion familiar terms.

It's… probably about nine o'clock in the morning along the southern coast of the Med…

The Great Inner Sea.

Like the Roman legions of Marc Antony and Octavius long ago, you have arrayed your forces in a contest for all the marbles. As it were.

As it is.

Same as it ever was.

Battles like this don't start until mid-morning and sometimes into early afternoon, or so many of the Rangers assure me from their careful study of the histories of warfare and... let's call it... all the marbles.

Those old Bronze Age armies never fought at night. Too much chaos, hard to control your troops, hard to tell who won. The day is for slaughter, the night is for figuring out what your next move is.

Yeah, there were rules, but there were also practicalities. And when you're moving around three understrength legions to line up against four crack legions, both sides are looking for all the advantages and for everything to be just right before the commanders order everyone forward and the slaughter commences in full.

The Accadions, under Captain Tyrus, who really should be a general according to his men, have the high ground and the best ground. Tyrus marched his men out before dawn and for three hours they've formed up into an old Roman fighting square, complete with palisades and spear.

Banners wave, NCOs move and hector. The legionnaires stand stock-still, shining armor gleaming in the rising morning sun on this day of slaughter.

Even with the fresh legion they are outnumbered and if *Surprise, Ranger Smash!* doesn't happen, they're going to be surrounded and slaughtered despite the high ground, the resolve, and their leader... the legendary Captain Tyrus.

His red cloak and high horsehair plume are easily visible from a distance. His armor shines like golden morning. His figure is the very essence of martial skill.

The enemy has targeted his point in the line for destruction. No doubt.

And that's why he stands forward and leading his men. Ready to meet the Saurian advance with shield, spear, and gladius at the front line of the battle.

This is the key element to *Surprise, Ranger Smash!*

The Saur have to think the battle is somewhere else other than where the Rangers want it to be. So, they have to go for Captain Tyrus.

Where are the Rangers?

I'll get to that in a second.

Let's discuss the disposition of enemy forces first.

Four legions. Crack elite lizard men, veterans of jungle warfare in the deep south. According to Vandahar they have gone deep into the darkest part of the continent, fought against overwhelming odds, and come back to tell the tale having stacked at the pro level.

Their pharaoh, Sût the Undying himself, has bet big on alliance with the Nether Sorcerer in the north. And the Black Prince of the Crow's March.

For all the marbles.

The bet cost the Lich Pharaoh big as the Rangers have advanced across the monster-howling madness of the Lost Coast and taken his key port city and made it their base of operations. The city Sût was sending his troops to for transport into the War Against the Stone Kings and Accadios herself.

This is epic-level stuff, and someone should write this down.

Oh yeah, that's my job. Ruin Herodotus. But with coffee!

The Rangers slaughtered that force and took the city for their own. Sût hired orcs of the desert wastes and they died trying against the Rangers.

Join the club, losers.

Take that, Herodotus!

That's another thing about this battlefield. It is not pristine right now. Between the opposing forces, lizard and human, is a rotting, foul, pestilent battlefield of bloating and hacked-to-pieces orc corpses who've died in the sands, leaving behind burned siege engines and ragged tent cities flapping like ghost ships on a sea of bloody sand.

The orcs are gone now.

The loss of their high priest and the defeat at the airfield has caused them to disappear so instantly, that if it were not for their abandoned dead and apocalyptic tent cities, and the small junky fortress they tried to erect in their crawl to the wall, structures smashed by Ranger mortar fire, it would be as though they were never here.

The four crack legions of Saur fly their green-and-gold standards as they approach the Legion position from three different angles. Their lesser generals are armored in gold beaten armor, carrying shining spears and wicked curved swords. Their troops are armored in bronze breastplates and white kilts with emerald trim.

They wear strapped sandals with nails in the bottom.

Drone recon is trying to find their medusa general who we've hedged our bets on ending this fast.

These Saur are not the lithe, almost fey troops we faced, and defeated, before at other times. Each of these, in varying degrees, could play that lizard thing that tried to kill Captain Kirk.

These dudes are straight-up jacked.

And whereas the legionnaires of Accadios are crisp, clean, and all armor and kit are identical to the man standing next to them... the Saur are not. They are wildly different beyond the bronze breastplate and white kilts. Many have necklaces of dangling skulls or other dire totems. Armor, helms, weapons, all are marked with scrawling runes and glyphs that may possibly either be magics, or just for good luck, or some lizard man equivalent of *Born to Kill*.

But with a lot of ssss and slurring hisssses.

The Accadions stand stock-still in the heat. Beyond the movement of their NCOs, or messengers running to and fro between the commanders of each of the legions, there is little movement at the center of their force. It's like watching a mass formation of statues, daring you to come and knock them down.

They know.

They have no illusions regarding what is about to happen.

On the other hand, once the Saurian legions began to gather in their formations, and they're still gathering, one legion is less than three miles back and moving at the double to join the battle according to drone recon, they began to hiss, beat their wooden shields, shriek their blaring disconcerting trumpets, and shake their fists at the Accadions.

So—where are the Rangers?

As if on cue...

The sound to attack comes from the Saurian line and all three legions of present Saur, with the fourth at the double and acting as a reserve force to exploit any weakness developed in the Accadion line, march forward, and the battle has begun.

The Rangers were there.

I was there.

CHAPTER TWENTY-SEVEN

DURING the three-week battle with the orc hordes, we had discovered the orcs were decent sappers. They'd tunneled all over the battlefield and that's what the captain and the scouts had been up to. During the night battles, the scouts went into the tunnels, cleared them out, then popped up and killed a bunch of orcs, destroyed some artillery pieces, or burned their command tents. And then disappeared back down into the dark.

They also mapped the tunnels.

Where were the Rangers as the Saurian advance commenced against the Accadion line?

We were in a tunnel just west of the left-most flanking Saurian legion as it advanced toward the Accadion line, ready to do battle.

We'd entered the tunnels inside the city where the orcs had achieved some degree of success before dying for their troubles. Then we crawled, hunch-walked, and at times moved as swiftly as we could carrying all the ammo and gear possible. All this while all the legions formed up to murder each other in super-sized doses.

Tanner and I got assigned to Hardt's scouts, which were the tip of the spear for the surprise attack. The scouts had taken some hits in recent days and along the way. No one was dead, but the two scouts we replaced...

Cousins and Texas…

They were caught in a cave-in and had to be dragged from the rubble with injuries that required them to be medically benched for a few weeks.

So as the scouts, led by Captain Knife Hand, crawled through the tunnels, a long snake of Rangers carrying tons of ammo, five-five-six, extra mags, belts of seven-six-two, Carl G rounds, and some mines, as much as the Forge had been able to crank out in just twelve hours, followed us and stacked in the narrow tunnels, wide halls, and shafts leading up to a smashed ballista emplacement the Ranger scouts had smashed on a previous attack.

We staged here and waited to make our surprise attack against the enemy flank.

The captain was near the entrance with Sims on RTO. Sims was in contact with the Air Force, through the comm operator, connected to our drone pilot. Pretty Blond Ponytail.

She was doing everything she could to spot the medusa general. We needed to know her location because we were going to drive on her and try to get the kill once we popped up out of the tunnels.

Sergeant Thor was forward with the scouts.

If we could get him a shot, he could do her at distance and we were hoping for the chaos of lack of leadership that would give Captain Tyrus the advantage on the field and thus let the Accadions basically make the Saur die on their emplaced spears, or advance and sweep the field once the Saur were in full rout.

"Contact!" whispered Sims in the darkness of the tunnel. "Got her, sir. She's just coming out from the lead legion, moving through her troops. Huntress says she's got her guard and... the black crows Gandalf apprised us of."

Huntress was the call sign for Pretty Blond Ponytail.

Gandalf was Vandahar.

The drone had two AGMs. Air-to-ground missiles.

But the Saur had magic.

The mortars had already tried to rain death on the Saur formations as they advanced through the dunes to reach the battlefield. From within their formation strange missiles like the magic meteor Kennedy and Vandahar could display, streaked up and knocked out the incoming mortar rounds like some kind of Patriot air defense missile system. Rounds got through, but then they impacted on ghostly green shields the Saur sorcerers could cast at the last second, or perhaps had already cast like some kind of ablative battery shield.

I don't know. I'm out of my depth here. Just guessing. Maybe it was that.

The mortar teams were now being held back, saving their rounds in case final protective fires were needed to cover the potential Accadion retreat back into the city if things went seriously sideways.

And then there were the crows all around her.

Vandahar warned us that the crows were actually demon servants of Sût. Entities the Lich Pharoah had summoned up from the pits of Abaddon in order to protect his champion from arrow fire in the thick of combat.

They were worthless in hand-to-hand combat, according to our wizards, other than they would gather around her and just caw at her enemies as she slaughtered them, then tear at their flesh once they were down. The crows were chanting, "Swallow your soul, swallow your soul," in their crow croak, but they could also intercept arrow fire.

So, we had to surmise that mortars targeted on her, and sniper fire, would be ineffective. We'd have to use the principle of mass to machine-gun her to death at close range.

So… that was the plan.

Vandahar also warned us regarding two more things about the medusa general.

Her sword was a blade of renown. Small and fast like the Accadion gladius, it supposedly flashed like lightning and made searing cuts in her enemy.

She was incredibly fast with it.

The second thing, and at this Vandahar had to do a kind of Kennedy preface, "What I tell you regarding the medusa general… is perhaps just mere fable, but the ancient texts indicate when a thrice-born medusa appears, and yes, she is the runt of the clutch, but unlike her sisters, the thrice-born may possess the ability to sing once every year."

Oh, I thought. *That's nice. She's going to sing while Thor domes her.* Then we all go home to coffee.

That was my hope, I'll be honest about that. Get close, Thor takes the shot. Blood and brain spray. Too bad. Everyone go home now.

I'd warred enough.

I needed a break.

That was my hope.

"Anyone who hears her voice," continued the old wizard, "and this is where the text gets… strange. Anyone who hears, or anyone she sings… at… will be turned to stone. Again, Rangers, this is fable, and it may bear no resemblance to what she can actually do, but if she begins to sing… then you must beware. I hope this is just fable. For your sakes, Rangers."

Sims confirmed her position now. Lead elements of the Saur were already pushing toward the Accadion palisades. Overhead, Saurian archers, following the three legions, began to fill the sky with their hissing arrows as their lead elements advanced to do battle.

The Legion NCOs shouted their defensive orders and as one, the three elements raised their shields overheard to defend from the onslaught of ten thousand arrows.

The captain then motioned us forward and we slipped from the ruined tunnel one by one and formed our wedges. Keeping low, we'd advance and try to get the third legion to disintegrate so we could attack the centermost where the medusa general would be fighting.

Overhead both Little Birds streaked across the battle-field, racing toward the formations.

The strap hangers looked ready to deal death.

And one of them was Vandahar.

He cast his first spell and a sudden cloud of death, like some Grim Reaper crop duster, billowed and rolled toward the indirect elements to the rear of the Saurian line. In moments they were choking to death as the Cloudkill spell spread everywhere across their lines, murdering Saurian archers and sorcerers alike.

CHAPTER TWENTY-EIGHT

WE got on line and started moving on the legion ahead of us. It was time to enter the battle.

The Rangers with Carls fired first according to the plan the captain had laid out during the briefing in the dawn dark, near the tunnel entrances we'd gathered at within the city. The anti-armor teams moved forward, called out, "back blast area clear," and sent rounds into the formations of Saur. The munitions exploded like sudden shotgun blasts of death and shredded ranks and columns of the fierce lizard warriors, tearing them apart and sending their bodies flying in every direction.

The Rangers surged forward, embodying violence of action as they lobbed grenades, fired their weapons, shifted forward, and tried to murder as many of the enemy as fast as they could.

The Saur reacted surprisingly swiftly. Ancient trumpets blared, signaling a readying to counterattack, but by that time the Ranger gun teams had set up and began to work the center mass of the bewildered Saurian element while the smaller wedges of Ranger fire teams conducted fire and movement, shooting down the lizard men that had survived the Carl rounds and the two-forty fire.

All commands between all elements, since we still didn't have radios due to the nano-plague breaking them down, and the batteries too, were shouted by the NCOs now as we moved. We had to listen to move, engage, and shift fire, while the three leading wedges overran the Saur and drew arrow and spear fire for the gun teams.

Lizard man pushes came and went as they closed, waving those cruel shining hooked swords. Some of the assaulters went hand to hand, but in reality it was easier to mag-dump and keep moving, calling out magazine changes.

The SAW gunners came in and hosed elements as we continued our push right into the guts of their formation.

Ahead of us, the remains of an orc command post fluttered like hanged men at the crossroads on a tiny hill overlooking the battle.

We were down and covering when the Little Birds swept in again and rained down fire from the miniguns, and a fireball from Vandahar smashed into the Saurian command element where pennants and banners of rank and command surged and bobbed in the chaos.

Saurian spellcasters shot brilliant beams of light, almost like lasers, up at the fast-moving helicopters, while other wizards called out words of doom on our lines.

We had no idea if these words of doom had any effect on us or if, as Kennedy might have put it, we made our save. Either way the Rangers were out for blood, and they weren't done by half as the sniper teams, roving through the formations, shot down sorcerers who managed to pop up and cast some spell or other at us.

One Ranger did get turned into a giant bat... but that spell died a few hours later. After he lost his marbles and freaked out, he started flying around attacking the Saur spellcasters by picking them up and dropping them from a decent height.

Then he'd check in with the team leaders, reminding them that no one was to shoot him.

Still, he was a little freaked out.

I sure would be.

Lizard men went up in flames, riddled by rounds, as both gun run and fireball savaged their line. More of them massed as almost the entire legion we were cutting into fractured and formed two elements to counterattack us right there.

Yes, our initial push had met overwhelming success. Now we were in it, and the enemy was intent on a real fight.

By that time we had no idea what was happening at the front with the Accadion legions the other Saurian elements were throwing themselves into.

For the next ten minutes it was pure brawl. I was shooting as fast as I could. Despite the spells and gun runs, there were still a lot of Saur pushing on us from two sides now, forming a pincer.

Still with Hardt's scouts, we followed the captain as he pushed into the remains of the ghostly orc tent command post on the small hill, shooting down Saur who dared come at him, waving at the combat wedges to follow him in. He gutted the first Saur who managed to get close, gutted that guy with his claws, switching effortlessly between hand-to-hand and carbine, then tiger-roared and began to shoot the other fast-movers stumbling in at us and lobbing spears from the "cover" of the tents on the hill.

One of the SAW gunners dumped a belt and shredded the major command post where a bunch of the Saur had just pushed in to lead the capture of the high ground in our sector.

One of the Rangers off to my right got run through by a flung spear, and he went down on one knee and kept shooting anyway.

No first aid was possible. Returning fire was first aid right now as more spears rained down on us.

I closed the gap between us, and saw Running Under the Moon moving up with her aid bag. I waved to her, and she spotted me instantly and dashed, heedless of spear and arrow fire, to the wounded Ranger. I laid down covering fire, but more Saur were contesting the hill. The best way to keep him covered was to push them off of it.

I swapped in a new mag, told her to keep low, and pushed forward, walking and firing, one foot after the other, heel toe to stay stable on uneven ground, drifting left to make it harder to hit me.

Tanner was moving ahead of me, and it was clear he saw what I was seeing. Taking a knee, then standing up aggressively and shooting Saur like it was a mechanical process, he worked his way forward, stepping gingerly over the dead Saur we'd already made.

Sergeant Hardt was behind us and working the grenade launcher, putting rounds over the rise where the command tents of the dead orcs had looked down onto a road leading into the battlefront near the wall. It was immediately clear this was a rise in the terrain, and we needed to own it if we were gonna continue to hammer the Saurian left flank while the Accadions worked the center.

Hardt looked around, saw me, and shouted, "Talker, get the two-forty teams forward and position them on that hill to suppress the enemy push!"

I acknowledged the order with a hand gesture and looked around for both gun team leaders. I spotted Soprano and Jabba carrying the two-forty forward and ran to them as spears stuck in the sand all around me, hitting the decaying bodies and bones of the orcs, shattering sometimes as they did so.

I reached Soprano.

"Hardt wants you on the hill to put fire on the push! Follow me!"

He didn't Mario-speak, he just hefted the gun, and Jabba followed both of us, overloaded with belts, the gob grumbling to himself about Moon God Potion.

I worked forward, sideslipping to the rear of what had been the Saurian legion's axis of advance. Now they were turning on us, but I could still move forward and to their left as we fired and pushed on the hill. I shot a few more Saur who spotted us and came surging through the sand, lobbing spears or slung stones. They were big brutes, and it took at least five rounds on target to get them to stay down.

Which meant ten rounds for me. I was breathing heavy, running and moving, shooting at the same time. My aim was all over the place as I tried to control my breathing. It was getting more difficult by the second.

I fired and moved forward, waving for the gun team to follow me as I cleared a path and swapped another mag.

We'd gotten a full combat load for this one. It was strange, after three weeks of battle, to finally have enough ammo to keep shooting.

Especially now.

At one point, Soprano went hip fire with the medium machine gun and dumped a hot spread all over some Saur that came in with short bows to fire at the Rangers behind us.

They didn't see us, crouching low and moving forward. They got ruined and those that didn't die immediately under the withering burst of gunfire fell back to the other side of the hill to save themselves from Soprano's relentless onslaught.

We reached the base and began to climb the small hill. I crouched, firing at some of the Saur who were swinging sling stones and firing at the Rangers behind us. They died and we made the top of the hill. Tanner was up there already, moving among the tents and killing everything he could find. He had arrows sticking out of him, but that didn't seem to bother him.

He's already dead.

I rendezvoused with him, turned over the gun team for emplacement per Hardt's orders, and raced back down the hill to get the other team forward.

I saw Kennedy, working the right flank with another squad, using his staff like a straight-up flamethrower to lay down a defensive line of hot fire so the Rangers could work around that and canalize the Saur into tighter kill zones they were already setting up while shooting, moving, and communicating.

I spotted the other gun team, got them moving in the right direction, and ran them up the hill under very little enemy fire.

It was clear we had the hill now, and the scouts were basically running a base of fire into the swarming mass of the disintegrating Saurian legion on the left flank. The captain was moving back to get more Rangers forward who'd bogged down in smaller fights along the flanks. He reoriented the other teams the way he wanted them headed, pushing them around the far side of the hill and cleaning up more Saur who seemed completely leaderless now.

The Rangers were now literally rolling on the enemy, and it looked like we wouldn't stop until we took the medusa general's head.

Up there, on the hill, I saw the whole battle in full.

Both Saurian legions were ramming smack into the Accadion formation beneath the walls. What was happening there looked like some kind of harvesting machine for lizard men as everyone was destroyed, cut to pieces, gouged, hacked, or stabbed, then scattered and tossed aside for a chance at more savage butchery. Dangerous spells rolled through the skies, creating shimmering lights, sudden thunderclaps, and hellish fireballs that tore through ranks like bowling balls of other beings not from this reality.

Burnt flesh and poison hung in the air as both sides went after each other hammer and tongs.

We'd pushed on the hill. We'd taken it. Now as the gun teams began to fire into both enemy legions ahead, within the next ten minutes, it would be clear that the battle was done.

Violence of action had smashed the left flank, and when both of the engaged Saurian elements needed to push to break through the Accadion line... there was nothing.

And now they were taking fire from us.

Even with the fourth legion now streaming into the battle to the rear, they were being rained death on by the fast-moving Little Birds and more of Vandahar's catastrophic spells cast from the strap.

The Saur had lost.

They just didn't know it yet.

Maybe.

Then all of a sudden…

The Bronze Age happened, and the battle almost consumed us all as ancient traditions and arcane rites soaked up all the momentum and stalled our victory.

Within the Saurian line, signal standards shot up, and all at once across all legions, enemy and friendly, combat ceased instantly and both parties backed away as some message we didn't understand… had been sent. And received.

"What's going on?" screamed Hardt for all of us as the battle suddenly went silent.

The gun teams continued to work, shooting down the Saur, even as both sides backed away, and in moments the Legion corporals were running for us on the hill, telling us to cease fire.

It was Chuzzo who shouted the loudest, pounding through the sand, running for the Rangers on the hill.

Shouting, *"Combattimento singolo! Combattimento singolo! Combattimento singolo!"*

Single combat! Single combat! Single combat!

"È stato dichiarato!"

It has been declared.

CHAPTER TWENTY-NINE

IT was the weirdest battle I'd ever fought in. The weirdest any of us had ever fought in.

As the Rangers held the small hill they'd taken, the NCOs refining and improving our positions as both sides backed away from each other, that weird Bronze Age stuff started to go down that had nothing to do with two sides killing each other... and a lot to do with tradition, sacrifices, and... well, combat from another age.

It was generally accepted among the Rangers that this was weird, and we should just start killing each other again.

Mainly them. Killing them.

What was revealed in the wide place between the legions of Saur and Accadions facing each other with knives and spells out, was becoming a sandy arena littered by the hacked-to-death recently dead.

Or burnt by fireballs.

Or choked by poison gas from a magical cloud.

Or riddled with magical meteors fired by wizards.

Or a dozen other horrid spell-based deaths that made the mind reel at the damage, and the wielder.

It was Corporal Chuzzo, whose broken English had gotten pretty good, who explained what was going on now between both sides to the Ranger captain.

The enemy general, the medusa, had asked for single combat to decide the matter.

The Legion was honor-bound to accept this offer due to ancient and arcane traditions founded and entrenched in Ruin human society.

Chuzzo explained to us that in times past, mainly among the human cities, life was so precious that it was not to be wasted in mass amounts of slaughter, so instead two warriors could be chosen to determine the outcome.

Every warm body was needed because the line was so thin for human survival.

This was, apparently, as old a rite in human civ as any, and it was considered bad juju to deny it. Civilization-ending juju in fact.

The clever medusa general knew a loophole when she saw one, and had played her hole card to stop the sudden attack on her formations.

Yes, we Rangers would have just gone on murdering everyone until they changed shape, or caught fire, which in some cases they were literally doing. But apparently, in the Ruin... stuff has to happen when *single combat* is declared. Weird... Bronze Age savages stuff.

First off, there's a lot of waiting. And this is bad because everything smells like death out here. Even for Rangers, this battlefield was getting pretty foul.

Bulls have to be sacrificed next.

The two sides watched each other as both sides brought forth their best animals. Standing at a distance their priests chanted, and then slaughtered the bulls.

Everyone looked at Sergeant Monroe.

He shrugged. Then muttered, "Stupid animals."

Then, I don't know, but it looked weird from this distance atop the hill the Rangers were planning to murder everyone from, but the priests started chanting and singing and holding the entrails up to the sky.

A lot of blood got sprayed around next.

I drank coffee. Cold brew and listened to the Rangers moan about how... their game of "Kill Everyone" had been ruined.

The smaj moved among them, reassuring them that more killing was probably gonna happen once enough bull blood got splattered all over the place.

The captain stood on the hill, gun teams ready, and watched the whole proceeding with a grim look on his face.

During the interim, Captain Tyrus crossed the bloody-body-littered sand from the legions to the hill and conferred with our commander.

The upshot, and I did the translating...

This had to happen, according to Captain Tyrus. His men would go fetal if it didn't.

Then, once the winner won, the Saur were probably gonna weasel and get back to the slaughter.

The Accadion Legion was bound to its traditions.

I heard the smaj mutter, "Then them traditions are stupid."

The captain said nothing. But I was pretty sure he thought they were stupid too.

It was the captain who next noticed the Saur were stacking more and more elements to their rear. More sorcerers were appearing out of the sandy distances, trailing their large retinues of slaves and sacrifices. Spells were being cast, and yes, the dead were beginning to rise out there in the dust and sand.

A field of zombies were beginning to rise, but they remained where they were.

"Ah, yes… that's the Saurian gift for vile necromancy," Vandahar chimed in grimly. "If they keep that up, they'll double their numbers by the time we have a champion."

The captain had that look.

"If it's going to be single combat, and the winner will decide who wins… why are they stacking more enemies?" he asked.

No one had a reply, but the sergeant major noted there were more jet-black griffins in the skies now. Circling high overhead, weaving in and out of the clouds.

The Little Birds hovered over the walls of the city, their rotors beating the air, sending off waves of heat in the almost noon sun.

If the battle resumed, all momentum was lost.

We'd lose.

The priests on both sides finished their songs and prayers, shouted something arcane, and returned to their armies.

"What happens now?" I asked in the graveyard silence. The world felt like two gunslingers from some spaghetti western were about to see who could look the meanest, then drop iron on each other.

Corporal Chuzzo answered as our two captains watched the enemy out there. One were-tiger. One legendary legionnaire.

"Now, we choose a champion," answered the corporal. "Then they fight to the death."

CHAPTER THIRTY

THE Little Bird carrying Vandahar came in hot after Sergeant Hardt got the temporary LZ set behind the hill we controlled right there in the middle of the battlefield.

The noonday sun beat down on the legions and the Rangers as ceremonies and rites were observed and we waited for the next arcane decision to be made so we could get back to killing each other.

Meanwhile, out there the clever Saur and their general were busy raising all the dead we'd slaughtered for three weeks straight and getting ready to announce their champion.

As far as the eye could see, dead orcs were beginning to shamble around, moving into masses near the Saur line.

"This is bad, Talk. Real bad. Big dead juju bad," Tanner moaned. "I can feel a lotta eyes on the other side watching this outcome go down. Favors gettin' called in at that Land of the Dead realm I can sometimes see. This is bad, man. Real bad."

Yeah. It looked bad. But I was outta coffee... so it was worse.

Like disaster-time bad.

We all have our apocalypses. Mine are more important than others. Trust me.

The Little Bird was down amid flying dust and sand to the rear and as soon as Vandahar hopped off the bird, it was back in the air and looking to get involved with the jet-black griffins who were circling lower and lower, their dire crow calls somehow like leviathans of some lost age before man.

The old wizard labored through the sand and flying dust, using his staff to pull him forward as the small light attack helicopter heaved itself into the air and spun away off over the battlefield.

An Uzi dangled from a sling across his robes.

"Oh…" said Tanner near the command group atop the hill where we waited. "He wanted to learn some of our weapon systems, so I started him off on the Uzi you and Joe brought back from that MACV-SOG cache. He's lousy with the carbines and sidearms, but the Uzi works for him. For some reason, he's fairly accurate with pray and spray… and he enjoys it. So… wizard with a machine gun. Who knew, man?"

Meanwhile, the command team was busy watching the enemy priests announce their champion as they hissed, raised savage standards, and from their midst the body-guards of the medusa general, all jacked Conan-actual lizard men carrying double-bladed battle axes, marched out into their side of the body-littered sandy arena.

A moment later they parted, and their commander, dressed more like a Greek Spartan, complete with the helm hiding her snakes, marched forth in a gold kilt and a shining otherworldly breastplate embossed with snakes and an image of the sun.

She planted her strapped sandals in the sand and drew her bright sword in one swift gesture, signaling she was ready to meet her challenger.

And yeah, her weapon flashed like lightning when it came out of its scabbard. Like the sun on fire, and her draw was one of the swiftest I'd ever seen.

Like… *Otoro fast.*

And then I was thinking about the wish and that… said just right… could fix that too. Bring back the gorilla samurai. He was good. The Ruin needs Otoro.

We need him.

Now he was most likely dead. But I didn't know.

The Ruin is a strange place. So, who knows.

The medusa general's praetorian guard withdrew from her, leaving one of their own to act as her second. And that guy was uglier, more jacked, and probably meaner than the rest of the other brute murder machines she ran with. His jaws opened lazily, and he snapped a row of crocodile fangs as he waited for what came next.

"Oh good," said Vandahar, breathing heavily as he arrived at the top of the hill and the command team. "I have come none too late. It seems they have chosen their champion and, as I suspected, it will be her. The medusa general. This is… not good, Rangers. Not good at all."

Captain Knife Hand rolled his shoulders, still in were-tiger form, and muttered, "I'll go."

Silence for the moment as we weighed the implications. "Once I kill her, get ready to push forward and join the Accadion lines with the assault teams. Gun teams hold the hill and provide—"

"No," interrupted Captain Tyrus. He too had learned our language, barely, though he never used it much, or spoke all that much for that matter. "I must go out and meet her in single combat. They have put forth their commander. I must go as the commander of my force. That is the way… it must be."

Knife Hand gave the man a look that said, *You sure about this? I'm a killer. I'll do her and be back to lead my men before the body hits the floor.*

Tyrus nodded once, staring stone-cold forward at the arena down there where he would fight to the death.

Captain Tyrus has scars, and muscles. A lot of them in fact. Though he looked average, a middle-aged man, like the captain, you could tell the difference between the rest of us, and them. The two captains. They weren't just professional killers… they were predators. You can just feel that when you're in their presence. Like they're dangerous wild animals on their best behavior. I remembered, at that moment, all the things the smaj, hints really, had dropped regarding our own commander.

That he'd been there and done that.

That there was more to him than anyone could know. Delta time. "He's been up some real dark alleys, Talker."

Unrated time in SOCOM.

The fact that he was a captain, when generally a Ranger company was commanded by a major.

The fact that he was now a were-tiger. That the Ruin had revealed that about him. A man sometimes, a murder machine, others. A jungle predator like no other.

I wondered sometimes about those *Dark Alleys*. But… I knew I'd never ask. For the record. Warts and all.

The Ruin reveals.

Captain Tyrus, of the Accadion Legion, was the same in many ways as our captain. Even to his own men he was a mystery. Not an Accadion. Not a general. In command of three Legions in a battle to determine the fate of Ruin civilization, nonetheless.

Also, killer through and through.

"If I may…" began Vandahar, edging forward to the two men staring at the growing force facing their troops.

The math of fatality was becoming clear, and it wasn't adding up for us.

"I would like to point out something that's very obvious to me…" said Vandahar, as if he were some accountant sitting down to explain to the boss why the company had no money and was about to go bankrupt. "But… to you two soldiers, you may not see… yet. In this… *combat…* whoever goes down there is most likely going to be slain. There are some eight snakes under that helmet of hers, and all are filled with a very deadly venom that will slay instantly. There is also her fabled blade, the *Sunsword.* The ancient books say it has never lost a battle. And, I might add, she is quite good with it. She's an able tactician. But beyond all that, I have no doubt, even if you somehow manage to defeat her… her entire army, sorcerers, priests, assassins, and almost two legions, they will charge forth and will slay you dead before you take two steps away from her body."

Vandahar cleared his throat.

"Which I don't think will happen… either of you slaying her, that is. You can see, if you had my eyes, the *hand of fate,* call it what you will, it still rests on her. She… she is a hero despite her current circumstances. And perhaps a tragic one at that. But nonetheless… she has not yet embraced her true destiny. Whoever faces her today… will die, warriors. For her road is not yet complete."

Captain Tyrus did not turn to the wizard. I could tell he was watching the terrain down there in the arena on the battlefield. Where a battle to the death would take place. Seeing where his advantages would be, and where he must avoid in order to survive.

I had a feeling Captain Tyrus had faced many *no-win* battles where death was assured... and walked away leaving a trail of dead bodies to mark down who was right, who was wrong, and who was just dead now.

Vandahar lowered his head, sensing his plea had failed to find an audience.

"Then who will go with you as your second? Who will go with you, out there, to die in the sand, warriors?"

Silence.

I felt the captain ready to say...

Then I beat him to it.

"I will. I'll go."

CHAPTER THIRTY-ONE

VANDAHAR went with us as we pushed down off the hill from the command post to reach the place where... apparently... I'd volunteered to act as second in a fight to the death.

Have I mentioned I have an achievement badge problem? Seriously. What the hell is wrong with me?

We passed Rangers covering behind rocks, ruined siege equipment, and the occasional pile of dead bodies.

Tanner came too. Picking up rear security and trying to talk to me as we marched to my imminent death.

I'd tried to look hard about the whole thing. The jury's still out if I pulled it off.

"Should be me, Talk. They can't kill me. I'm already dead."

"No," I whispered to Tanner. "G...ot a plan," I gasped.

My voice was dry. I was out of coffee. And yeah, I was scared. My plans hadn't always... gone according to... well... plan.

The captain marched ahead of us, his legionnaires in the Accadion line shouting, cheering, beating their shields. Proud of their war leader the way we used to cheer pro quarterbacks coming onto the field. Or that cleanup hitter, bottom of the ninth, two outs, bases loaded. World Series do or die.

But with lizard men who were going to eat us if we failed. About twelve thousand of them, and the dead orcs they were raising from the dead right and left.

Out there on either side of the bowl, along the enemy line, the lizards hissed and ululated chilling war cries that seemed almost totally alien.

Bronze Age weirdness abounded.

And yeah, it felt like we were walking to our own execution. And we were supposed to be motivated about it.

That's the thing they don't tell you about fights to the death in gladiator-style arenas in a world you once knew gone total Bronze Age madness: the crowds are there for blood and they expect a certain amount of motivation on your part.

"The light of fate flickers on you now, Talker," whispered the wizard close and near as we moved toward the fight, leaning down to me so only I could hear what he was trying to tell me. "Like the medusa… you too are… *fated*. I have suspected this from the beginning. So perhaps… I know nothing, but I suspect even now the Hidden King moves as he wills and there is something in this he wants to accomplish. Even if it is your death."

Sweet!

Vandahar pulled me to a halt and searched the sky, licking one long finger as he did so. He held it up into the air.

"No wind."

"And what's that mean?" I asked, desperate for some good news. And yeah, my voice cracked a little.

"Perhaps nothing, Ranger. But it is said the Hidden King moves when the wind moves. And that we are to know it's him when such things happen and expect… victory."

"There's no wind, Vandahar."

"Yes," agreed the wizard. "There is that. Still, I suspect you are about something, Talker. You have a plan, no doubt?"

It felt like one a few minutes ago. Now… I was having trouble focusing.

"Kinda. Maybe. Maybe it's a lotta things coming to gather in my… head. Things you told us about her, the medusa… general. A conversation I had with another medusa… my powers. Maybe… I'd like to tell ya I got this, Vandahar… but… not so sure. Right now."

Chief Rapp appeared, moving from a covered position in his operator kit to meet us as we came out on the sandy track that led to the impromptu arena.

He took off his FAST helmet and raised his assault-gloved hand to the hot blue sky.

"God, give my man here everything he needs out there today, if you could do that for us. Amen."

He looked me in the eye and said, "Get some, Talker." Then he moved back to his position, helmet back on and ready to deal death, and save the wounded.

I felt… better.

Kennedy says clerics, in his game, can bless their allies. He also says the game might not match the reality of the Ruin.

Vandahar turned me around. "Talker… you got this."

Then he was gone, robes flapping, staff pulling, wizard hat bobbing up and down as he made his way to the defenses and waited for the outcome of the impending fight to the death.

"Are you ready now, Ranger?" said Captain Tyrus, staring into the arena. His voice was a quiet, yet powerful, whisper. His calloused hand on the hilt of his plain, unadorned, razor-sharp gladius. "Let us go out there now. Destiny is waiting."

CHAPTER THIRTY-TWO

JUST before I passed the last Ranger forward and entered the sand and dead bodies that formed the "arena," a kid I barely knew, young, still a private, moved toward me from cover. He was carrying a SAW.

His name was Holt.

He shrugged out of the M249 and thrust it at me.

"Goes down out there, you better be ready to lay the hate, Corporal. Dust that big bastard over there."

I said nothing.

My mouth wouldn't work, and I was trying to turn on my psionics for what I needed to do to accomplish what might get us out of this mess.

Dying trying was an option on the table.

I took the SAW and handed him my MK18 and mags. My hands were shaking, and they didn't want to work but I made them anyway.

I strapped the SAW, flipped the belt out so it would feed, and nodded at Holt, which was all I could do.

"It was Brumm's, man," he said as we tapped fists. "Carl G don't care."

And then… I wasn't afraid anymore.

CHAPTER THIRTY-THREE

I followed the captain, Captain Tyrus, out into the arena of bloody sand and rotting orc bodies. The enemy general was there, still helmed, and so was her swole second. Behind them and beyond was a sea of inhuman lizard warriors and priests ready to murder us at the drop of a hat, or the death of our champion.

For some reason... it had to happen this way.

Sigh... Bronze Age.

I stopped at the same distance as her second did, and man, I was already trying to work my psionic voodoo.

Whatever it is.

The demon crows flapped away from here but still stayed close, resting on her elite guard, the bodies of the dead orcs nearby, rotting in the sand, their eyes pecked out.

But that didn't stop the crows from continuing the work as they waited for the coming slaughter.

At first I couldn't get it going. Then I took a deep breath, patted the SAW, heard Kurtz hating on me to be a better Ranger... and it switched on like that.

Okay... what was I trying to do here?

I asked myself.

On the hill, two things had occurred to me. Something Vandahar had said during the briefing just a few days ago.

This medusa was a prisoner. A political prisoner traded by her sister, to get her out of the way.

And… I'd talked with her other sister when we went to smoke the dragon, and then we'd blown her up with the SEAL monkey IED. I remembered that conversation.

In fact, I'd thought about it often.

Specifically… her words. The ones about being seen. Being beautiful. But no one could see you because, as a medusa… you'd turn them to stone. Having to have blind slaves just to feel the touch of another person.

And maybe the psionics was kicking me and hinting at something I might be able to pull off regarding medusas and real human interaction.

I took a few steps closer to the captain as both he and the fierce girl Spartan who was actually a medusa began to circle each other, swords out and looking to make a cut. And a kill.

Now everything was real. More real than I'd expected it to be.

For some reason she hadn't taken off her helm.

I had to wonder…

Did she want the honor of killing Captain Tyrus without the advantage of her serpents?

Was she that kind of warrior? A real warrior just like Captain Tyrus who easily could have been a Ranger?

She chanced a cut and Captain Tyrus moved like a pro, never crossing his feet, just shifting out of the way of her lightning strike. In reply, he struck out once the blade had passed him. Her round circular shield, embossed with an angry medusa, came out and caught the blow.

I forgot to mention that. She had a shield. Big for her and made of what had to be bronze.

Bronze Age games in full effect.

She was smaller than him. She caught the blow and danced backward as he followed up and hammered the shield three more times. Each strike was a thunderbolt, ringing out in the desert silence.

She gave ground, and then, like a deadly viper disturbed, struck out and slashed at the Legion captain.

If he'd been where the blade passed... he would have been dead.

But he wasn't.

I got into her mind by that time.

I saw her life. On fast forward.

She was driven by her duty to the Medusa Throne even though it, her sister the queen, had hated her greatly because of her obvious skill, talent... and honest beauty. Using her for her petty deals.

Still, this medusa served a greater cause than her own wants. Traded for collateral, she'd become a soldier in the armies of Sût.

A soldier without peer.

She sheathed her deadly blade, keeping behind her shield and dancing away, shifting her feet and circling the big legion captain.

With her free gloved hand she ripped off her Spartan helmet and threw it in the sand.

Two things.

The writhing snakes almost danced away from her, and it was clear they had some kind of hypnotic effect as they weaved and bobbed.

And... yes, she was beautiful. In a small, almost delicate way. But her eyes... they were fierce like the eyes of an angry avenging dark angel.

Oh yeah, and a third thing… the snakes' eyes glowed an otherworldly blue as they focused on the captain and began to dart and strike out at him with any opportunity they were given.

Tyrus backed away, blade between him and her.

As both warriors faced each other, I realized I had one chance to stop what was about to happen. And I was pretty sure that no matter what happened, even if the Legion captain killed her, and he'd need to be close to do that, those snakes would strike and kill him.

Her blade came out, flashing in the sunlight, and again she moved forward, blade held out and ready to strike whenever she could.

Across the stinking, rotting desert, filled with the dead, a small breeze picked up, shifting the enemy banners and bells atop their standards. The hair in the death orcs ruffled, and the feathers some of the Saur wore danced about.

And my mind cleared, no longer smelling death, and seeing now… possibilities.

I was calm.

There's a place inside people. Inside every one of us… a place that wants to know more about themselves. That's always asking for external validation.

It's always asking…

Am I this…?

Am I that…?

Do you value me?

Maybe it's the psionics, maybe it's me just writing down the stories of the Rangers, sometimes their personal stories, for the log.

Maybe it's languages.

And maybe... okay, Vandahar... maybe it's the *Hand of Fate*. Call it what you will. Maybe this Hidden King...

That was a new one for me from the wily old wizard.

She had that place. Just like we all do. But, as a medusa among the Saur, as nothing but a mere asset to be traded for gain... she'd closed it off. She'd learned to not ask anyone... what her worth was.

What a tragedy.

Ask the one you love... ask them what you mean to them.

Ask a child.

I've found we don't know how valuable we are to the people who love us. That when asked, they'll often say something like... *I would just die without you. I'd be lost.*

I'd felt like that since Autumn. Since Brumm and Kurtz.

Lost.

I know that now.

But... she was a woman. Women value themselves, no matter what they say... on a certain aspect.

"Tell her she's beautiful, Captain," I hissed suddenly, getting closer so he could hear me.

The big lizard across from me and behind her saw me, rumbled, and began to shift into a fighting stance, switching claws with his battle axe. Ready to get involved if that was the way I wanted it.

Listen, lizard chungo... I'm operating on levels you can't even comprehend. To paraphrase Ranger Wizard Kennedy... *I'm a psionics guy.* Whatever that is.

I don't know what they call them. But I bet it's a cool name I don't know yet. Wizard... but like... better.

I'm sure his hisses were a warning to back off.

Meanwhile, the legions on both sides bayed and howled, or hissed and shrieked, for slaughter and blood.

I felt the two-four-nine.

Yeah… if this didn't work… I was gonna lay some serious hate.

"What?" hissed the captain, backing away from her next attack. The deadly vipers opened their fangs and struck out at empty hot desert air.

"Trust me. Just say it!"

He said nothing and snapped an attack off and out so fast, it would have taken her right in her long slender neck if her shield hadn't come up so fast to block.

One of the vipers whipped out in reply like an uncoiling bullwhip and landed on his armor, but the bite didn't penetrate the shining breastplate.

He backed away and the dance of death continued.

"She's beautiful, isn't she?" I practically shouted at him while trying to keep my voice low, shift my feet to back away from him, and not trip him up. But still keep close enough to keep that space in her mind I was prying open with my psionics ready to receive…

I saw his head bob, like he was nodding that she was actually beautiful, or he was avoiding her cutting his throat with that flashing blade of hers.

"Say it, Legionnaire. Bite off more than you can chew! Say it now!" I ordered.

Then, backing away from her, he said it with no flair, no flourish. No game, if you woulda asked Tanner.

"You're beautiful."

Plain and simple.

But he was such a rock, such a constant in the galaxy… that it was the truth. He was that kind of… eternal warrior.

Just the truth. Nothing more, nothing less.

I bore down, gave myself the ice cream headache of all time, saw double, and pushed what he'd just said right into a deep dark place she'd cut off from the entire Ruin in order to survive.

I gave her a thought to chew on while trying not to trip us both up in the sand and dried blood mixed with dead orcs.

He sees you. The real you.

I felt a sudden shocking cold run through her. Not bad cold... but electric cold mountain water cold. Long time in the desert finally standing in a cold pool cold.

Her face, just behind her shield, scowled... and the snakes went wild.

Her full lips pursed as angry dark eyes bored into the captain... trying to find the lie he was telling.

Confused that she couldn't.

Then, like a little flower, or a small child in a window staring out at rain that would never end, seeing a break in the clouds... I found the hope inside of her. A little at first. Then I pushed everything I had right in there. For all I was worth and everything I could beg, borrow, and steal from the universe.

And even what I told myself I could not trade...

Autumn.

"You are... beautiful," said the captain again, and he was smart enough to know he'd gained some advantage over her for a moment.

She stood there, shining blade out, shield ready, crouched and more than willing to spring and kill.

This could go horribly wrong in half a second, I knew that. *Or...*

"It will be a shame to kill you, General," said the captain matter-of-factly.

She laughed. And she had never laughed, *really laughed...* in as long as she could remember. Never. Ever. I could see that. Inside her mind.

But this laugh was... well, as the Rangers say... *you know.*

She was... vulnerable now.

She was... listening. Now.

The question was, to me, would he kill her in this moment of hesitation?

"Who says it'll be me that's dead, Legionnaire?" she said, her voice a coy, dark whisper.

Captain Tyrus stood there, blade ready to deal death, towering over her.

And then... I could feel his mind.

He had a thing for her.

Suddenly I pushed thoughts in her mind that we could free her, that she could join forces with us. That her sister was dead and the Medusa Throne no more.

Her obligations were... *null.*

The two warriors watched each other, trying to find what was false, what was true... and what was... new...

Then the captain lunged at her, pushing her shield aside, grasping her, still holding his sword—moving like lightning, like I never would have expected of him... and he kissed her.

The snakes could have struck. But they didn't. They were frozen. Bewildered.

She could have stabbed him.

She didn't.

Her eyes were open. She'd never been kissed. Never been... desired.

She closed her eyes, leaned back, and he dove into her soul with his lips. His will. Who he was.

Who she was.

It was like... Mark Antony and Cleopatra... except without all the craziness and cobra venom.

The snakes hovered and danced.

He pulled away from her lips and watched her deep dark brown eyes.

The legions were silent.

She watched him with those dark eyes. Searching...

"Allies..." she murmured.

Tyrus nodded.

She watched him, and then slowly... nodded once. As though the two of them had spoken lifetimes in just a second.

In just a kiss.

Perhaps a kiss... is not just a kiss.

She turned, opened her mouth... a high soprano note, the highest, clearest, striking turn-you-to-stone note rang out from her tiny heart-shaped mouth and she glared at her army, her sorcerers, her priests... her jailers.

They turned to stone. Some exploded, withering under her wrath. Wherever she looked, huge swaths of the Saur were suddenly frozen and turned to stone, or even shattered as they fell back from her wrath, trying to get away from the monster she had become to them.

And then it was on.

The Legion surged forward, Captain Tyrus and the medusa leading, cutting down the Saur who had survived her gaze, driving and slashing into the sudden chaos. The

Rangers opened fire from the hill, and we drove the legions of Saur off the desert before Sûstagul that day.

Even the griffins got rocked by the air defense munitions fired from the Carls as they tried to swoop in.

One turned to stone and smashed into the enemy legions, killing several all at once in a huge explosion of sand and stone that shook the ground.

The Little Birds swooped in, making gun runs on the spreading, running Saur, fleeing the battle as their zombie orcs just fell over, dead again.

It took a few more hours, but the battle was over by dark.

And thus ended the Second Battle of Sûstagul.

I have seen strange things.

And beautiful things.

I will forget nothin', as Robert Rogers ordered those first Rangers, long ago.

CHAPTER THIRTY-FOUR

WE made it back to the city by dark. It had been a long hard day in the desert, and I had seen too many things to process out there in the bloody sand.

The Saur were done as a military force.

We'd won.

Next, after rearming from the Forge, we would recon the south, find Sût... and kill him.

But that was for another day, not today, and more pages in the log. Other stories...

Right now, I was beat. I felt like I was starting to fall asleep even as we threaded the dark and ancient city.

Some Rangers got cut loose for the night. Chow, clean weapons, sleep. Others got sent to the port to unload a galley that was just beating into the port and would dock in a few hours.

More supplies.

But we had the Forge now.

Tanner and I walked back through the quiet streets heading for our rucks and the small encampments we'd made near the area we were always supposed to be found in.

There'd been some leeway allowed for this during the second battle for the city.

I'd found a small, quaint hut long unused but strangely clean and in good repair. Books I'd found in the city, during the battle, or trips through the market, I'd stashed here, intending to translate them someday.

I'd left my gear there too.

Now, we were on our way there. Tanner didn't really sleep, he actually just kind of wandered the streets and graveyards all night long.

He said it was very restful. In another way.

We were close now, and the streets here were dark and quiet even though there were celebrations among the locals at other points across the desert port city.

"It's time, Talk…" said Tanner in that dead trance voice he sometimes uses when he goes… there.

"Time for what, Tanner?" I groaned, too tired to think.

"Time for you to meet the guy that wants to talk to you… about that wish."

I stopped.

I had the wish. I was… ready, ready or not, to make it. I would just ask for Brumm and Kurtz to come back. I had it in my head. But over the next few days I'd write it down. Then…

Well…

Was I really?

But I knew the answer and it scared the hell out of me when I actually thought I'd do it.

"Where is he?"

Tanner pointed toward an alley. It was dark down there. Further down there were… soft lights. Blue.

"He's in there, Talk. I'll lead the way."

"You sure? You sure I need to do this now, Tanner?"

He nodded and then began to shamble that way.

Maybe because he's dead now. Or maybe because it had been a long day, fighting and chasing Saur in the desert, but he shambled like a dead thing and I was reminded that... he was fading from the living day by day, sometimes faster than I wanted.

And I still had that headache.

"Okay," I murmured as though I was in a trance. Or just more tired than I'd ever been in my entire life. Still, I followed Tanner into the alley, and into the fog...

There's no fog in Sûstagul.

And it wasn't an alley.

We walked, and walked, and the alley got close and tight and then... it wasn't there, and we were just walking through the fog. Soon the ground was soft, like swamp, or the ground near a river.

I heard crickets in the night.

Then... soft silver moonlight through willows and pines. I smelled magnolia. And pines. Clear and fresh like they are at night.

I knew this place, and I didn't. Not yet. And that thought kinda scared me, except I was too tired to be rung by its implications.

But it was nice there.

"I'll wait here for a while, man," said Tanner in that dead voice. "He's over there, near the river. Guy you need to talk to, Talk. It's okay... you know him."

It was... countryside. Forest. Fields. A lazy burbling river in the moonlight.

And there, near its edge, was a rangy figure, about my size. Wearing a cowboy hat I knew all too well.

My dad. My father. A horse whisperer who'd died of cancer one summer during my regularly allowed visits.

I stopped. Felt like I stopped, but I was walking toward him anyway. I tried to say… "Dad" but nothing came out.

When I got close, in that slow drawl of his, he said, "Son."

I was on my knees.

Yeah, sobbing.

He bent down, and I reached out for him. To grab on to him.

He hugged me once and I wanted it to last forever, but he pushed me away. Gently.

"Can't now, son. Not why I'm here for ya. Can't cling to me just yet. Okay?"

"But…"

"Okay?"

I was glad just for this. To see him as he was. And not as he died of cancer, wasting away that last, worst summer.

"I'm here son because what you're gonna do… you can't do it."

"The wish?"

He nodded. "Yeah. That. Can't do it, okay?"

"But… my friends… my buddies… it wasn't right. I… can… bring them back, Dad. I can fix it…"

He shook his head.

"Can't. Okay?"

I nodded and just watched him.

"Where are we, Dad?"

"I'll explain later, son. We gotta walk for a while now. Lemme show you something, okay?"

I followed him along the quiet river in the silver moonlight, and it was like a dream. Yeah… it was just like that. I never wanted it to end. Never wanted to… go back. Soon we came to a small campfire, and at first I almost didn't see them, but there were two small figures there, sleeping by the fire in old green sleeping bags.

And there was a pallet for me too. I knew that and no one needed to tell me. It just… was.

My dad pointed to it.

"You need rest now, son. I'll come back tomorrow night and take you home after you've spent the day here. Just rest here now, okay?"

Couldn't argue with that. I dropped to the ground. I weighed one million tons.

"Okay," I mumbled and dropped my gear too, crawling onto the soft warm pallet of old country quilts and blankets.

"Will you stay…" I mumbled, fading from consciousness. Hoping for dreams of good things. Autumn. So tired I didn't care…

"For a while, son. Until you sleep. Then I'll be gone till tomorrow."

But by then I was gone.

* * *

I woke on the ground in the morning in the forest. Golden light filtered through the green trees all around. Two little boys, one dark and solid, the other taller, blond, and lean, stared at me as I rubbed sleep from my eyes.

"Who are you?" asked the taller one. The blond.

I pushed up off the pallet. Completely refreshed.

"Talker," I answered.

He nodded, staring at me, watching me. Studying me intensely.

"We gotta fish for breakfast now. You wanna go fishing?"

I nodded.

Smiles broke out across their grim faces. I got up. In the night I had taken off my shirt, but I was still wearing my Crye Precision bottoms.

And boots.

"What're those?" asked the darker, smaller one. His voice a deep rumble even for a kid.

"Army clothes," I answered.

He nodded, accepting the idea.

"We fight Indian Boys here, when we do war. That's later. You good at throwin' dirt clods?"

I nodded that I was.

"That's good," he said seriously. Too seriously. He looked at his brother. "We need a good thrower for the raid."

"We'll see," said the taller blond brother.

And then we were off to the river. They had sticks. Not fishing poles. And yeah, we got fish. We cleaned them and fried them in a small fire with an old cast-iron pan.

Then we swam.

They laughed and swung from ropes out into the river. I did too.

Later we hiked, or what they called "war scouting."

They showed me trees they thought were special, or weird. A cave where a "big ol' bear" lived. And cliffs they wanted to jump off or climb and places where treasure "was hid" by old conquistadores and prospectors.

They warmed up to me as the day went on, eventually telling me jokes later, or asking me dozens of questions about the stars, or rivers, or bugs and animals and places I'd been.

I tried to answer what I could.

Whatever they did, I did.

Later we fought the Indian Boys, after we put on mud camo and striped our faces with berries we found. Then we snuck into "their territory" further along the river and threw dirt clods at them.

The Indian Boys returned fire and eventually hand-to-hand combat broke out, but it was all in fun.

Someone found a leather ball and a game of soccer-football-dodgeball broke out in a pasture near the river. We played forever and the rules constantly evolved, and everyone agreed it was one of the best games ever.

Later the Indian Boys, they had war paint too like they'd expected our attack, had to go and we shook hands, and they told me their names before they went.

I can't remember the names.

We found honey and ate it. Then fished again near the pirate fort the two boys were building in secret. It was a treehouse in an old, wide, twisting, leaning tree that hung way over the river. Later, below the tree, we worked on their pirate ship, which was a raft on old tires and inner tubes, strapped with frayed rope.

They were trying to find a sail and a mast, so we scouted into the deep woods and found an old pole and later a ragged canvas around an abandoned shack that was supposedly, according to them, haunted by ghosts.

We didn't see any.

We took the found sail and mast back to the pirate ship and rigged it all up, and the taller blond boy was proud of it and the younger darker more solid boy was proud that his brother, who was his hero, was proud of what had been accomplished.

We gathered wood as the day ended and the gloaming came on. Stars came out, we made a bonfire and did Indian dances, and they showed me a secret code they were making.

The moon crossed the night and I listened to stories they made up about the moon, and the river, and their plans to sail the pirate ship into other strange and exotic lands because there was someone they needed to find someday.

I rummaged through my pack and found hot chocolate packs. We made chocolate and drank it in old tin cans they used to drink from, and soon it was time to go to bed.

The younger darker one fell asleep, secure that his brother was keeping first watch for the night.

And for a while, the older blond boy and I sat there in the dark, saying nothing and just watching the night sky, and the stars, calling out the bats as they passed, whispering in their hunts.

And yeah... I knew who they were.

Kurtz as a ten-year-old boy looked at me. Serious. Just like he would be as a Ranger.

"We knew you once, didn't we... a long time ago?"

I nodded.

He watched me.

Then, "You were our brother, Talker, when we were soldiers then?"

I nodded.

He stared off into the dark, and the night above.

"We don't remember that here. Not now. Maybe later."

I thought that was it. That was all he was going to say to me.

I just watched him.

"You're good here?" I whispered finally.

He nodded.

My dad was near the fire now, coming in from the trees.

"Time to go, son," he said softly.

I stood, gathering my ruck. Kurtz watched me. Brumm slept, the look on his little, still serious face, peaceful now. Dreaming dreams of pirate gold and Indian attacks.

Lost boys.

We started to leave, and Kurtz suddenly spoke before we went.

"I think… you are a good soldier, Talker. Me and my brother could count on you. We knew that. You are good. Goodbye. Today was fun."

"It was," I croaked at the NCO who had taught me how to Ranger. "It was… the best day," I whispered in the late night.

Then I followed my dad and left that place.

He talked as we walked and told me their story as I followed him in the darkness.

"Imagine two boys, son," he said. "Imagine them being separated by bad marriages and a dad who was always gone saving the world for the US Army. They had a tough life. Bad people always with the moms. Summers… well, they had a safe place like this they could be… safe in. Like kids should be, son. Together in. Good grandparents. Then they just had to survive until the next year. The next summer. That was their life."

"Where is this place, Dad?"

"Where is it, son? Don't know. I'm just ranchin' here right now. But... let's call it... summer. Remember our summers?"

I do. How can I forget?

I wanted to cry now because I knew our walk was almost over.

"They're healing here, son. Ain't forever. But for just a while now."

"And you, Dad?"

He turned. The entrance to the alley and the fog was all around us now.

"Just a little further on up the trail, son. That's all. I need you to know... they're fine now. They're safe now. You don't need... to save them, son. Gotta save yourself, okay?"

I watched him for a long moment.

"Dad... I got a horse now."

He smiled. He loved horses.

"That's good, son. Horses is good for the soul."

I reached out and put my hand on his shoulder, feeling the flannel. The life there.

"I understand, Dad."

EPILOGUE

TANNER left me and went off to wander the streets until dawn. I entered the shack, tired from either the day on the battlefield, or summer.

I lit the small candle I'd bought in the markets and just watched the piles of old books I'd found and left there. Like friends I'd promised I'd return to and that times would be good, better, and even… hopeful.

They were beautiful by candlelight.

I wondered how much they'd tell me about the Ruin. How big the world was. What tomorrow would bring.

I rolled out my bag and got ready to rack.

There was a soft knock at the flimsy door to the shack and I grabbed my sidearm and answered it, finding Running Under the Moon waiting there at the threshold, head bowed.

Our Shadow Elven medic spoke in her halting English. Whispering.

"Excuse please… My mistress begs audience with you this late night…"

Before I could say anything, Autumn was there, wrapped in a dark hooded cloak she pulled back to reveal her beautiful face gazing at me like I was a good thing lost, and found again.

She held on to me. I smelled the night, and the salt and sea of the galley she'd just arrived on.

I held her.

I felt her tears on my chest.

"The king…" she began. Her voice a whisper so that what was said would only be heard by us. Running Under the Moon had closed the door quietly and gone, as we held each other in the candlelit shack. "He cannot… provide… an heir… for our people. He has agreed… you must… stand. This must be secret… between us… and the Shadow Maidens. It is for my people…"

She waited, trying to find the right words.

"And me… my love."

She looked up at me, her eyes shining with tears, that smile I had known on her face.

"How long… do I have you?" I asked, holding her and knowing I could never, ever, let go. Of her.

And that I would not, as I had. Even if we were apart and I marched with the Rangers to the other side of the world and back.

And even to hell… and back again.

"Forever… and tonight… only. Ship… it leaves with tide in the morn."

I smelled her hair and understood that you can carry moments with you… if you are willing, and true, and faithful.

"Then," I said softly. "We have forever, now."

* * *

I woke in the morning, the soft light of desert dawn coming in through the cracks in the walls of the tiny shack.

She was gone. The ship would already be beyond the lighthouse and the harbor, beating for open seas now. Raising sails and gone to the west.

But we were us now. Forever.

We had spoken much, never sleeping until the last hours before dawn, talking when we could all through the night like desert wanderers finding an oasis in each other. Drinking deep.

And seeing a tomorrow, or tomorrows, when there had been none before because they were all lost and gone.

I left the shack in search of coffee. It was going to be a good day. A better tomorrow.

What more did I need?

The End

ALSO BY JASON ANSPACH & NICK COLE

Galaxy's Edge: Legionnaire
Galaxy's Edge: Savage Wars
Galaxy's Edge: Requiem For Medusa
Galaxy's Edge: Order of the Centurion

ALSO BY JASON ANSPACH

Wayward Galaxy
King's League
'til Death

ALSO BY NICK COLE

American Wasteland:
The Complete Wasteland Trilogy
SodaPop Soldier
Strange Company